## PRAISE FOR
## THE COMFORT FOOD MYSTERIES

### *A Second Helping of Murder*

"Like good old-fashioned comfort food, *Second Helping of Murder* will satisfy your mystery-loving taste buds. Trixie Matkowski is a frisky, sassy sleuth with a heart of gold."
—Daryl Wood Gerber, national bestselling author
of the Cookbook Nook Mystery series

### *Do or Diner*

"The first Comfort Food mystery is a real treat! Well plotted, it'll keep you guessing right up to the last chapter. Trixie's involvement as an amateur sleuth is well motivated, and her witty sense of humor makes her instantly likable."
—*RT Book Reviews* (top pick)

"Culinary mystery fans have a new series to sample." —The Poisoned Martini

"A comfort foodie and cozy reader's delight."
—Escape with Dollycas into a Good Book

The Comfort Food Mystery Series

*A Second Helping of Murder*
*Do or Diner*

# A Second Helping of Murder

## A Comfort Food Mystery

# CHRISTINE WENGER

AN OBSIDIAN BOOK

OBSIDIAN
Published by the Penguin Group
Penguin Group (USA) LLC, 375 Hudson Street,
New York, New York 10014

USA | Canada | UK | Ireland | Australia | New Zealand | India | South Africa | China
penguin. com
A Penguin Random House Company

First published by Obsidian, an imprint of New American Library,
a division of Penguin Group (USA) LLC

First Printing, April 2014

ISBN 978-0-451-41509-7

Printed in the United States of America
10   9   8   7   6   5   4   3   2

This book is for the Packeteers: Ginny Aubertine, Laurie Bishop, Gayle Callen (who also writes as Emma Cane), Terry Kovian, Michele Masarech, and Peg Benson (who writes as Maggie Shayne).

For Packeteers Emeritus Jenna Mindel and Lisa Hilleren, who have moved away but aren't far away in my heart.

And for Packeteer Amber Schalk, whose love of books can't be measured. I miss you dearly, Amber, and I often think you are still with us when we laugh and joke.

We've been together since 1992, and all of you have believed in me and have supported me, especially when I proposed my first cozy mystery. I totally love you all and always will!

And for Jim, the love of my life.

# Chapter 1

*M*y diner was hopping and so was I!

I'd just dropped the larger-than-a-manhole-cover, cast-iron frying pan on my foot. It bounced off my big toe and landed on the floor with a thud. Thank goodness there wasn't anything in it yet.

I took a couple of deep breaths and willed myself to calm down. I had a big breakfast (served twenty-four hours a day) order to get ready with a variety of eggs and an even greater variety of toast.

Wiping the sweat from my forehead with a towel that I kept draped over the shoulder of my new tomato red chef's jacket, I took the pan over to the sink and grabbed another that was equally as big and heavy and emptied a couple dozen patties of breakfast sausage, handmade by yours truly, into it, along with a half pound of bacon, and set it on the stove, on low.

Then I readied another order and rang the little brass ship's bell that I had bought because it was nautical and sounded better than the little school bell that reminded me of Sister Mary Mary's constant attempts to get our attention in fourth grade.

Chelsea Young, one of my waitresses, appeared in the kitchen looking more than exhausted. It had been an extraordinarily busy graveyard shift at my Silver Bullet Diner.

"You rang, Trixie?" Chelsea yawned, walking slowly toward the prep table.

"Hang in there, sweetie. We're almost done."

I handed her the plates over the steam table. "One cowboy on a raft, one hounds on an island, a large Cobb with Thousand Island, three meat-loaf specials with the works, and two kiddie specials."

I had become very fluent in "Dinerese," the special language that diner staff used to communicate orders. It took me a while to get the hang of Dinerese, but I kind of enjoyed it now. Truth be told, I even made up my own as I went along, which sometimes stymied my waitresses or got us all laughing.

"Don't forget the free udder juice that goes with the kiddie specials, Chelsea."

"The wha—?" She wrinkled her face. "If you're referring to milk, that's pretty lame, Trix."

"I know!"

Chelsea set the western omelet on toast, the franks and beans and everything else on a large serving tray. "I've never seen the diner so packed at two o'clock in the morning."

I eyed the pile of orders wrapped with a rubber

band that the day cooks, Juanita Holgado and Cindy Sherlock, had filled on the morning shift. Later, I'd enter the orders on a spreadsheet, somehow looking for a pattern as to what customers liked and what supplies I needed to order.

"It's been like this all shift." I plucked a couple of orders from the wheel and studied them. There were a lot of orders for the daily specials—cream of chicken soup, my salsa-infused meat loaf with mashed potatoes and gravy—and for those looking forward to a summer picnic, I offered the Silver Bullet Summer Clambake: a dozen steamed cherrystones, an ear of corn, broiled or fried haddock, and salt potatoes. Thankfully, I could do some of those orders at the same time. "I love it when we are busy, though. Time goes by so fast."

And with the extra business, I could make the next balloon payment to Aunt Stella!

I'd bought the diner on the installment plan from my aunt; it had been in our family for years now, and I hadn't been about to let it go under when Aunt Stella decided to retire.

I'd grown up inside this diner, spending summers here with my family, learning how to cook from Uncle Porky and Aunt Stella. My aunt and uncle didn't have any children, and had always wished to keep the property in the family, so when Aunt Stella wanted to sell and my awful divorce from Deputy Doug, my cheating ex-husband, made me want out of Philly, I jumped at the chance to buy.

"By the way, Trix, I love your new outfit," Chelsea said, balancing the tray on the palm of her hand and hoisting it to shoulder level.

I looked down at my red jacket and matching baggy pants covered with a never-ending tomato print and grinned. I'd ordered both items from a new little shop on Cedar Street called Sew What, which was across from the Sandy Harbor Library. The three senior owners, Barbara, Diane, and Elaine, who were cousins from Buffalo, had huge commercial sewing machines arranged in a circle for conversation. The little shop had three walls loaded with bolts of material that looked as if they were about to fall over on the Sew What owners or customers. I'd invited them to lunch at the Silver Bullet so I could get to know them better.

"Thanks. I love my new outfit, too. I've decided that since I'm a chef, I ought to look the part." I brushed some panko crumbs from my embroidered pocket, which read TRIXIE MATKOWSKI, OWNER, SILVER BULLET DINER, SANDY HARBOR, NEW YORK.

I had added the embroidery in black script when I ordered the jacket. Classy.

Chelsea scooted off with her order, and I pulled an assortment of plates from the shelf for the next order.

Smiling, I thought about how the diner would soon get even busier since it was almost the official start of the tourist season in Sandy Harbor: Memorial Day. The fishermen arrived even before all the ice melted on Lake Ontario. Soon the sun worshippers would arrive at the state beaches, so would the recreational boaters, and those who had camps.

My heart raced when I realized that in addition to the Silver Bullet Diner, circa 1952, I was ready to open the doors to my twelve cottages that dotted my "point," a type of peninsula that jutted out into the lake.

I'd be doubly busy when the cottages opened!

Thank goodness, my handymen, Clyde and Max, had slapped a fresh coat of white paint on the cottages and freshened up their shutters and trim in forest green.

They did the same to my Victorian farmhouse, which I called "the Big House," not that it looked like a prison in the least, but because it was way too big for one person.

The Big House was to the left of the diner. Now everything matched. I chuckled, thinking that it looked as if the big Victorian gave birth to a litter of little cottages.

I'd bought everything from my aunt Stella, whose interest in the diner plummeted after Uncle Porky died.

I remembered giving Aunt Stella a down payment after we worked out the numbers on a Silver Bullet place mat. Aunt Stella had handed me a fistful of keys, given me a quick kiss, and headed for a long cruise to Alaska. Then she slid right into retirement in Boca Raton with a gaggle of her friends.

I had always loved cooking, but to own and manage the Silver Bullet (OPEN 24 HOURS A DAY, 7 DAYS A WEEK, AIR-CONDITIONED, WELCOME) and twelve housekeeping cottages seemed overwhelming at times. However, keeping busy took my mind off my divorce from Deputy Doug and his very fertile trophy bride.

But why was I thinking about ancient history? I'd like to believe that I moved on from Doug. I took back my maiden name—Matkowski—and was making a new life for myself in Sandy Harbor, so what was my problem?

I rang the ship's bell, placing the major breakfast orders under the heat lamps. Chelsea needed to hurry, or the eggs would keep cooking.

"Chelsea, order up."

Wipe off hands on towel, fling towel over shoulder, make up another order. Ring bell. Repeat.

I helped Chelsea stack the orders onto two more trays and met her at the kitchen door to relay the orders to her.

Back at the prep table, I mentally ran through a checklist of all the things I had to do to prepare for our busy summer season as I made four large antipastos, six small house salads, and two Cobbs for what looked like a party of twelve.

Then it dawned on me that I probably needed to hire more maids . . . er, . . . housekeeping attendants . . . to clean the cottages. All of the cottages were designated as "bring your own stuff," but some customers opted for daily service.

I pulled my ever-faithful notebook from the pocket of my tomato-printed pants and scribbled *Hire more housekeepers. Put an ad in the* Sandy Harbor Lure.

Most of the cottages were rented for the entire season and beyond with the same families returning year after year. That was just what my family had done. Cottage Number Six had been the Matkowski family's standard rental.

"Where's Chelsea?" I wondered, looking at all the antipastos and salads for the party of twelve, which were now languishing on the shelf. I rang the ship's bell again.

Then I looked over at the pass-through window. Not that I ever used it for passing orders through, but it gave me a look into the dining area of my diner.

Chelsea was leaning over the counter along with my two handymen and a dozen or so regulars. They were all reading what seemed to be the morning edition of the *Sandy Harbor Lure*.

Deputy Ty Brisco, my studly neighbor who lived above the bait shop next door, was holding court and gulping down coffee. He was with the two other cops who made up the entire Sandy Harbor Sheriff's Department.

"It's been a long time," said Mrs. Leddy, the president of the Sandy Harbor Historical Society. "I've always wondered what happened to her."

Who were they talking about?

"'Several local children had been exploring Rocky

Bluffs and stumbled on a cavelike place,'" read Clyde, my maintenance man. He turned to the gathering, waving his hands. "And there she was. It probably scared the pants off them."

Who was in a cavelike place?

I looked over to where the party of twelve should be sitting and waiting for their salads. Half of them were missing, and probably were part of the crowd gathered around the deputies and my staff.

"Chelsea, your order is up," I said, louder than usual.

She gave a nod in my direction and reluctantly tore herself away from the group who were now all talking at once.

I could only catch pieces of the conversation, but I was dying to find out what the hot topic was. Ty Brisco suddenly looked up and smiled.

My face heated up as if I'd just opened the big pizza oven. Why did the former Houston cop have to be such eye candy? And why did he have to be a deputy like my ex?

Not that I was interested in the least.

I gave a half wave to Ty and returned to my spot behind a massive aluminum table just as Chelsea walked in. Time to get the big order started.

Time to cross-examine Chelsea.

"Chels, what's going on?"

"Some kids were climbing the rocks by the bluff, and somehow they discovered a cave. Inside the cave was a body." Chelsea's eyes grew as big as saucers. "The newspaper said that according to Hal Manning, the Sandy Harbor coroner, it's the body of a woman. Hal identified her, but I forgot who— He checked the remains against dental records." She shuddered. "Everyone knows her. Oh, I forgot her name . . . um . . . uh . . ."

"Claire Jacobson." I could barely breathe. I remembered Claire from when I was about ten years old. Claire was the prettiest and coolest high schooler that I'd ever met, and she was so nice to me.

"That's the name." Chelsea hoisted the tray full of salads. "She disappeared from here a zillion years ago, from Cottage Eight, the one that everyone thinks is haunted."

After Claire's disappearance, I always thought Cottage Eight was haunted, too. Aunt Stella said that it was always the last cottage to be rented, and not to old customers, but to new customers who hadn't heard the story—yet.

The back door of the diner opened and I knew it was Juanita Holgado, one of the day cooks. She seemed to appear right out of the fog and darkness. Or maybe I was just feeling overdramatic because of the news about Claire.

"*Hola*, Trixie!" She walked around the steam table and gave me a hug. Juanita was definitely a morning person. She always arrived happy and cheerful. "Look at you! Nice tomatoes!" She eyed my baggy chef's pants, grinning.

Suddenly I remembered Juanita telling me she'd worked for my aunt and uncle for a long time.

She'd been working as a housekeeping attendant at the cottages during that fateful summer twenty-five years ago when Claire Jacobson went missing. A lot of the staff had helped in the search for her, and Juanita had, too.

It had been a big deal that had shaken our small community to the core.

But the recent news about Claire could wait. No need to bring down my cook's morning cheer yet.

"Hey, Juanita. Good morning. I have a surprise for you."

I handed her a gift bag and enjoyed watching my friend's face as she opened it.

Juanita pulled out a red chef's coat that matched mine, but her chef's pants were covered in red and green peppers. Juanita loved her peppers, the hotter the better.

"I love it. I just love it!" Juanita grabbed me in a big bear hug. "And my name is embroidered on the jacket. We are really chefs now. We can have our own show on TV."

Juanita hurried to the storage room, probably to change. I had another gift bag for Cindy Sherlock, another full-time member of my kitchen staff. It was a red coat and pants covered with colorful slices of pizza. Aunt Stella and Uncle Porky, in all their wisdom, had really invested in quality appliances for the diner. The wood-fired pizza oven was a big point of pride for me. Cindy was known for making the best pizza at the Silver Bullet.

Then there was Bob, the missing fourth chef,

who was supposed to be helping me on the graveyard shift. I hadn't yet met or even talked to the elusive Bob in my several months as owner. He was always on sick leave and his doctors were suspiciously in either Vegas, Atlantic City, or New Orleans.

I didn't buy him anything. Matter of fact, if he ever showed up, I probably would fire him.

I went back to preparing the order for the party of twelve. Sometimes it felt as if I were dancing in the diner, doing what I called the Silver Bullet Diner Shuffle. I twirled to the fridge and grabbed a steak. I tangoed to the freezer, scooping up an order of fried clams. I pirouetted to the toaster and loaded buns and bread onto the Ferris wheel.

Three tens from the judges.

I rang the bell, and Chelsea took it all away without any more news from the group still gathered around Deputy Brisco.

Not that I'd looked at him again. No way.

I cut up more lettuce and tomatoes and restocked the freshly baked loaves of bread and rolls that Juanita had set to raise, and I had baked when I started my shift. The diner patrons just loved the smell of baking bread. Who didn't?

Soon Juanita appeared, twirling around the kitchen. "I just love the peppers!"

"I knew you would." I hated to spoil Juanita's good mood, but I had to tell her about Claire. "Juanita, they found Claire Jacobson."

"*Madre de Dios.*" Juanita reached out and steadied herself on the cast-iron dough mixer. "I remember her. What a sweet girl. Where?"

"Rocky Bluff."

Juanita shook her head. "But everyone searched that area. I remember. I helped."

"The waves, the ice, the flooding, storms . . . the rocks must have shifted."

Juanita nodded. *"Sí."*

"If you're ready to take over, I think I'll grab a cup of coffee and talk to Ty and the other deputies and see what I can find out."

"Go ahead. Then you can tell me. And thank you again for the peppers, Trixie Matkowski. You are a good friend and a good boss."

"Boss?" I chuckled as I headed for the double doors that led to the dining room. "Nah. We're all a team—team Silver Bullet Diner and Sandy Harbor Cottages. Jump, salmon! Swim, you lake trout! Come, tourists!"

Juanita pumped an arm into the air. "Go, team!"

Walking behind the counter, I poured myself a sorely needed cup of coffee and then decided that I had to have an apple hand pie made by Mrs. Sarah Stolfus, my Amish friend and an extraordinary baker. I put it on a dish and set it on the counter in front of a vacant stool next to Ty Brisco.

It only became vacant when I raised a blond, nonplucked eyebrow to my handyman Clyde. Clyde cleared his throat and headed out the front door to either work or find a place to sleep. I hoped it was the former.

I sat down on the stool and swiveled to my coffee and hand pie. The crowd had gone back to their tables, the other two deputies had left, and I had Ty to myself. I sure could break up a crowd.

"Catch me up, Ty. I remember Claire Jacobson. I remember how we used to sit on the beach and talk and she taught me how to float on my back. I thought she was the greatest. She reminded me of Olivia Newton-John in *Grease*."

Ty showed me the headlines of the *Sandy Harbor Lure*: BODY OF MISSING TEEN FOUND AFTER 25 YEARS. I skimmed the article. I'd rather hear the news from Ty, spoken with his delicious cowboy twang, than read the long tome.

"Is it really Claire?"

He nodded. "Her dental records happened to still be here from the initial search. Hal Manning, our resident coroner and funeral director with the biggest mouth in North and South America, said that the remains are those of Claire, but we are going to verify his findings with the State Police Lab. Hal should know better, but I guess he's dating the new editor of the *Sandy Harbor Lure* and she was with him when everything hit the fan."

"Wow. Claire Jacobson, after twenty-five years, and she was only about a mile down the beach entombed on the bluff, in the rocks."

Ty nodded.

"I've always wondered what happened to her. I always hoped that she ran away to Europe with her Prince Charming and was ruling some country." I took a bite of my apple hand pie and a sip of coffee. Delicious. "Can you tell me anything more?"

"Not much." He sighed. "There was a kind of cave where she was found, and we believe that some of the rocks that were placed in front of the cave's opening got dislodged throughout the years. Then the kids who were climbing on the rocks dislodged more, making the cave visible."

I sat for a while, thinking. I was taking a sip of coffee when it dawned on me. "Ty, someone had to have known that there was a cave on the bluff. Seems to me that only a local or regular summer vacationer would know to hide her body there! Don't you see? Maybe a local person even killed her."

Ty nodded slowly. "I was thinking the same thing."

"Is there no chance that it was an accident?" I asked hopefully. It was terrible to think someone might have killed poor Claire and gotten away with it for so long.

"No chance."

"Why do you say that, Ty?"

"I can't tell you. Confidential information."

"I understand," I said, but I really didn't mean it. I wanted to know . . . everything. Claire was special to me. She made time to pay attention to a little girl who wanted to be grown-up and beautiful like her.

I remembered the day that I heard the news about Claire missing. I was baking sugar cookies with Aunt Stella in the kitchen of the diner, rolling the cookies into little balls and then squishing them into circles with a sugarcoated glass. It smelled so nice and sugary in the kitchen. Even though it was July, it smelled like Christmas.

Uncle Porky was the chef that day. He was singing like always—some navy song. When he pounded on the little bell for a waitress, it was to the tune of his song.

It was the perfect way to spend a July day.

Then a man in uniform walked into the kitchen. "Hey, Porky, I have some information for you."

"Tell me, Willie. I have a big order to make up."

Willie lowered his voice, but I could still hear from where I stood. "There's a search on for Claire Jacobson. She's been missing for two days. It doesn't look good."

Suddenly Uncle Porky looked serious. "I'll join you in the search."

Uncle Porky walked over to me, gave me a pat on the head, and told me to go and have a soda in the diner. I nodded and sat in my favorite stool at the counter.

"What can I get you, Trixie?" Bettylou, the waitress, had asked me.

"Nothing. Thank you."

I remembering feeling sick, sick. Claire wouldn't just disappear; she wasn't the type.

Claire promised me that we were going to make the biggest and best sand castle on the beach, but I hadn't seen her since.

Claire wouldn't break a promise. Something

was very wrong. I burst into tears, and I remember putting my head down on the counter and sobbing. Not too long after, my mother took my hand and we walked to a picnic table by our cottage. We sat down on the same side, and my mother put her arms around me and let me just cry for my friend until I was all cried out.

"Wh-wh-what if sh-she's dead, Mom?" I sobbed.

"Trixie, we don't know that for sure. Everyone is looking for her. I hope that they'll find her alive and well."

I blinked and brought myself back to the present.

There was a steady stream of customers walking in, and everyone was talking.

"The killer could be someone we know," I said to myself, scanning the people in the dining area. Some were strangers, but most of them I knew from the community or because they frequented my diner.

Could I know Claire's killer? Could I have talked to him or her? Maybe we were even friends.

A shiver went up my spine and then turned into a nagging headache that I couldn't shake for several hours.

# Chapter 2

It was after midnight and I was back cooking at the diner. As I prepared the orders, I kept thinking about the unusual call that I received yesterday.

He'd said his name was David Burrows, and he insisted on reserving Cottage Number Eight— Claire Jacobson's cottage. No other cottage would do. He wanted to rent it for the entire summer, maybe even until October, when we closed for the season. He wanted housekeeping once a week, only on Saturday morning, eight thirty sharp.

If Cottage Eight was rented, he wanted me to relocate the renters, stating, "I'll make it worth your while."

I didn't have to check my laptop, because I knew that Number Eight was free. Most of the cottages were rented, but Eight remained available.

The haunted cottage.

I wasn't going to relocate anyone who had already requested Cottage Eight, no matter how much money Mr. Burrows offered, so it was good that Eight was available.

But why did he insist on renting that particular cottage?

He'd made it more than clear that he was to be left alone, other than he wanted his meals delivered.

For breakfast he wanted a ham steak and scrambled eggs with buttered rye toast and grape jelly delivered exactly at eight in the morning.

For lunch he wanted a rare cheeseburger with the works on an onion roll, steak fries, and a small chef with Italian dressing delivered at exactly one o'clock.

For supper, he wanted a roast beef dinner with mashed potatoes and extra gravy, both corn and peas, and a piece of apple pie delivered at six o'clock promptly.

Mr. Burrows wired more than enough money for the cottage, meals, and tip. I probably owed him money, and as soon as I had a chance to figure out his bill, I would reimburse him.

There were so many good things on the Silver Bullet menu, I couldn't imagine eating the same thing for the entire summer. I called that to his attention, but he insisted that he'd be fine and again insisted on being left alone. He said that he had a lot of work to do.

What kind of work?

"The elusive Mr. Burrows is checking in today," I said out loud, just to remind myself. I checked my

Mickey Mouse watch. "At seven thirty this morning, sharp."

Normally, check-in time was two in the afternoon, but since he was the first and only occupant, it really didn't matter.

I couldn't stop wondering why he wanted to be such a recluse with beautiful Lake Ontario in front of him. He could swim, watch the sun rise and set, read a book on a lounge chair. I could even arrange a fishing trip with Ty Brisco or Mr. Farnsworth, the owner of the bait shop next door.

Maybe I'd ask Mr. Burrows if he was interested in going fishing.

I rang the ship bell and put all the salads on a serving tray. Chelsea was quick to pick up. I started on the actual meals.

Finally the rack was free of orders. I checked my watch. Seven o'clock in the morning. Where did the time go? Juanita should be arriving soon to relieve me, and I could get Mr. Burrows settled.

Just then, Juanita came through the back door of the kitchen.

"Juanita, I'm so glad you're here. I forgot that I have an early check-in. Cottage Number Eight. He's going to be with us all summer long. I'll tell you about his breakfast, lunch, and dinner order later. He wants his meals delivered, so you'll have to send Clyde or Max to his cottage, and apparently punctuality is mandatory!"

Juanita nodded. "No problem, Trixie."

"It's the strangest thing, Juanita. David Burrows insists on staying in Cottage Eight."

"Claire Jacobson's cottage? Why?"

"Beats me."

"*Madre de Dios.*" Juanita wrinkled her nose. "You know, some people are just creepy."

"He certainly is a strange guy," I conceded, stepping aside to let Juanita take over the kitchen. "As soon as I meet him, I'll tell you more. I already Googled him and didn't find anything."

Juanita shrugged. "Well, adios."

"Adios," I echoed. I glanced over at the pass-through window and saw Ty Brisco staring at me. I gave him a wave, he gave me a lazy salute, and then I hurried out the back door. I still had a copy of the *Sandy Harbor Lure* in my pocket, so I was going to take it back to my Victorian and thoroughly read the article about Claire.

Dodging some potholes in the parking lot, I called Max on my cell.

"Max, when you have some spare time, like now, would you toss some gravel into the potholes in the parking lot? A couple of them look like they could swallow up a VW. Thanks."

The whole parking lot should probably be tarred over, but it'd have to wait until the off-season—that tricky time after the majority of the fishermen leave and before the first snowfall.

A couple of perfect sunny days with high temperatures so the tar would stick would be lovely, too.

So would the money to pay for it.

I crossed my fingers and lifted my face to the narrow slit in the clouds where the sun was trying to shine through. This was going to be a good summer season—I just knew it in my bones. So far, I had a couple of big clambakes scheduled, a wedding, and a bar mitzvah.

What I was most excited about was the fact that I was going to bring back the Silver Bullet Saturday Dance Fest. I planned on renting a big tent, charging for a huge buffet, and hiring a live band for dancing. There would be a big bonfire, too.

Uncle Porky and Aunt Stella's Saturday night dances were legendary around this area—at least they were until Uncle Porky got sick and Aunt Stella called them off.

I stopped halfway up the stairs to my Victorian, remembering. It was during one of their Saturday night dances that Claire Jacobson had disappeared. Her parents and her younger brother were at the dance, and somehow Claire slipped away to join the Sandy Harbor High School's clandestine party down the beach.

I sat down on my newly painted forest green top step and unfolded the *Sandy Harbor Lure* to the front page and read a recap of the old story:

*According to several students, Claire Jacobson was invited to attend a celebratory party/bonfire that some graduating seniors had planned near Rocky Bluffs along with various non–Sandy Harbor High School individuals.*

Sometime during the evening, salutatorian and former class president Richard "Ricky" Tingsley reported that he looked for Ms. Jacobson, but he couldn't find her. He assumed that she simply walked back to the cottage where she was staying with her family, Cottage Eight at Porky and Stella Matkowski's Sandy Harbor Housekeeping Cottages.

Ricky Tingsley admitted that he had told Ms. Jacobson about the party. He said that he'd known her for several years in that she and her family always summered at the cottages, and that he and several members of the graduating class also knew her, liked her, and thought she'd like to join them.

Salvatore Brownelli, graduating senior and valedictorian, stated that he was playing the guitar and Ms. Jacobson was singing along with the rest of the partiers who were gathered around the bonfire. However, after a while, approximately before midnight, he didn't remember seeing her anymore.

Laura VanPlank, head cheerleader of the class, reported that she remembered Ms. Jacobson saying that she had to get back to the Silver Bullet's Saturday Dance Fest before her parents missed her.

Marvin P. Cogswell III, four-year president of the Chess Club, claims that he noticed Ms. Jacobson arrive by herself by way of the beach and mostly talking to Antoinette Chloe Switzer about ladies' fashion.

*New York State Police Troop "D" Commander John Mulberry and Sandy Harbor Sheriff Vern McCoy both stated on separate occasions that each individual who attended the party will be required to give formal affidavits of the night's events at the Sandy Harbor Sheriff's Department.*

*The Grab and Go on Route 343A is also being investigated for selling alcohol to minors.*

The article went on and on, talking about how the event wasn't school-sanctioned and how events like that were just a magnet for all kinds of illegal behavior on the part of Sandy Harbor youth. It ended with a fervent message that anyone who had any information on Claire Jacobson's whereabouts needed to contact state or local law enforcement immediately.

It was as if I'd lost my friend again—not that I knew Claire Jacobson to any great extent—but I just idolized her. It was almost as if she was a living and breathing Barbie doll with a Barbie doll life.

At the Saturday night dances, Claire never sat down. As soon as she finished one dance, she was asked again. Her smile was electrifying, her reddish brown hair was shiny and bouncy, and she treated all the boys the same no matter their shape or appearance.

From a ten-year-old's perspective, none of the girls seemed jealous of her either, even though she wasn't a "townie."

Everyone seemed to like Claire.

But someone hadn't.

I took a deep breath and skimmed the paper again. The cast of characters mentioned were still living and breathing the Sandy Harbor air. Well, not quite.

Marvin P. Cogswell was deceased, and Antoinette Chloe's husband, Salvatore Brownelli, was serving a life term in Auburn Correctional Facility for his participation in Cogswell's death.

Antoinette Chloe Switzer married Salvatore Brownelli back in 1990 and became Antoinette Chloe Brown, or ACB. After Sal was sentenced to life in state prison, ACB jumped on the back of Sal's brother's motorcycle and hadn't returned to Sandy Harbor to run her business, Brown's Family Restaurant, yet.

ACB was a little strange, and wore over-the-top muumuus, wild jewelry, and wilder hair things, but I liked her anyway.

The former Laura VanPlank had married real estate agent and small-town mayor Rick Tingsley. For the most part, Laura, who dressed and wore her hair like Jackie Kennedy Onassis, ran the Crossroads Restaurant. Rumor had it, via my pal and cook Juanita, that Rick Tingsley was going to run for governor of New York State—something that Laura had spent years waiting for. Laura had made it known that he'd eventually be running for the presidency. Yes, the president of the United States! The fact that the U.S. president could one day be a local boy made a lot of residents really proud.

But I'd never vote for Rick Tingsley. I didn't like the man. He was pushy and arrogant and had tried to strong-arm the purchase of everything on "the point" from my aunt Stella after Uncle Porky died, a time when she was very vulnerable.

Aunt Stella knew that she wanted to keep the Silver Bullet Diner and the Sandy Harbor Cottages in the family. Luckily, she held out for me, and I jumped on buying everything from her. It was a time in my life that I needed to keep busy and do what I loved doing: cooking and baking.

Come to think of it, Rick Tingsley had also been a bit rude in trying to get me to sell the diner to him.

A horn blew loudly, waking me out of my reverie. A car pulled up in front of my Victorian into one of the parking spaces with new signage proclaiming CHECK-IN.

No doubt this was Mr. David Burrows.

I squinted into the burst of sunlight above. Burrows didn't seem to want to get out of his car. Did he expect me to roller-skate to him like a carhop?

I didn't move from the top step, feeling very inhospitable for someone in the hospitality business. He'd better make a move, because there was a possibility that my new chef's pants were sticking to the newly painted step.

He finally got out of the car and walked slowly toward me. He was tall and thin with a head of closely cropped white hair with a prominent cowlick on his crown. He wore thick black glasses.

As he got closer, I saw that his eyes were red-rimmed, and he looked tired, as if he had been driving for a week straight without any sleep.

I stood up and heard my pants peel from the step. If I'd ruined these pants, I'd scream so loud they'd hear me in Syracuse.

"Mr. Burrows?"

"Yes."

"I'm Trixie Matkowski, the new owner of the Sandy Harbor Housekeeping Cottages. We spoke on the phone. You're checking in today?"

"Of course." He checked his watch. "Seven thirty, prompt."

"Yes. You are very prompt." I forced a smile. "And what brings you to the cottages?"

He hesitated. "If you have to know, I'm a writer. I'm writing."

"Oh. I see. I'll get the key and show you the way."

"No need."

"You've been here before?" I'd never even thought of that. But of course, when he contacted me, Mr. Burrows knew that we had numbered cottages and specifically asked for Cottage Eight. Interesting.

"Uh, I—I was here, a long time ago." He rolled his eyes. "May I have the key now?"

"Sure, but I have to go inside and get the required form. You know, the usual: name, address, car, license plate number. And if you'll give me your credit card, I'll run it through for future expenses."

"That's not necessary. I'll pay cash for any additional expenditures."

"Yes, but, having your credit card on file is just standard operating procedure."

"Miss Matkowski." He spoke very slowly as if I were a child. "I said that I'll pay cash for any additional expenses."

"I think I even owe you some money."

"Then why do you want my credit card?"

"In case there are more charges, so—" We were going in circles.

"Let me repeat myself: there won't be any additional expenses."

He raised his head to the sky as if he was saying a prayer for patience.

He needed to say one for me, too!

"One moment, please, Mr. Burrows."

I hurried up the step. Got the form, put it on a clipboard, grabbed a pen and the key to Cottage Eight.

Back outside, I handed him the clipboard and the pen. He ignored my pen and slipped one from his shirt pocket.

I bit back a giggle.

Here was my first guest, and I couldn't warm up to him.

"Your meals will be delivered as instructed."

"See that they are."

"Starting this morning, Mr. Burrows?"

He looked at me as if I had snakes crawling out of my ears. "Of course."

He finally looked at me, and I saw that he had pale blue eyes. They matched his pale blue Windbreaker and pale blue shirt. He had on pale blue polyester pants. He probably wore pale blue underwear.

He handed me the clipboard, and I handed him the key.

"You can drive around to the front of the cottage," I said.

"I know."

"If you have any guests, they have to park in the parking lot."

"I'm not expecting any guests." He glanced toward his pale blue car. "Is there anything else?"

"Well, yes, there is." I took a deep breath. "May I ask why you wanted to specifically rent Cottage Eight?"

"No, you may not."

I pulled on my earlobe. Did I hear him right?

"I may not . . . what?" I asked.

He looked down his nose at me, and I went up a couple of steps, backward, to be eye level with him. "You may not ask me that question."

"But it is my business. It's my cottage. If anything illegal is—"

"I am not up to anything illegal. I am a writer."

"Okay, Mr. Burrows." I plastered on a smile. "Your breakfast will be delivered at eight o'clock sharp. Happy writing, Mr. Burrows."

"Happy?" He snorted. "Happy writing? I doubt it."

With that strange comment, I'd just checked in my first guest.

## Chapter 3

*I* immediately phoned Juanita at the Silver Bullet and informed her as to what Mr. Burrows's standard breakfast order would be.

"Juanita, please make sure that Clyde or Max delivers it promptly to Cottage Eight at eight o'clock. Eight at eight. That should be easy for them to remember."

"Got it," Juanita said.

I hurried up the stairs, anxious for a shower and some sleep. Blondie, my rescued golden retriever, greeted me and gave me a look that meant she had to go outside.

I put her leash on and hustled her outdoors. From my side yard, I could see the backs of the twelve white cottages all lined up like chubby soldiers along the shoreline.

In the space between Cottage Seven and Eight, I could see that Mr. Burrows had parked his car and was unloading things from the trunk.

It looked as though he was lugging in an old typewriter. No, it couldn't be. Hadn't he ever heard of a laptop or any one of a dozen gadgets that would do the same thing without causing back problems?

As Blondie did her business, Clyde did his. I mean that I saw him hustle over to Mr. Burrows, and Clyde never hustled. Juanita must have read him the riot act.

Clyde handed Burrows a plastic bag. I checked my watch. Eight at eight. One down, many more meals to go.

It seemed that Clyde tried talking to Burrows but then left, shaking his head. Clyde loved to talk and he was probably disappointed that Burrows wasn't interested in being a fresh pair of ears for his old army stories.

Just as Blondie and I were about to go back into the house, I heard the whine of diesel engines switching gears. On the road that led to the diner, I could see three huge tourist buses rolling in.

I wasn't expecting any buses!

I scooted Blondie into the house and hurried to meet the first one in line. The door opened and the driver came down the stairs.

"I'm Trixie Matkowski, the owner of the diner and cottages. Can I help you?"

"We had reservations at Brown's, but . . . uh . . ."

"No one's there?"

"Yeah." He shook his head. "We are looking to

eat, and one of the cops in town—one with a cowboy hat—said to come here. Any chance you could accommodate all of us?"

The cop with the cowboy hat had to be Ty Brisco. "How many people?"

"Eighty-two."

"How about a buffet instead of individual meals?" I asked, mentally calculating my inventory of eggs, ham, sausage, juice, and bread items. We'd restocked recently and just might be able to pull this off!

He grinned. "Perfect."

"Stall a little . . ." I looked at his name tag. "Stall a little, Ronald, and we'll supply them with coffee, tea, and juice to make them happy while we get things ready."

"You don't know how much we all appreciate this, Trixie. Five Star Journeys will be notified of how you helped."

I smiled and ran as fast as I could—which isn't fast at all—to the back door of the diner. Juanita, Sandy, and I could pull this off and have fun in the meantime.

I took out my cell and telephoned Max. "Max, I need two tables set up in the side room of the diner. Tablecloths, too." I went inside the diner and motioned Chelsea and Nancy aside.

"Get a boatload of coffee going and hot water, and bring out as much juice as you can. And we need to get a buffet set up, too. We are doing a breakfast buffet for eighty-two people."

Announcing the same to Cindy and Juanita, we sprang into action.

"I heard the buses, Trixie," Juanita said. "Did you forget to tell us?"

Hey, I wasn't that forgetful. Was I?

"No. They were supposed to be at Brown's, but ACB must be motorcycling with her ex-husband's brother, or maybe she just forgot."

"That can't be good for business," Cindy said.

I nodded. "But it is for our business, isn't it, team?"

"Team Silver Bullet!" we all cheered together.

"So, let's do this," I said. "Juanita, you and Cindy get all the meat cooking. I'll get the scrambled eggs going. Think you two can fry up some pancakes in between?"

"No problem, Trix," Cindy said, reaching for the handle of the refrigerator.

Juanita was already pulling boxes of sliced ham, link sausage, and bacon out of the walk-in cooler, so I couldn't hear her mumbled answer.

My heart was pumping as we all did the Diner Shuffle with the three of us behind the prep table, vying for room at the huge commercial stove. Funny, how it didn't seem so huge with the three of us cooking at it.

I quickly looked out of the pass-through window and saw that Clyde was making coffee. Max was even walking around with two pots in his hands—regular and decaffeinated.

They were part of my team, too. Clyde and Max,

jacks-of–all-trades. They deserved a raise—or maybe an embroidered uniform shirt. Maybe both.

Some nonbus customers wanted to order off the menu, so we had to make those up. Most of them were thrilled to find a buffet and asked if they could order that.

"Absolutely," I told Chelsea when she asked me.

All the interest made me think about adding a breakfast buffet on Sundays.

I made a mental note to ask Juanita's and Cindy's opinion.

"What do we have for something sweet? Danish? Pies?"

Cindy glanced at me, then returned her attention to the stove. "Mrs. Stolfus just made a delivery, so we are flush with pies and sweets, but there won't be anything left for tomorrow."

"I'll give her a call! Oh, wait." I kept forgetting that Mrs. Stolfus was Amish, and she didn't have a phone. "I'll stop at her house."

"I'll do it, Trixie," Chelsea said. "I can go by her house on the way home. Just write down what you want me to order."

"Hmm. Tell her that I'd like the same items that she just delivered today."

We laughed. It was wonderful to have friends. Friends that I enjoyed working with. Cindy was quite a bit younger than Juanita and I. For heaven's sake, she'd just graduated from high school, but the girl was mature beyond her years. That probably came from helping her single mother raise her eight brothers and sisters.

Cindy even had to bring all her siblings to her job interview with me. Remembering how I had had them all order off the menu and then had Cindy make up the orders, I smiled. I had hired her on the spot and given her whatever hours she could handle around her babysitting duties.

We carried out a couple of aluminum rectangular pans full of steaming food. I lit the cans of liquid fuel on the two stands that I could find and set the pans on top. Underneath I laid out some serving utensils on plates in front of each pan and gave a signal to the waitresses that everything was ready.

The customers could serve themselves from both sides of the tables for quicker service.

The three bus drivers served themselves last. On his way, Ronald gave me a thumbs-up, and I grinned.

I was feeling good, up until the time several bus customers took a copy of the *Sandy Harbor Lure* off the wire rack by the door.

I held my breath. I knew what was likely to come next. Amazement, disbelief, horror rippled across the diner like waves on the lake. Then, when they realized that they were on the very location from which Claire Jacobson disappeared, the ripple became a tsunami.

It started as a whisper, like the game of gossip; then necks became rubber, faces were pressed against the windows of the diner, and fingers pointed outside. Some of the customers actually went out the door and counted off the cottages. Then they told others.

What on earth? Did they think that my Cottage Eight was some kind of tourist attraction?

I poured myself a cup of coffee, then walked over to Ronald to express my concern that something was cooking with his bus passengers, and it wasn't another pan of link sausage.

"Well, this *is* a bus tour for mystery fans," he said, and I almost choked on my coffee. He pointed to the paper in front of him. "And they like this kind of stuff. Maybe they think it's part of the tour."

A group of five walked out the door. I could see them walking across the lawn to the cottages. Oh no!

"Ronald, please tell them that this diner, cottages, and grounds are not part of their mystery tour." I hurried out the door to round up the five individuals on the loose and turn them back to the Silver Bullet.

But I was too late. They had already knocked on the door and met the friendly and charming Mr. Burrows.

"What the hell do you all want?" he asked in his friendly and charming way.

"We want to investigate Cottage Eight," one woman said, pulling a magnifying glass out of the pocket of her Windbreaker. "Are you one of our clues?"

"Am I what? What clue?" Burrows yelled. "I wish to be left alone!"

I stepped between Mr. Burrows and the five bus renegades. "Will you all please go back to the buffet? There's a new pan of piping-hot sausage coming out and fresh coffee is available. This property is not part of your bus tour."

"What bus tour?" Burrows yelled.

I peeked into Cottage Eight. Although I'd said the bus tour participants shouldn't look, surely there was no harm in my curiosity?

There was his big monolith of a typewriter on the wooden kitchen table. It was dark gray, at least from the back. A piece of white paper was hanging from the roller like a white waterfall. The typewriter belonged in a museum.

There were two reams of paper on the side of the table and what appeared to be a big scrapbook, opened to yellowed construction paper pages with pictures and newspaper clippings taped to it.

Burrows caught me looking inside, and with a grunt, he stepped out on the little porch and closed the door behind him.

"This should be part of our bus tour," said a tall, thin man with a tan raincoat. "This is the best mystery setup that we've had all week. The newspaper article that was planted in the diner was pure genius."

"It wasn't planted," I said, stretching my arms out wide to move them toward the diner. "It's the real news."

"Then that's even more exciting!" said a woman with a navy blue beret and a purse wider than she was. "Are we supposed to help the police?"

"What police?" Burrows looked right and left, then glared at me.

"There're no police here, Mr. Burrows. Why don't you go back into your cottage? I'll see that you're not disturbed again."

I had to wonder why he was so adamant about not being disturbed. Maybe it took all of his concentration to push down the keys of his relic of a typewriter so he wouldn't make a mistake, or lose a finger between the keys in the process.

I shouldn't be that harsh on him. It's understandable that he wouldn't want people barging in to inspect his cottage, but he still seemed a little too cranky, secretive, and over-the-top.

Managing to get the five mystery buffs walking in the direction of the Silver Bullet, I told them again that this was not part of their mystery tour.

"I'm going to request that it's included next year," said the lady with the magnifying glass.

"It's going to be the first thing that I suggest on my comment card," said Beige Raincoat. "This area would be a gold mine of clues."

The case was over two decades old. All the clues in the gold mine had to be gone by now.

When she walked through the door of my diner, the first thing that Blue Beret with the big purse brought up for a vote with the other bus people was returning with Five Star Journeys to solve the mystery of Claire Jacobson's murder.

They could return all right, as guests, not mystery solvers. I didn't want to wait another year for Claire's death to go unsolved.

And I wanted to be the one to solve the mystery of Claire's murder. For some strange reason, I felt I owed it to Claire for being my friend every summer.

If I only knew where to start.

Maybe the bus people had the right idea. Start at Cottage Eight.

I helped cash out the bus people, and we got them on their bus before a crack of thunder scared me out of my sneaks. In my hurry to cook, I hadn't seen the storm front rolling in over the water.

"Juanita, can you and everyone else get everything cleaned up and put everything away? I hate to leave you with such a mess, but I just have to get some sleep before my shift starts again."

Both Juanita and Cindy shooed me away.

I hurried home just as the rain started falling in sheets. It stung my skin as I raced for the Big House. I kicked off my wet sneakers and got a clean towel from the laundry room, blotting the water from everywhere.

"Blondie!" I yelled, wondering why she didn't greet me at the door. "Blondie, where are you?"

I found her cowering in a corner between a chair and the wall, scared of the noise outside.

"Oh, you poor sweetie. C'mon, let's go to sleep."

I motioned to the stairs, but she wouldn't move. I figured that she'd follow me up sooner or later.

I peeled off my wet clothes, tossed them into the bathtub, slipped into a nightshirt, and fell onto the bed like a chain-sawed Christmas tree. I squished up the pillow under my head, and with a sigh, I was just about to fall asleep when I felt the bed bounce.

Blondie.

She spread out on my right side, and we probably snored in unison.

Until another bang of thunder and lightning flashes woke me up. Blondie jumped off the bed and curled up into a ball on the side of my dresser.

I checked my alarm clock. Eleven o'clock. I had to start work in another hour, so I might as well take a shower and get ready.

Peeking out my bedroom window, I noticed that the parking lot was mostly empty. It was going to be a long night unless business picked up.

No one but cops and various other service personnel would be out on a night like this, so it would be a long, slow night. Maybe I could do some yeast baking—bread, rolls, and the like.

I had a craving for my grandma Matyjasik's Easter babka.

I heard another clap of thunder, but this sounded different from the usual. It sounded more like a . . . sharp, quick blast . . . um . . . like a gunshot.

But that was ridiculous.

Clearly the murder mystery tour group was getting to my head.

The motion lights that hung from my wraparound porch flashed on. Through the curtain of rain, I could see some kind of movement by Cottage Eight. Was it someone running?

The first person I thought of was David Burrows.

Why would David Burrows be running in the foul weather?

He didn't want to leave his cottage, for heaven's sake—it couldn't be him.

I didn't know why, but I felt the need to check.

I ran a brush through my hair and slipped Uncle Porky's yellow raincoat over my nightshirt. I couldn't stand the thought of putting on my wet sneaks and went outside in my bare feet instead, sliding on the squishy, muddy grass.

In the distance, I thought I heard a car start up, but no lights flashed on in my parking lot. Strange.

The door to Cottage Eight was ajar, and the lights weren't on inside.

I pushed on the door. "Mr. Burrows? Mr. Burrows, are you okay?"

There was no answer, so I flicked on the switch at the side of the door.

Mr. Burrows lay on his back. Spreading onto his blue-striped pajamas, in the middle of his chest, was a circle of red blood.

His ice blue eyes were open, and they stared up at me, blank, lifeless.

I knew he was dead.

I screamed so loudly that I scared myself. Then I screamed again and again. I had to be heard over the thunder because I couldn't move. Whoever came to investigate would have to peel my cold, bare feet off the wooden floor and push me out the door.

While I waited, I tried not to look at Mr. Burrows, but I did register that the cottage was in shambles. Mr. Burrow's typewriter was on the floor, upside down. There were no signs of the scrapbook that I'd seen earlier, no sign of any paper or typewritten pages.

"Freeze! Get your hands in the air! Now!"

"I'm already frozen, Ty!"

It was Ty Brisco, of the Sandy Harbor Sheriff's Department, and in his hand was a big black gun.

"Trixie?"

"Thank goodness! Ty, get me out of here. I can't seem to move."

He whistled, long and low. He lowered his gun to point at the floor but didn't make a move to put it away.

"Ty, for heaven's sake, put your gun away. I didn't kill Mr. Burrows!"

# Chapter 4

*H*e finally holstered his gun and squatted down on the side of Mr. Burrows. He put two fingers behind the man's ear, probably to find a pulse.

Good luck.

"I was at the diner, and thought I heard a gunshot," he said. "I went outside, wondering where to go first in the pouring rain, and then I heard you scream. I think you scared the bats away. I had to leave my hot roast beef sandwich with the candied apples and stuffing on the side. Delicious."

How could the man blithely talk about food as he was crouching over a man's dead, bloody body?

"That's nice, Ty. Glad you liked today's special." I shook my head. "Now, will you get me out of here?"

"Did you touch anything, Trixie?"

"I didn't even scratch my nose."

"You're free to go, Trixie. I'll question you later at the diner."

"I. Can't. Move."

Mr. Burrows was still looking at me. There'd be no more deliveries to Cottage Eight. No more tiptoeing around him. No more detouring of bus people. No more of his crankiness.

I took a deep breath. "First, Claire Jacobson disappeared from Cottage Eight. Now Mr. Burrows dies in the same cottage. Everyone thinks that it's either jinxed or haunted. I should just level it."

"Mr. Burrows didn't just die. He was murdered, Trixie."

"Sorry. I stand corrected. And I'm still standing in the same spot, I'd like to add."

Ty started to dial his cell phone. "Huh?"

"It's not important." My legs and feet were numb.

Ty called the other two members of the sheriff's department to the scene. Then he punched in another set of numbers.

"Hal, it's Ty Brisco. We need you and your coroner skills over at Trixie's cottages. Number Eight. And hurry, please."

More numbers were punched. I could guess by the conversation that he'd contacted the New York State Police Bureau of Criminal Investigation.

My property was going to be crawling with law enforcement types, and other than poor Mr. Burrows, the first thing I thought of was feeding and watering them!

I needed to call Cindy and ask her to put on

more coffee and set out more pies, cakes, and pastries in the pastry carousel out front.

"Ty, I have to get to the diner. It's my shift."

"Sure. Go ahead. We'll talk later." He switched the light on in the bathroom. "Nothing disturbed in here. Matter of fact, Burrows was quite neat."

"Ty, give me a push." I still couldn't take my eyes off Mr. Burrows's eyes. He was still staring at me as if he was trying to tell me something. What?

Something about his icy blue eyes seemed so familiar, but I couldn't think. Not now.

Ty did better than give me a push; he gathered me into a big hug. "Are you okay?"

"Not really."

"Don't worry. This won't hurt your business. It might increase it. People like to rubberneck, you know."

"Ty, I'm not that shallow," I said into the shoulder of his damp New York Giants Windbreaker. "I'm not worried about my business. I'm worried about finding Mr. Burrows's killer. And Claire Jacobson's killer."

"I apologize," he said. "I shouldn't have said that. Sometimes I go into cop mode and don't pay attention to the rest of the world."

"And here's my statement: I thought I heard a gunshot. My outside sensor light went on, and I saw a movement from my upstairs bathroom window. It looked like someone running away. Then I heard a car start, but it didn't come from my parking lot. Then I saw that the door to Cottage Eight was partially open. I walked in to investigate, turned the light on, and I've been standing in this exact same spot since. End of my statement."

Ty rubbed my back, just a couple of circles, but it felt so good, so calming, and I needed that. At least for a moment it seemed that he'd stepped out of cop mode and realized I was feeling upset. I leaned in closer . . . but a flash of red and white lights had Ty stepping back and hustling out of the cottage to direct the investigation.

There I stood, just Mr. Burrows and me. Alone again.

"Mr. Burrows, you're the first real tenant of my Sandy Harbor Housekeeping Cottages, and I'm sorry this happened to you. I'll find out who shot you. I will. I promise."

I was able to move now. I stepped out of the infamous Cottage Eight with one bare foot in front of the other and dodged my way through a sea of cops back to the Big House. Ty had obviously spoken up on my behalf as an innocent bystander.

I needed shoes and something to wear other than my nightshirt.

Yeah, it was going to be a long night, but I was going to work on my plan of action. I did my best thinking when I cooked and my absolute best planning when I baked.

Tonight—well, this morning—I was going to do both.

\*        \*        \*

I should have known better than to try to bake. I must have given my statement one million times to one million cops.

Okay, three times. I gave it three times, and then I had to promise to go to the Sandy Harbor Sheriff's Department just as soon as my shift was over.

Ty was going to type it in the computer then.

Sheesh. From past experience, I knew how he typed—with two fingers and one thumb. It'd be like medieval torture. Maybe I could talk him into letting me type it.

Until then, I saw to it that the cops were never without strong, hot coffee and sweets.

They had to be wired. I certainly was.

In between orders, I couldn't stay away from the kitchen window that overlooked the Big House and the cottages. I had to wipe off the condensation to get a good view of what was happening.

The various sheriffs, troopers, and other people for evidence gathering and whatnot milled around the grounds and the diner, clustered in groups or huddled like a football team. They all wore a type of rain bonnet on their hats, and when they dipped their heads at huddle time, it must have seemed like Niagara Falls.

I couldn't help looking for Ty to see what he was doing. He always seemed to be the tallest and definitely the one with the most defined swagger. I knew from TV shows and spending too much time with Ty over coffee that it was standard procedure for the first officer to arrive at a crime scene to be charged with protecting that crime scene, and Ty would take his charge very seriously.

Thank goodness, I didn't touch a thing. I was too busy acting like petrified wood.

I called Ty on his cell phone. In spite of the fact that my ex-husband was the least faithful man on the planet, he'd taught me that law enforcement had a really difficult job. I could see in the slump of his shoulders when he returned from a very horrible crime scene. I could see the pain etched on his face when he dealt with child abuse, and I could tell the weariness in his bones when he had to be outside in cold, rainy, or snowy weather. He was always grateful for a hot drink in cold weather and a cold drink in the blazing sun. So I tried to help the cops out with food-and-drink appreciation as much as possible.

"Ty, I know you're busy, but pass the word to everyone that the hot roast beef special is free to everyone as soon as they have time. If they want to order off the menu instead, it'll be half price."

"Okay. I'll let them know."

"Can I ask how it's going?"

"The BCI boys are taking pictures now. Just as soon as they are done, Hal Manning can . . . uh . . . do his thing. I gotta go, Trixie."

"Sure. Okay," I said, but he was gone.

I felt queasy when Ty said that Hal Manning was going to do "his thing." Hal's "thing" would be to take the body away and do an autopsy.

Anyone with half a brain would know that Mr. Burrows died from a bullet to the chest at close range.

Oh! I wondered what Hal's findings had been when he autopsied Claire Jacobson.

Maybe I could get the results out of Ty—or maybe even Hal himself. His new girlfriend, who was the new editor of the *Lure*, the one who'd written the story on Claire, was rumored to have loosened Hal's lips in more than one way.

Just then, Bettylou, the waitress on duty with Nancy, walked in. "Someone in the diner wants to talk to you. Her name is Joan Paris, and she's the new editor of the *Lure*."

*I was just thinking of her!*

"What does she want with me?"

"She said that she heard you were the one who discovered Mr. Burrows." Bettylou shuddered.

The first thing I'd learned when I moved from Philly to little Sandy Harbor was that news travels faster than a speeding bullet in Sandy Harbor.

A speeding bullet? Eew!

I finished off the order for two triple-decker club sandwiches and heaped a bunch of home-made potato chips that I'd just fried in the middle of the plate. I speared the sandwich wedges with fancy toothpicks, positioned them around the chips, and added a radish rose and a sliced dill pickle to the plate.

Very nice.

Wiping my hands, I walked out to meet Joan Paris. She was the only woman with a briefcase at the counter.

"Joan?" I asked.

"Yes." She held out her hand to shake mine. "And you must be Trixie Matkowski."

"Guilty." Oh, bad word choice again. I blamed the lack of sleep.

Her smile didn't quite ring true, but I took a seat next to her. I didn't want to say anything until I cleared it with Ty. Actually I didn't want to be quoted in the *Lure* at all.

But then again, Joan might have some current information about Claire that maybe she'd slip in during the interview.

"Welcome to Sandy Harbor, Joan. I'm fairly new here, too. This is my first summer as the owner of the Silver Bullet and the cottages."

"I haven't even been here long enough to publish my second issue and already two dead bodies have turned up. After working at the *New York Post*, I thought this job would be like a vacation. Instead Sandy Harbor is like Sandy Horror."

I tried not to crack a smile, I really did, but I couldn't help myself. It felt wonderful to release some tension. We laughed together. Then I felt it was my duty to say that Sandy Harbor was actually a beautiful town with lovely people, and this was just an unfortunate coincidence.

"So, tell me what happened tonight," she said. "Starting with how you discovered the body."

"How about a cup of coffee, Joan? Or a soft drink? Maybe cocoa or tea?" I motioned to Bettylou.

"I'd love some tea," she said.

Bettylou stood before us. "What can I get you ladies?" She poured me a cup of coffee without me even asking her, pulled out two creamers from the pocket of her apron, and moved the sugar dispenser closer to me. A good diner employee remembers how you like your coffee.

"I'd love a cup or a pot of black tea," Joan said. "Even though it's pretty cozy in here, my feet are soaked and I'm chilled to the bone."

"Coming right up," Bettylou said. "How about a slice of banana cream pie? It's homemade by our Amish friend Mrs. Stolfus."

"I'd love it," Joan said.

I took a sip of coffee. It was like the mud at the bottom of the nearby swamp. The cops would love it. Ty would be thrilled since he took his coffee hot and thick. See what I mean about a good diner employee?

"So thick that a horseshoe could float on top," Ty always said.

"Make it two slices of pie, Bettylou," I said.

Joan and I sat in comfortable silence for a while. Then I decided to jump in with both feet. "Claire Jacobson was a friend of mine. I always wondered what happened to her. You did a great research article about her in the paper."

"Thank you."

"Did Hal finish his autopsy?" I asked.

She nodded. "Since the remains were so old, he worked with the state police to confirm his findings."

"Are you going to put the findings in the paper?"

"I can't just yet."

"You mean I have to wait longer still? I really want to know." And I did. When God passed out patience, I was too impatient to wait in line. Maybe I could turn on the charm.

Bettylou took that moment to deliver our pie and Joan's pot of tea. Joan dug right in.

"I can't remember the last time I ate today," she said.

Can't remember the last time she ate? Was she some kind of alien or did she have an eating disorder? I never, ever forgot a meal.

"For heaven's sake, let me make you something. I don't want you to pass out."

"No. The pie will be fine, but thanks for worrying about me." She leaned close to me. "Claire Jacobson was shot."

Even though I was fishing for information from Joan, I wasn't prepared for that.

"Shot, huh?" I mumbled. "Just like Mr. Burrows."

"Oh, Mr. Burrows was shot, too?"

Dammit. I had a big mouth, but she'd probably discover that herself, probably tonight, since she was dating Hal.

I nodded. "Yes. He was shot in the chest, but don't quote me, Joan. Let Hal or someone official tell you."

"Of course." She took a mouthful of banana cream pie. "This is delicious."

"I know, but I can't take the credit for it."

"I saw your ad in the *Lure*. You feature Amish-made baked goods. I like to support the Amish. I used to live by them in Lancaster. Some of my good friends are Amish."

"One of my good friends who I met here, Sarah Stolfus, bakes for us. And I bake, too. And so does Juanita Holgado. And Cindy makes delicious cinnamon rolls. We do everything here, but we are also an outlet for Mrs. Stolfus's goods."

"Nice."

"And I try to use local produce and dairy products."

Joan took out a pen and scribbled something on a steno pad. "I'm going to do a story about that."

*How did we get so far away from Claire Jacobson, and how do I turn the conversation back?*

"Joan, I can't help wondering how Hal managed to discover that Claire was shot so long ago."

"He's good. He's really good." She grinned, and it seemed that she was talking about something other than his coroner skills. "She wasn't in great condition either. The cave was pretty wet, but Hal's good."

"Where was she shot?"

"In the chest."

"Oh." My mind was whirling. Two bodies. Both shot in the chest. Was it a coincidence?

The same wound.

The same cabin.

No. No way. The murders were too far apart. There couldn't be a connection—not in little Podunk, New York.

I shouldn't be so quick to rule it out. Maybe . . .

I'd wanted to discuss the possibility of the murders being connected with Joan, but Ty Brisco would be a better bet.

Just then, Ty pulled open the door of the diner and was shrugging out of his yellow raincoat. He hung it from a peg by the front door. His hat followed.

So did two dozen or more cops, all shedding their rain gear and heading for the side room of my diner where I had tables instead of booths.

"Joan, I'm sorry. I wish we could talk more, but it looks like I have some cooking to do." Standing up, I ate the last bite of my pie. "Maybe we could meet again?"

"I'd like that. I don't have many friends in Sandy Harbor."

"I know how that feels. It's tough to be a new person in a closely knit community. We'll have to get together. I've been thinking of starting a book club. We could meet at the diner once a month or every two weeks. What do you think?"

"I'd love to. Can we make it a mystery book club?"

That was the last thing that I'd want to do. I felt as if I'd been living in a mystery.

"That's fine," I said. "Whatever everyone wants. I was thinking of the books on the bestseller list, no matter what genre."

"That sounds great, too," she said, waving to me as she hurried out the diner, still chewing something. No doubt, she wanted to catch up to Hal Manning.

Ty smiled at me as he passed by. "There're another dozen or so coming behind us."

I mentally ticked off how many hot roast beef specials I could prepare before running out. I thought I'd be okay.

The orders came fast. I was faster. Chelsea had arrived early to help the waitresses. Juanita had arrived early to help me and to get the gossip.

"How did you know?" I asked.

"Police scanner," said Chelsea. "My brother's obsessed with all kinds of cop stuff, but that's a story for another time."

"My nephew John called me," Juanita said. "He works at the gas station where many of the state police fill up their patrol cars. They were talking about Mr. Burrows and the Silver Bullet and how you gave them coffee and pastries. Then he said that you invited all of them to eat the roast beef special for free. I said to John that it's just like you to do something like that, and that I'd better go help you."

Juanita took a breath, then added, "How are you doing, Trixie, considering everything?"

"I'm okay, now that you both are here." I hugged them both. "You both are fabulous. Thanks so much. Of course, I'll pay you double time."

"That's not why I'm here, Trixie," Chelsea said. Juanita sniffed. "Me either, and you know it."

Tears stung my eyes. I hate when that happens. "I'm going to cry. Stop it!"

"Let's get to work," Chelsea said. "Bettylou looks like she's dead on her feet."

I wished Chelsea had picked another word rather than *dead*, but I got her drift.

Juanita and I heated up more gravy, whipped up more mashed potatoes that I just took off the stove, pulled a big pan of stuffing out of the fridge, and blasted it in the pizza oven to heat it in a hurry.

"Family-style salad," I said. "That'll buy us some time, Juanita." Then I realized how ridiculous that sounded. Cops eating salad? Possibly some of the health-conscious ones did. "Nope. Let's give them big bowls of homemade chips. Peels on. You start cutting and I'll start frying."

I peeked out the pass-through window. The cops were seated in groups of four to twelve. Tables were moved around and the noise level was high. After the gruesome scene that they'd just witnessed, and all the caffeine they'd consumed, they seemed ready to let loose.

I decided to make salads after all while the chips were frying. We made several large house salads with various types of baby lettuce and spinach, carrot curls, grape tomatoes, radish roses, and cukes. I shook a healthy portion of Uncle Porky's special house Italian dressing on them, set them on three large trays, and rang the ship's bell for the waitresses.

"They are going to love these," said Bettylou, clipping several orders to the carrel. "But they'll love the chips even more."

She hoisted a tray of salad onto her shoulder. "Most all of those orders are for the hot roast beef, Trixie, but I have a couple of orders for western omelets and burgers and fries."

We pulled out the fries and divided them into plastic baskets that we lined with absorbent paper. Juanita rang the bell.

"I'll get the stuffing out of the oven," I said, pulling the stuffing pan out of the pizza oven. I tested it with a thermometer. "Perfect." Then I slid the pan into the steam table. "The stuffing is good to go, Juanita."

We had time to get organized while everyone ate their salads and munched on the chips.

More orders came in for the special. Others wanted steak, spaghetti and meatballs, club sandwiches, and various omelets. Three people wanted pancakes.

Juanita was already pulling plates from the rack and setting them on the prep table. Two burgers were frying and minced onions and peppers for western omelets were already getting soft in another pan. Two orders of fries were sizzling in a basket of hot vegetable oil.

"I got it," she said. "You take the specials, and I'll do the other orders."

"Okay," I said, spooning stuffing onto the plate, covering it with hot slices of beef and a side of mashed potatoes. For garnish, I put some spiced apples and dill pickles on a lettuce leaf. Unless the order stated otherwise, I ladled gravy over the sandwich and potatoes.

Juanita and I did the Diner Shuffle in the kitchen for over an hour, until Ty Brisco walked in and stood to the side of the steam table.

The man always took my breath away whenever I saw him, but I wasn't looking. No way.

I was still shell-shocked from my divorce from Deputy Doug. It isn't easy to be dumped for a very fertile twentysomething.

But Ty's smile was contagious, and when he smiled at me, I always felt better, no matter what I'd been worrying about.

"Worrying is like rockin' in a rockin' chair. It gives you something to do, but you don't get anywhere," he'd told me a couple of times in that sweet, low Texas drawl of his.

"Trixie, can you spare a moment to come out front? It'll only take a second," Ty said.

"Is everything okay?" I asked, wiping my hands on a towel. I always expected the negative. I was working on changing that, but it was hard when dead bodies seemed to be turning up everywhere.

"Everything's fine," Ty said. "Come on out."

I walked toward him, and he placed his hand on the small of my back.

Not that I noticed. No way.

He led me to the middle of the diner and stopped.

"Ladies and gentlemen, this is Trixie Matkowski, the owner of the Silver Bullet. Let's show her our appreciation for her generosity."

Ty started to clap, and everyone chimed in. Then they started singing. They all knew the words, like some fraternity song. I was too embarrassed to catch a lot of the words, but it was something about the sweetest gal in the precinct, who cooked like a dream and was always waiting for her cop to come home. A little sexist, but okay . . . maybe it was an old song before the women's movement.

As I caught more of the words, I decided that it was a little tongue-in-cheek. In fact, several of the cops couldn't get the words out as they were laughing too hard, probably thinking of how their wife or significant other would react.

At the end of the song, they clapped, and I clapped back at them. They had come into the diner wet and tired, and now they were leaving drier, fed, and maybe less stressed.

I bowed and motioned to Juanita, who was looking through the pass-through window, to join me.

"I'm not the only one who deserves your thanks. My two excellent employees, Juanita and Chelsea, hurried down here to help."

I pointed to Chelsea, who was caught flirting with a cute state trooper. She lowered her head and turned crimson.

"And an extra thanks to Bettylou and Nancy, your waitresses." I took a deep breath. "And I hope that you find out soon what happened to Mr. Burrows, and Claire Jacobson, too."

"We will," Ty said confidently, speaking for the crowd.

I didn't doubt that Ty would move heaven, earth, and especially Sandy Harbor to find the killer or killers.

Little did he know that I was going to do the same thing.

# Chapter 5

*R*eality was setting in. The body of beautiful Claire Jacobson was found not far from my property. Another body was discovered in my cottage, the Jacobson cottage. People were going to catch wind of this and not want to stay.

Or my only customers would be reporters.

Reporters were flocking to the sheriff's department and to the *Sandy Harbor Lure* in droves. It wasn't going to be long before they came to the Point.

I planned to put Clyde and Max in charge of paparazzi removal.

Ty walked me back to the double doors leading into the kitchen, his hand warm on my back.

"Ty, I'm wondering . . . Do you think that Mr. Burrows and Claire Jacobson were killed by the same person? I mean, they both were connected to Cottage Eight. That couldn't be a coincidence, could it?"

His hand dropped from my back, and, if he had false teeth, those would have dropped, too.

"That's kind of a stretch." He shrugged. "Maybe there's a connection. We don't know yet."

"Would you tell me when you find out?"

He hesitated. "Trixie—"

"Ty, I owe Claire. She was years older than I when she went missing, but I owe her. She was good to me. I want to find out what happened to her."

"I hope you don't plan on doing anything stupid. Leave the investigating to the professionals."

He stepped closer to me, and I had to crane my neck to look up. I'm not a short person. I'm five foot eight. But he was trying to intimidate me.

Good luck with that.

"Trixie, you manage your diner, and I'll look for the killer or killers."

"Are you saying that the little woman should keep to the kitchen?" I crossed my arms in front of my chest. Okay, that was a cheap shot, but it was a good shot.

"I didn't say that, and you know it," he snapped.

"Let me help you investigate." I'd made a promise in that cabin when I came across Burrows, and I intended to keep it.

"Do you see all those people out there? The ones that you fed and who mainlined your coffee all night? They will all work on this case. And Claire's case, too. What can you offer?"

"I care, Ty. I care."

"They do, too."

"Not as much as I do."

"Stay out of it. And you'd better not interfere with the official investigation." He spoke through gritted teeth, a habit of his now and then.

I'd just have to do it alone. On my own. I walked away from him, back to the kitchen. It looked as though he was going home.

Since I got married to a cheater at the tender age of twenty-one, I'd been on my own.

And alone. Even when I was married to Deputy Doug, I felt alone.

Finding one or two murderers should be a piece of cake.

"Trixie, let me walk you out," Juanita said. "Cindy Sherlock is here. I just saw her car. She can help us clean up this mess. You deserve some rest."

Cindy, the other cook, had come, too. I just loved my staff!

How could I leave when there were dirty dishes everywhere, stacked in precarious piles by the industrial dishwasher? The machine would be working overtime tonight.

"I should help with the dishes."

"No. We'll take care of everything. I insist," Juanita said. "You go and rest. You're frazzled from the diner's extra customers and from stumbling onto a crime scene. You're not thinking clearly."

Once outside, Juanita stopped. "Trixie, how

about hiring someone to bus tables? Then that person could load and run the dishwasher."

"I totally agree, Juanita. Wish I'd thought of it. I'll call Joan Paris and put an ad in the *Lure* for a bus person/dishwasher." That would give me an excuse to press her for more information and make plans for the book club.

"Wonderful. Clyde and Max do help with the dishes most of the time, but they are going to be busy when all the cottages are full."

I nodded. "I'll take care of it immediately."

Juanita went back into the diner, and instead of going right to the Big House, I walked to Cottage Eight.

The sun was shining. The lake was sparkling and was a perfect turquoise color. The recent rain had made the sand on the beach perfectly flat. There were no footprints on it.

I stopped in my tracks. Cottage Eight was wrapped like a Christmas present in bright yellow tape with big black letters that said CRIME SCENE, DO NOT CROSS.

Now, that ought to attract a plethora of renters—not!

Who on earth would want to bring their family on a vacation with a "crime scene cottage" smack dab in the middle of their campground?

It'd certainly put a damper on their fun.

I got my cell phone out of my pocket and phoned Ty Brisco.

"Yeah, Trixie?"

"How long will the crime scene tape be wrapped around Cottage Eight?"

"No idea."

"C'mon, Ty. Give me some sort of time frame. I have renters coming in."

"Sorry. I don't have a clue. The tape will be there until it's decided that we have every bit of evidence from it that we need."

"Wow. Way to go with information, Ty."

"Your help will not speed up the investigation, so find some patience behind Door Number Three and let the professionals do it."

I wanted to toss my phone into Lake Ontario. No, I wanted to toss Ty Brisco into Lake Ontario.

"Yeah, right," I said like a Valley girl, and clicked him off.

I looked at Mr. Farnsworth's bait shop that was next to the diner. Ty was renting the upstairs apartment, and I could see him looking out of the big window toward me.

Glancing up, I saw Ty wave at me. I was so ticked that I didn't even feel like lifting my hand in response.

As I walked to the Big House, I got to thinking. To be fair, I should notify the upcoming renters about the murder that took place and about the taped-up crime scene cottage.

My stomach sank. I didn't want to do that.

The next thing I should do was get started on the investigation, but what?

I walked the grass in the vicinity of my motion

sensor light, thinking that I could discover footprints where I'd seen someone running. Or maybe
even tire tracks. I knew I'd heard a car start that
night. Maybe it was the getaway car.

Maybe I shouldn't disturb any tracks.

I'd be careful.

Walking past the end of my property, I saw
grass matted down in two tracks—tracks that a
car would make. I walked farther, searching the
area for who knows what, but hoping that I'd find
a clue.

The car had driven through a field that was adja-
cent to my property. Wildflowers were blooming—
sweet peas and wild daisies—but mostly there was
just thick grass. I followed the tracks, and I didn't
have to walk far to see that the car had driven
through the field up to the highway.

I walked back to where the person would have
gotten into the car and crouched down to look at
the wet mud. The police weren't here that I knew
of, having concentrated their efforts mostly on the
cottage.

If I found something the police had missed, I
could take it as a sign that I was supposed to continue my investigation, no matter what Ty said.

Carefully, I stepped, looking for something . . .
anything.

Finally I saw something.

I could see the bottom prints of the shoes that
she wore; I'd decided it was a "she" because the

footprint was too small to be that of a man. They weren't heels, and I ruled out jogging shoes because there weren't any treads. My guess was they were flats. And the woman wasn't very large, because she didn't sink very far into the mud.

That was my nonprofessional opinion.

Carefully, I walked around the shoe prints.

"Trixie Matkowski, what the hell are you doing?"

I jumped and let out a scream that would make the seagulls drop from the sky in terror. I was going to have a sore throat tomorrow from all this.

"Ty, you scared the snot out of me."

"Good. You have no business over here."

"I was just going for a walk."

"Yeah, right."

"And you, Deputy Brisco, were watching me out your apartment window."

He slipped his thumbs into the loops of his jeans and stood there looking casual, yet intimidating, yet gorgeous.

And totally sexy. Not that I noticed.

"Okay," he said. "Tell me what you're doing here."

"I thought I saw a person running away last night. The motion sensor lights on my porch went on, but because of the sheets of rain that fell, it was too dark to see anything much. Then I thought I heard a car start, but no headlights went on."

"And you found the tracks of the car."

"And a woman's footprints." I pointed. "They

are too small to be a man's. She wore flats without treads."

"And you walked around, disturbing the scene."

"Not really. I gave the scene a wide berth."

"But this *is* the scene, Trixie. Didn't you see the tape I put up around this area?"

I wisely kept my mouth shut.

He took out his cell phone and ordered a litany of cop stuff, from the crime scene van to cops who could make casts of car tracks and footprints.

"The rain last night might work in our favor. Then again, it might not. We'll have to see what the cast guys can turn up."

"Okay. Fine. I'll tell Juanita and Cindy to get the coffee going."

He sighed. "That's not necessary. They won't be here that long."

"Okay."

"And in the meantime, I'll take your official statement at the office. I should have done it last night, since you found the body. That was my mistake, and I hope to rectify it as soon as possible. I'll drive us both downtown."

"I told you all about this last night."

"I know, but I never expected you to duck under my crime scene tape and walk around here before I got the crime scene people back during the daylight."

I groaned, thinking about watching him type. "I need to let Blondie out."

"I'll let her out. In fact, let's take her with us. I haven't seen her in a while."

Shoot. It was hard to stay mad at someone who loved my dog as much as I did.

We walked toward the Big House, and I got Blondie's leash and handed it to Ty. Ty and I had pretty much shared Blondie since she showed up at the back door of the diner one night along with a blizzard. She had been so wet and cold that ice had formed on her fur.

She was hungry and thirsty, and we took care of her. Finally Ty adopted her. Somehow Blondie then adopted me. Probably because she knew that I needed her.

That was okay with Ty, but he always found time to play with her and take her for walks.

"Let me freshen up," I said.

"That's fine. I'll direct the crime scene people to the field in the meantime."

I washed my face, ran a brush through my hair, put some makeup on, and added a spritz of gardenia perfume, my favorite scent. Maybe that would help detract from the circles under my eyes from being up all night.

Just as soon as I was ready, his big black SUV pulled up in front of the Big House. Blondie was in the backseat. I climbed up into the passenger side.

We drove for a while; then I had to ask before I burst like a Macy's Thanksgiving balloon. "Would you please tell me something about the Burrows case?"

"He was shot."

"Oh, really, Wyatt Earp? Like I couldn't tell that?"

I waited for a couple of beats. "How about Claire Jacobson's case?"

"Nothing yet."

"Come on, Ty. I'm going to go bankrupt without cottage renters, and no one is going to want to look at all that crime scene tape and know that there was a murder there."

"Didn't you just ding me for being shallow when I said something like that?" he asked.

"Yeah." Oops.

"We are working on both murders, but these things take time."

"I don't have a lot of time. There're only two weeks before Memorial Day. That's when the season officially begins. Throw me a bone, will you, please?"

"Okay, okay." He took a deep breath. "We think that someone didn't like what he was writing."

"Oh, come on, Deputy. That's totally obvious. Besides, his scrapbook and all his papers were gone." I didn't realize until this moment how much of the scene I'd observed while standing frozen in the cottage.

"Scrapbook? What scrapbook?"

"I saw it earlier, when I got the bus people away from him, but that's another story."

"I want to hear that story. Did you see what was in the scrapbook?"

"Not really. I was in the doorway looking in. I

did see a lot of newspaper clippings, and they were really yellow. It was your typical old scrapbook with big beige construction paper pages."

"That's interesting, but what was he doing?"

"Writing. And he wanted peace and quiet and to be left alone."

"Did you see that typewriter of his? What's that about?" Ty asked.

"I saw him lug it into the cottage. It should be in a museum."

"It ended up upside down on the floor. The murderer must have done that."

I nodded. "When I peeked into the cottage earlier, I saw that he had a piece of paper hanging down from the roller. It was gone. Every piece of paper was gone."

"If we could somehow discover what he was writing about, that might help us find who killed him since they seemed to have targeted it."

"And since the evidence is gone, that's going to be tough," I supplied.

He nodded and made a left turn onto Main Street. The Sandy Harbor Sheriff's Department was just ahead on the left. The construction of the building was like the library, all white and gleaming with two large pillars in the front.

It was an imposing building for only three sheriff's deputies, so they put other county offices in it.

I'd been there before and loved how my footsteps clinked on the marble floors and how they echoed throughout the building.

Unfortunately, I had rubber soles on my shoes. Darn.

Ty's footsteps would have to do. He wore cowboy boots, and the echo was divine.

He unlocked the door to his office, and I couldn't procrastinate any longer.

"Ty, please let me type my statement as I speak. I don't have the time or patience to watch you type with your two fingers and a thumb."

"Hey, I'm pretty fast," he said, in his slow Texas drawl.

"You stink. I haven't got all day. I have to walk over to the *Lure*'s office and put in an ad for a bus person for the Silver Bullet."

"A bus person?"

"To bus tables and run the dishwasher. Then they have to put the silver, glasses, and dishes away."

"I've got the perfect kid in mind for you. Let me call him later, and you can interview him."

"Great!" Well, this would solve one of my problems, but I still wanted to see if Joan had any more information from Hal.

"He's had some difficulties, but he'll be ideal once he learns the job. You just have to be patient with him, Trixie. You'd be perfect for him, also. So would the other ladies who work in the diner."

"I'll give anyone a chance. What's his name?"

"Ray Meyerson. And his parents will be thrilled. Ray's been getting into a little trouble lately—just

petty stuff. Dad's a farmer, and Ray just doesn't cotton to it. Mom doesn't work outside the home."

I tried to set aside Ty's sexy Texas accent and get to the heart of what I wanted to know. "What kind of petty stuff did he do?"

"He's a juvenile and that information is not for public knowledge."

"Ty!"

"Sorry. I'll let him tell you himself if he wants to, but it was nothing assaultive or of a sexual nature."

"Fine."

Ty did let me type as I talked, and I went into detail about how I'd watched Mr. Burrows move into Eight and seen him carrying the ancient typewriter in.

Ty prompted me with questions.

Then I related the scenario about the bus people who thought that the article in the *Lure* and Cottage Eight were grand clues on their mystery tour. Then I typed officially what I'd noticed when I peeked into Mr. Burrows's cottage.

Last was the part about me looking out my bathroom window and what I saw and didn't see the night of his murder.

Finally we were done. I signed the affidavit and he signed as witness.

I took a deep breath and stretched.

The phone rang, and Ty reached for it. "Sandy Harbor Sheriff's Department, Deputy Ty Brisco."

So official. So cop-ish.

He reached for a yellow legal pad on his desk, and couldn't quite get it from his standing position, since I hadn't yet moved from his desk.

I handed it to him along with a pen.

"Uh-huh. Yep. I see." He scribbled on the yellow paper. The pen didn't work. I handed him another as if I were an ER nurse and he were the surgeon.

"Yeah. Um . . ." He wrote, and I didn't move.

I knew he was noncommittal because I was there, and he was getting information about one of the cases.

Casually, I tried to look at his notes, but he moved the pad away from me.

Busted.

*C'mon, Ty. Talk!*

I stood and walked around the room, looking at the bulletin board—boring—but I had an ulterior motive in mind: I wanted to see the caller ID on the phone console, but I'd need binoculars.

Oh! A box of tissues. I leaned over and casually pulled out a tissue, throwing in a sniffle for good acting measure. Score! The call was from the New York State Police BCI—Bureau of Criminal Investigation—the major forensic folks in Albany, New York.

Ty raised a perfect black eyebrow. Okay, so he knew what I was doing with the tissue ploy.

I shrugged. My fingers were itching to slip that yellow legal pad out of his hand.

"Hang on a sec, Lieutenant. Just hang on." Ty

said, turning to me. "Trixie, would you mind waiting in the waiting room?"

"I don't want to wait in the waiting room."

He pointed to his handcuffs on his belt. "Go."

Okay, I went to the waiting room and took a seat on a totally uncomfortable metal chair. Maybe I could eavesdrop.

The big tall ceilings and the marble floors and walls that I had loved so much before were an acoustical disaster. Ty was chirping away to the lieutenant from BCI, but I couldn't make out a word.

I listened at the keyhole. There was probably some law against putting an ear, complete with fake gold earrings in the shape of slices of pizza, on an official keyhole of the Sandy Harbor Sheriff's Department, but I did it anyway.

Yes, I stooped that low. All I could think of was Cottage Eight wrapped in yellow tape, and the tenants who would cancel when they found out about the recent murder there.

And then I thought of Claire and my promise to Burrows.

The mumbling stopped, and Ty finally hung up. I stood up and tried to get the circulation back in my numb butt.

The door opened and Ty walked out. I studied his face, but I couldn't figure out anything.

This day was turning out to be a bust.

"Well?" I asked.

"Well what?"

Suddenly I was sick of playing games with him. I understood that there were some things that he had to keep confidential, but sooner or later, the small-town tongues would wag and I'd find out.

I just wanted to find out now and right from the source.

"Never mind. I'm tired of nagging you for information. I'll hear it on the grapevine like everyone else. Let's go. Take me home."

I gave him the frozen treatment. I didn't talk. I looked out the window of his SUV and watched the scenery go by.

Realizing that I couldn't depend on Ty for information, I decided I'd have to make time to talk to my new friend, Joan Paris. Maybe Hal Manning talked to the BCI and did some pillow-talking with Joan.

I'd ask her to lunch. Regardless of the case, she needed a friend, and I liked her. I could show her around and introduce her to some of my new friends in the area. We could see if Antoinette Chloe Brown's place was open yet. I could tell ACB that I served her mystery bus people and we could plan for the book club.

Or we could always go to the Crossroads Restaurant, Laura Tingsley's place. Laura was the mayor's wife, she was a gracious First Lady, and the restaurant was her White House.

I felt so helpless about these crimes, and I didn't like that feeling.

There was one thing I could do . . . but it would

probably be at least a misdemeanor, maybe even a felony if I got caught. And since Ty tended to pop up wherever I went, I might as well pack my toothbrush now for when Judge Cunningham of County Court sentenced me to the real Big House.

State prison or not, I was going to slip under the crime scene tape. I'd take it apart board by board if I had to, but I was going to find out if Cottage Eight held any secrets.

# Chapter 6

$B$y the time we turned off Main Street, the sky had darkened and the wind blew. Once we were out of downtown, the thunder rolled in and the lightning flashed, the wind picked up more and the rain hit. Just as we turned off the highway onto the no-name road that led to the diner, the rain was looking like Niagara Falls.

Lake Ontario was choppy. If this wind kept up, the waves were going to be three feet high.

I loved watching storms over the lake. The sky never looked the same twice, and right now it was an angry grayish purple.

I was definitely looking forward to snuggling under my favorite comforter and sitting on my porch and watching the storm.

But first, I had to make a run for it to the Big House.

Ty stopped his SUV to let me off. I wasn't going to say anything to him, fully content in keeping the deep freeze going, but then I decided I was being juvenile.

"Thank you for the ride." Icicles could hang from my every word.

"Thanks for all the typing, Trixie. It saved us both a ton of time." He nodded in that sincere cowboy way he had, as if he were nodding for his bull to be let out of the chute.

"No problem."

"What are you going to do now?" he asked.

"Watch the storm from my porch. Maybe I'll even fall asleep."

He said something, but the rumble of thunder drowned out his words.

"What?" I asked. "I couldn't hear you."

"I said that it sounds great. If I bring the coffee, can I join you?"

It was hard to say no when he asked so sweetly and volunteered to bring coffee, which he'd just get from the Silver Bullet anyway.

He obviously didn't get my frozen message.

Maybe I had to be even more blunt.

"For Pete's sake, Ty, I'm freaking mad at you."

"Because I won't spill everything to you about the investigations?"

This man was an investigator? A deputy sheriff? *Someone, quick, buy him a clue!*

"I don't want to read about things that concern me in the *Sandy Harbor Lure*! I'm not asking for all the confidential details . . . just a couple of them so I can get my business going again."

"I'll get us some coffee and a couple of donuts, and we'll talk."

I looked at him suspiciously. "Really? We'll talk?"

"What I can tell you, I'll tell you. But it isn't going to be much."

"Hurry up, then, Ty."

He left to go up to the diner. I got a couple of comforters and headed out to the back porch, or should I call it the front porch because it faced the water and had a separate entrance?

Anyway, it had a fabulous view of Lake Ontario and the waves that were now rolling in. The rain rapped on the roof and the brick pavers that led to the back . . . er . . . front porch. The air smelled wet and earthy with a touch of fish or maybe it was a touch of worms.

The flag flying from the pole in the middle of the lawn was whipping in the wind. The purple gazing ball, in the middle of a raised garden where I'd just planted petunias and marigolds, looked like a shiny golf ball on a tee. In this wind, it could soar off any second for a par.

I got comfortable in my Adirondack chair and tucked the comforter around me. Taking several deep breaths, I closed my eyes and meditated, my breath keeping time with the waves.

I don't know how long I drifted off, but when I awoke there was a large covered take-out cup on the end table next to me, along with a white bag containing my donuts.

Ty wasn't there.

I took a sip of coffee. It was ice-cold. How long was I out? So much for our talk.

Gathering up my comforter, I somehow got myself out of the Adirondack chair and stood on the porch for a while to get my thirtysomething bones time to lock into place.

I looked at Cottage Eight for a while, then looked up at Ty's apartment above the bait shop. I couldn't see him in the expansive windows that he liked to look out from or his porch that jutted out onto the lakeside.

Maybe he went back to work.

That meant it was time for me to break into Cottage Eight.

I went inside, microwaved the coffee to heat it, and took a couple of sips. Nice. I peeked at the donuts—chocolate with cream filling. Perfect.

I took another sip and reluctantly set the coffee down to drink later. I didn't want to take it with me and spill coffee on the crime scene.

Out of the corner of my eye, I saw my answering machine blinking. I hadn't checked it for a while, so I hit the button even though I expected it wouldn't be good news.

It wasn't.

Two messages, two cancellations. Cottage Ten and Cottage Three. They knew about Mr. Burrows's murder. One man "didn't want to expose his children to that kind of thing" and another, a woman, said that she was scared of the restless ghosts of murder victims.

This was just what I was afraid of. Well, I wasn't afraid of restless ghosts, but I was afraid of more cancellations.

Time for me to spring into action.

I scrounged up another key to Cottage Eight, as either Ty or the state police had taken Mr. Burrows's. I grabbed a flashlight, remembering that the newly painted forest green shutters had all been closed and hooked shut by the cops.

Instead of walking right to Eight, I went to the end of the line of cottages. If Ty was watching, he would think that I was going to Twelve. If I walked close to the front of all the cottages, maybe he couldn't see me heading for Eight.

Why didn't I just head for the back of Eight and then the left side of it to get to the front?

I grunted at my lack of Nancy Drew genes.

I ran up the three steps to Eight and hoped the crime scene tape would stretch as I opened the door.

My heart pounded when a couple of the strands of yellow tape snapped. I held my breath and sucked my stomach in to squeeze in. If only I could do something with my D-cup boobs.

I was inside.

I closed the door and clicked on the flashlight, glad that I'd brought it. I looked around at the mess, particularly the grayish dust all over. What on earth?

Oh! Fingerprint dust.

The cops had left the typewriter on the floor where I saw it before, lying facedown. I stared at the bloodstain, my inner neat freak wondering how I'd ever get it off the plank floor.

Poor Mr. Burrows.

I hadn't noticed before when I was standing in the cottage, paralyzed, that there were no dirty dishes around. Probably Clyde or Max had taken them away or maybe the police had. I sure hoped that Mr. Burrows's last dinner was enjoyable.

Looking around the little cottage, I tried to see it with fresh eyes. The biggest room held a full kitchen against the wall, a wooden table, and four chairs, and there was a twin bed in the corner.

A small bedroom held a queen bed, a nightstand, and a dresser.

Another bedroom had two double bunk beds.

The bathroom had a shower stall with a blue curtain, no tub, another dresser, a closet, a toilet, a sink, and a medicine cabinet. It was the old-style medicine cabinet with a mirror on the front and made of white metal.

And it, too, was covered in fingerprint dust.

I opened the medicine cabinet by the corner. There were just some cheap plastic shavers, a can of shaving gel, and a plastic container of deodorant.

The medicine cabinet was rusty on the bottom, and it looked as though someone had pushed the rust with either a finger or some kind of tool.

Or maybe it was the natural way of rust, but I didn't think so.

This medicine cabinet needed to be replaced. I wished that Juanita's cousin who had prepared the cottages for me would have said something.

I shut the mirrored door, and the whole thing slanted. It must be missing a screw.

I made a mental note to tell Clyde to replace it before it fell off the wall and someone got hurt. Then again, there was no rush. Who'd want to rent this cottage when the word got out that a murder had been committed here?

Going back into the main room, I pulled out a chair from the table and sat down.

The old typewriter was still on the floor upside down. I wanted to put it upright or even move it onto the table the way Mr. Burrows had had it, but I didn't dare.

I studied the inside of the cottage. It was paneled in white wainscoting and throughout the years guests had etched messages into the walls—mostly their initials or their last name and a date. There were some hearts with initials.

I remember Uncle Porky hating that his tenants scratched up his cottages, but Aunt Stella thought it was fun. She said that it was a tradition—a type of history. She said, "Look at all the pioneers who wrote on Signature Rock in Wyoming. Our cottages are a history of those who stayed with us."

Uncle Porky didn't agree, so he had Clyde and Max paint the wainscoting every couple of years.

Smiling, I remembered etching *Trixie M. loves Tim P.* underneath the sink in Cottage Four. That was Timmy Preston, our paperboy, who had been at least a freshman in high school, an older man. I had such a crush on him.

I wondered if Claire Jacobson ever scratched her initials onto this cottage.

With my trusty flashlight, I started inspecting the wall by the door. The mystery bus woman was right to carry around a magnifying glass. I'd have to find one.

With any luck, the hardware or hunting store in town carried magnifying glasses, or maybe the dollar store would have them. If not, I'd have to drive to Watertown or Syracuse, where there were more stores.

Until then, I read every scratch, square inch by square inch. *G. K. loves J. C. JACK & ROSE married 1940. Marry me, Ginny B. Michele loves Martin. I hate you, Mary C. Peg loves Lance 1997* . . . On and on it went.

I kept reading and made it to the kitchen window before I sat down again. My eyes were getting tired. Maybe the daylight would be better, but that wasn't going to happen until the cops released the cottage.

What could the cops have missed?

Would Mr. Burrows have etched something into the wall?

No way. He didn't seem the type. It was more of a kid thing anyway.

I gasped. My heart started racing. Would Mr. Burrows have stayed in this cottage when he was a kid? Was that why he asked for Eight?

A lot of people who returned requested the same cottage year after year. Maybe Mr. Burrows really did stay here when he was young. That would explain his obsession with the cottage.

I'd look for his initials, too. Or maybe he'd left a message.

Maybe it was a dumb thing to do, but what else did I have to go on?

I got up, flashlight in hand, and went back to the bathroom. The loose, rusty medicine cabinet was niggling at my brain. I didn't remember the rust being so worn down when I'd inspected the cottage for tourist season.

Did I dare move it? It was already dusted for prints, so I thought it was okay to touch. I removed Mr. Burrows's stuff from the cabinet and set it on the dresser. Then I gave the cabinet a little push to the right, then a bigger push to the right. The cabinet that used to hang vertical was now horizontal.

There was a hole in the wall! And etchings.

I studied the printing from several angles, moving my flashlight in different directions.

There it was: CJ. It had to be Claire Jacobson!

I looked for more, ran my finger over the wood. *C.J. loves B.*

*Damn. I couldn't make out the initial of the last name. It was painted over! Who did Claire love back then?*

"B" who?

I kept looking for more, but nothing. Then I shone my flashlight down the hole. Nope. Couldn't see a thing.

"Beatrix Matkowski, what the hell are you doing in here?"

I jumped, scared out of my wits. My heart pounded in my chest like the dough mixer on high.

Why did he keep doing that?

Turning, I looked into the furious face of Deputy Sheriff Ty Brisco. His hands were on his hips, his legs were spread apart, and he was biting his lip. The vein in his neck seemed ready to pop out of his skin.

"No one calls me Beatrix except my aunt, Aunt Beatrix."

"I don't give a damn." He took a couple of deep breaths, looking up at the rough-hewn beams and boards of the ceiling.

I think he was praying.

"Ty, I couldn't sit still and do nothing."

"I believe that we had this discussion before. I can't believe that you crossed this crime scene tape, too. Didn't we just have this discussion? Have you lost your mind?"

"I'm losing business. That's what I'm losing." Yeah, okay, that was true, but in my heart of hearts I wanted to get to the bottom of both murders.

His nostrils flared like a rodeo bull's. He pointed to the door. "Out."

"I found something, Ty. Listen to me. I found initials behind the medicine cabinet. And there's a hole in the wall. I wonder if something was hidden there. Maybe something was dropped down the hole."

He didn't budge, but his shoulders relaxed a bit.

"Don't you want to see what I found? It's amazing. I think it could be a clue."

"Burrows?"

"I don't know. Maybe." I shrugged. "But maybe Claire Jacobson."

"Let's see what you found." He walked toward me.

I moved the medicine cabinet and showed him Claire's initials, and the lone *B*. He didn't seem impressed. He was more impressed by the ragged hole in the wall.

"Why would she put her initials behind the cabinet?" he asked.

"Maybe the cabinet wasn't there twenty-five years ago. Maybe it was hung later. Or maybe Claire thought it was a secretive, fun thing to do. She probably didn't want anyone to see her name linked with a guy. You know how parents can be or siblings . . . They tease, or so I hear."

What did I know? I was an only child.

"Did Claire Jacobson have any siblings?" Ty asked. "I can't remember from all the reports." He pointed at my flashlight. "Can I borrow that?"

I handed it to him. "Hmm . . . you know, I think she had a brother, a younger brother. I remember . . ."

I paused, reaching way back to a cobwebbed corner of my memory. "Yes, a younger brother." It was all coming back to me. "His name was Phillip, I think, but they called him Phil. That last summer, he was six or seven, I'd guess. Phil would rather sit at the picnic table and scribble or color, and he hated to walk on sand with bare feet, and he didn't particularly like the water. He'd only go in the lake if he could get onto a vinyl raft on the shore so he wouldn't get wet, and Claire would float him in."

Ty peered down the hole in the wall. "Interesting. What kid doesn't like splashing in the water?"

"Phil didn't. He was kind of fussy and liked to be by himself."

"Poor boy. He missed out on being a kid."

"That's what Claire thought, too. She tried to get him out of his shell. She was so good with him. It was almost like she was his mother instead of his sister."

Ty tried another angle with the flashlight as he looked down the hole. "Didn't his parents pay any attention to Phil?"

"They were quite a bit older and were always off fishing."

"Too bad, but it seems like Claire was a great older sister."

"She was, and Phil adored her." I leaned against the dresser. "You know, Phil had the strangest eyes. They were such a pale light blue. I've never seen eyes that color except for—"

Why hadn't I made the connection before?

I sank to the floor.

Ty must have heard the thump when my butt connected with the wooden floor. He spun around. "Trixie, wha—? Are you okay?"

"Pale blue eyes. David Burrows and Phil Jacobson. They have—had—the same color eyes."

"Coincidental. Probably a good chunk of the population has light blue eyes."

"Pale blue!"

"Okay, pale blue."

"And Mr. Burrows was fussy and private, and he'd been here before."

"So have I," Ty said. "That's another coincidence. My family vacationed here since I was seven years old until my baby brother started college. Then I returned at least once a year for the salmon."

Coincidences? It was more than that. Little things were starting to add up.

"I think that David Burrows was really Phil Jacobson."

"I can check it out."

"Will you let me know, Ty?"

"I think I can give you that information, but I'm not quite sure. I'll have to wait until it's officially released."

Wyatt Earp was getting on my last nerve. Law enforcement work was so darn slow.

"What about his car, Ty? I'm sure you ran the registration and everything on his car."

"It was a rental. He rented it under David Burrows."

"But doesn't the rental company make you show your license. Didn't he do that?"

Ty hesitated. "Yeah, we checked all that. He was licensed under David Burrows."

"But anyone can get a fake license, right?"

"Not just anyone."

"But it can be done."

He shrugged. "Of course it can be done."

"And David Burrows appeared just when Claire's body was found, or should I say that Phil Jacobson appeared right when his sister Claire's body was found? And he specifically asked for Cottage Eight, Ty. More coincidences?"

"Maybe not."

Hurrah! "I think you're starting to think like me."

"That'll be the day." He grinned in that cowboy way of his, all white teeth and twinkling turquoise eyes.

"I think that Phil was investigating Claire's death, and obviously someone wanted to stop him." I paused as I realized what I was suggesting. "The killer. One killer."

"I think so, too."

"You do?"

"Yeah, but it's just a gut feeling. There's no real proof yet."

I was on a roll. Looking at the hole in the wall, I couldn't contain myself any longer. If I ruined the crime scene, I might as well pack for Bedford Hills, but this was my cottage and my hole, and the whole hole was missed by the cops.

Moving Ty aside, I put both of my hands on the ragged edges of the wainscoting and gave four yanks.

"Uh, Trixie . . . ," Ty warned, but it was half-hearted. He wanted to see what was in the wall as much as I did. He probably could have done the same thing that I was doing, but Ty did everything by the book and would call back the crime scene people.

But not me.

I gave another yank but couldn't move the wood. Frustrated, I kicked it with my sneakered foot and it splintered.

Ty pushed me aside and gave it a kick himself. The boards splintered more and we both pulled, tossing the mess of wood onto the floor.

"There's nothing there," he said. "Damn."

"Hand me the flashlight, please."

He handed me the flashlight and I knelt down. There was a little piece of paper in the corner of one of the vertical two-by-six boards where it met the floor.

Nervously, I picked up the paper.

"It's a picture, Ty. A picture!" I looked at it, and Ty looked over my shoulder. "What on earth?"

"Is that what I think it is?" Ty whistled long and low.

# Chapter 7

"A sonogram," Ty said.

It was faded and had some water damage, but there was no doubt that it was a sonogram. Claire had been pregnant?

I shook my head. "It was hidden in the wall. Probably Claire hid it. Maybe she was going to retrieve it later but never got the chance." I was still staring at the photo in my hand.

"That's my guess."

"I don't think so, Ty. Maybe a guy hid it in the wall."

He shook his head. "It isn't something that a guy would do. He might show the picture around to show off that he's a stud, but it's a girl thing to hide it like that."

"There's something written on the back. I can barely make it out. It looks like Dr. Edward Francis, August eight—no, it's August three—nine a.m."

"Must be her next appointment," Ty said.

"Then all we have to do is find out who had an

appointment with Dr. Francis at nine on August third, twenty-five years ago."

"You're thinking that Claire Jacobson might have been pregnant when she died, aren't you?"

"Yes." I thought back. The Claire of my childhood fantasies would have saved herself for Prince Charming. But hadn't I learned the real world is never as perfect as you thought when you were a child?

Maybe she'd met someone and loved him. No. She was so sweet and trusting, he probably seduced her.

I was probably reacting to my very Catholic upbringing that was drummed into our heads by an army of St. Mary Marys: No rolling up the waistband of your school uniform to make your skirt shorter. Your green knee socks must go to the knee. You will be fined a quarter for the mission if you don't wear the standard black and white saddle shoes, and make sure you polish them. And no sex without marriage.

"I'll phone Hal Manning and see if he had a clue about Claire being pregnant during the autopsy. If he did, he would have told me about it," Ty said.

If that sonogram belonged to Claire, she would have been seventeen, pregnant, and all alone. Yet she never stopped smiling. She had to be in love.

The roll of thunder made me jump. Another storm was coming in. Thunder flashed through the cottage, and I heard a noisy creak of wood. It was probably the shutters outside, but I suddenly felt uneasy. I was with the toughest cop in the whole state, but not even Ty Brisco could stop a speeding bullet.

Suddenly I wanted to get out of Cottage Eight and all of its secrets.

"I'm out of here, Ty."

"I'll second that." He opened the door for me and lifted the yellow tape. I ducked under it. He tried to make it taut against the door, but he didn't have the tools.

"What are you going to do now?" he asked.

"Tired of watching me?"

"Yes, actually, I am. I was just hoping you'd save me the trouble."

"I think I'm going to make an appointment with Dr. Francis. I suddenly feel sick."

"I've never heard of Dr. Francis, but I think I'll go with you."

"I work alone," I said.

"The hell you do."

"It was worth a try."

We walked to his SUV and drove back downtown.

The one and only doctor's office in town was on Broadway Street and had a white and black sign out front: Dr. Fayton Huff. It was located in an old Victorian house, not unlike mine, but it had more gingerbread trim and was painted in various hues of lavender and yellow. Pretty.

"I've heard of Dr. Huff, but I haven't met him. I haven't found it necessary to go to a doctor," Ty said.

"Me either. Thank goodness."

"Did Dr. Huff replace Dr. Francis?" Ty flashed his badge to the young receptionist with the moussed crown of hair on her head.

"In a way. Dr. Francis passed away several years ago. Then Dr. Morgan took over. Then Dr. Fineburg. Then Dr. Huff took over that practice."

"Is Dr. Huff available?" Ty asked, looking around at the very empty waiting room.

"No, he's not. Sorry. Right now he's golfing at Twin Trees. Today's his day off."

Ty leaned on the counter and turned on the charm. "Well, darlin', you seem like you run this place by your little self. I'd like to look at one of Dr. Francis's old files. The name is Claire Jacobson."

"I can't do that, Deputy Brisco. Our files are confidential. You know that. I'd need a court order."

"It's impossible to find a judge now." He checked his watch. "It's almost four o'clock on a Friday. I couldn't get a judge until probably Monday." He sighed, and I knew that Ty wanted to follow this clue—and fast.

But I wanted to follow it up even faster.

I read the receptionist's name tag. Shannon Shannon?

I cleared my throat just to get her attention away from Ty. "Miss Shannon, Claire Jacobson is deceased. Surely, she won't object."

She ignored me and smiled at Ty. "I'll have to ask Dr. Huff, but I can assure you that he won't release anything without a court order."

"Then why ask him?" Honestly, I hated rules when they got in my way to get something done quickly. "Are all your records digitized?"

"Huh?" said the diligent Miss Shannon.

"Are they all on the computer?"

"Not the old ones. They're still on paper. In files. In filing cabinets." She still hadn't taken her eyes off Ty.

Ty leaned over and grinned, flashing two perfect rows of whiter-than-white teeth. "Where are the old ones, darlin'?"

"Um . . . ," she said. "I don't know if I should tell you that." But she immediately looked at the door to her left. On the door was a sign that read RESTROOMS ARE DOWNSTAIRS.

I decided that I had to go to the restroom.

Nudging Ty, I said, "Officer Brisco, please excuse me. I'll be right back. I have to hit the ladies' room, if Miss Shannon doesn't mind."

She waved me away as her phone rang. I could hear that it was a personal call—something about a trip to New York City to visit a vampire club to drink umbrella drinks with a twist of animal blood.

Eew!

I hustled down the stairs and headed right for the rows of file cabinets that were lined up against the wall like gray metal soldiers.

They were locked.

I found 1989, the year that Claire Jacobson would have visited Dr. Francis. And found her exact drawer. It was marked ɪ–ᴋ.

I yanked on the drawer. Nothing happened. I tried to pop up the lock. No luck. I yanked again.

I was about to give up when I saw a key in another lock. With any luck, the same key would fit this file cabinet.

I tried the key, and the lock popped up. A thrill of excitement ran up my spine, and I felt ready to begin a career as a safecracker should I fail to fill the cottages this summer.

I pulled the file drawer open, walked my fingers through the names, and found Claire's file.

Stuffing it into the waistband of my jeans, I zipped up my jacket.

Sliding back the drawer, I pushed the lock in and put the key back in the other file cabinet.

Time to get the hell out of here.

I hurried up the stairs and was breathless when I got to the top.

Ty took one look at me, and his eyes grew as wide as platters. He took me by the arm, gave Miss Shannon times two a "Good-bye, darlin'," and we were off.

"Tell me you didn't steal her file."

"That would be illegal."

"That's never stopped you before. And why are you walking funny?"

"No reason."

We climbed into his hulk of an SUV, or at least he did. I tried to climb up without losing my five-to-fifteen-years-at-a-women's-prison-worth of stolen property.

Finally I plopped down on the beige leather seat, the manila folder digging into my back.

"Hand it over, Trixie."

"Just drive, will you? This is the getaway SUV."

"So you did steal the folder! Dammit, Trixie. It could have waited until Monday, when I could get the court order."

"Look, Deputy, I don't want to get you in trouble."

"Well, like you said, I'm driving the getaway SUV. Plus, I'm harboring a criminal. I'm in this deep." He shook his head, but when he looked at me, there was a twinkle in his eye.

Ty Brisco might be a by-the-book cop, but he was willing to skip a few pages.

"Bedford Hills is women only. You'll have to find another prison of your own," I informed him.

"How do you know about Bedford Hills?" he asked.

"My ex-husband's niece, who was a math teacher in one of the western New York high schools, decided she was in love with one of her students. Unfortunately, she didn't know math good enough to calculate that he was underage. She was sentenced to Bedford Hills, and she kept writing my ex because she seemed to think that a Philadelphia traffic cop could help her get out of Bedford Hills in New York."

He laughed. "Let's go to your place and take a look at the folder that I don't know you have. Do you want to stop somewhere for takeout?"

"Yeah. Let's go to the Crossroads. They have excellent burgers. They aren't as good as mine, but they're okay. Besides, I'd like to chat with Laura Tingsley about the two murders. She always has something to say."

Ty nodded. "Good idea, but she might not talk if I'm there."

"Then you wait in the getaway SUV and hide from the cops. I won't be long." I pulled the file out of my clothes and handed it to him. "This will be good reading while I'm gone."

"Thanks. Take your time."

From the outside, the Crossroads looked like Daniel Boone's log cabin on steroids. The inside was knotty pine. It was divided in half by a planter with silk vegetation. One half was the restaurant area, and the other half contained a bar with red vinyl and silver barstools and booths around the perimeter.

I knew that Laura Tingsley, the former Laura VanPlank, bought the Crossroads from a very outdoorsy couple for a low price several years ago, but the informal, rustic appearance of the place really didn't suit her. However, it did suit the locals and the Sandy Harbor visitors.

I didn't plan on staying very long with the wannabe Jackie Kennedy Onassis. She always managed to slip several campaign-type sound bites for her husband, Mayor Rick Tingsley, into any conversation.

Laura was sitting at a table with an older woman, who looked just like Nancy Reagan. Jackie O. and Nancy Reagan were eating Cobb salads and drinking red wine.

"Hi, Laura. How are you?" I smiled at both ladies. "Nice rainy day, isn't it?"

"Hello, Trixie. I'd like you to meet my mother, Mrs. Carla VanPlank."

Mrs. VanPlank held out a limp hand so loaded with diamonds, no wonder she couldn't hold it up.

I took it and pumped away.

Local gossip (my maintenance man Clyde) said that Laura's parents were wildly wealthy, and now I believed it. Gossip also had it that they were the ones who were bankrolling Rick Tingsley's runs for office.

"Nice to meet you. How long are you visiting, Mrs. VanPlank?"

It would have been nice if she told me to call her by her first name.

"Oh, I don't know. Our plans are flexible. It's just so nice to visit my daughter and Mayor Tingsley."

Was it me, or wasn't it creepy that she referred to her son-in-law so formally?

"With the recent discovery of Claire Jacobson's body and the even more recent murder of Mr. Burrows, it must be a public relations and tourism nightmare for Mayor Tingsley," I said.

Laura sniffed. "He can handle it."

"Of course he can handle it. He can handle anything," Mrs. VanPlank snapped. "After all, he's senator material. And after he's senator for a term, he'll be elected president."

I'd heard the same declaration from Laura several times before, but now her mother was throwing his hat into the ring, too.

"Of the United States," Mom added.

I snapped my fingers as if this question just occurred to me. "Laura, you knew Claire, didn't you?"

"Barely. She was not part of Sandy Harbor proper. She was just a summer visitor."

"Just like me," I said. *Sandy Harbor proper?* What on earth?

"Not like you anymore. You've graduated to being a regular Sandy Harbor resident since you're a property owner here now," Laura said, as if she were quoting from a rule book.

"Graduated, huh?" I'd call it being in debt up to my hair roots.

Laura turned to her mother. "Trixie owns the Silver Bullet Diner and Sandy Harbor Cottages. She bought it all from Stella, her aunt."

Carla VanPlank patted her white coiffure, even though not a hair had escaped its varnish. "In the past, Mr. VanPlank and I attended several of your aunt and uncle's Dance Fests when we were living here."

She didn't seem like a Dance Fest kind of person, and it seemed as if she called her husband "Mr." all the time.

I shifted on my feet, which I'd just realized were killing me. Apparently, I wasn't going to be asked to sit.

I decided to press on to see if they might have any information that could help me in my investigation. After all, they might remember important things after all these years. Laura had been there, and her parents had lived in Sandy Harbor at the time, too.

"Speaking of graduation," I began, "I read in the *Sandy Harbor Lure* where the mayor—obviously, he wasn't the mayor then—said that he was the one who invited Claire to the bonfire the night of their graduation party. I guess that you and the mayor weren't dating then. Right, Laura?"

"Of course we were dating!" She turned her eyes to the bare rafters as if her next sentence were written up there. "We were a couple all through high school. The mayor was just trying to be nice when he invited her." Laura crossed her arms over her chest, daring me to contradict her. "He probably felt sorry for her. He's sensitive like that."

*Sensitive* is the last adjective I'd attribute to Rick Tingsley.

"Really?" I feigned surprise. "My mistake. The way the paper read, I must have misunderstood. I thought that the mayor was with Claire—like a date."

"Don't be ridiculous. The mayor was always

enchanted with my Laura." Mrs. VanPlank set down her fork, quite ladylike. However, judging by the sour expression on her face, she'd rather throw the fork at me, prongs first. "The mayor was just trying to be nice to Miss Jacobson, just like my daughter said."

I leaned over the table and whispered, "Do either of you have a guess as to who killed her?"

"For heaven's sake." Mrs. VanPlank sniffed. "This isn't very pleasant lunch conversation."

"Are you getting takeout, Trixie?" Laura asked. "Or are you lunching alone?"

Yikes. I can take a hint. This conversation was over. I'd pushed too hard.

"Takeout. I came here for your delicious burgers."

"Give your order to Charlie, the bartender. He'll help you," Laura said, picking up her fork.

That was an absolute dismissal. She didn't have to hit me over the head with a serving platter. I got the message.

"Ladies, I'd like to invite you both to the Silver Bullet Diner for lunch or dinner, on me. Please do come."

I heard myself babbling, and couldn't believe I was inviting the First Ladies to dine with me. But maybe I could get more information out of them on my home turf.

"Thank you, but our schedule is quite full," Laura said, fingering her pink pearls.

"I'd like to go, Laura," said Mrs. VanPlank, surprising me. "I'd enjoy seeing Trixie's diner and cottages. I'd like to take a tour."

"Then it's a date," I said. "How about tomorrow for lunch?"

"I presume that'll be okay. I do have to check my appointment book to be sure." Laura shifted on her seat to cross her legs. "If I don't call you to cancel, we'll see you at noon."

Mrs. VanPlank nodded.

I waved good-bye and decided to skip the takeout from here after all. I'd phone Juanita and order some bacon cheeseburgers on homemade sourdough bread and some curly fries with balsamic vinegar. It would be ready by the time we got there.

When I walked to where Ty had parked his black monolith, I found him completely absorbed in reading Claire's file. Walking around to the passenger side, I climbed in.

"What did you find out from Claire's file, the one that you know nothing about and have never seen?" I asked.

"Claire was pregnant. Two months along when she saw Dr. Francis."

Pausing for a while, I let that sink in. She had to be truly in love, head-over-flip-flops, white-lace-and-promises in love with whoever her boyfriend was.

And Claire was always happy, even more so just before she went missing. Her eyes always twinkled and the smile on her face was even bigger. I'd studied her every movement back then, her hand gestures, the way she walked, talked, and laughed. I would have known if something was wrong with her.

"Who went with her to the appointment?" I asked.

"No one."

"Twenty-five years ago, did a seventeen-year-old have to have a parent or guardian with her to see a doctor?" I wondered.

"I don't think so, and Dr. Francis didn't seem to care. He even made a note in the folder that he thought she was younger than twenty-one. That was the age she gave him."

"Really?" That surprised me. "Who did she name as father?"

Ty stared a hole through the folder. "She didn't. She said that the father was unknown."

"She knew who the father was. Claire wasn't the type to sleep around."

"Being that you were ten years old, how did you know?"

"Let's call it preteen intuition. Admittedly, she was my heroine, so my opinion was very tainted, but I just had a feeling that Claire was in love— and she seemed like the type to fall hard for one person," I insisted. "What else did you find out from the folder that you don't have in your possession?"

"When her family came to Sandy Harbor for that summer in June—it was June first, if I remember correctly from the reports—she saw Doc Francis on August third and was already four months pregnant. She died three days later, the night of the bonfire."

"I'd assumed that the father was a townie or summer vacationer, but if she came here already two months pregnant, that isn't likely."

"True."

"But somehow the murderer found out. Maybe it was the father of the baby. Maybe it was 'B.'" My heart started pumping. Maybe this was the right track.

"Who?" Ty asked, then snapped his fingers. "Oh yeah, the initial she carved behind the medicine cabinet."

"Maybe he didn't like the fact that he was going to be a father at age seventeen."

I was on a roll, playing off Ty.

"Trixie, you're assuming that the father of Claire's baby was a high schooler. What if he was my age at the time? What if he was older?"

"Claire wouldn't go for someone as ancient as you when there were hot high school boys around."

"Thanks a lot." He ran his fingers through his thick dark hair. "By the way, where's our food?"

"I decided to skip ordering from here. I didn't want to hang around and wait. I'm calling Juanita now. I figure that it'll be ready just as soon as we get back. Cheeseburger and fries okay with you?"

"Perfect."

He started the car as I called Juanita with our order.

"Oh, could we stop at Brown's? I want to see if ACB is back. You can wait in the car. I just wanted to tell her about the three buses of mystery people that she missed and make sure she's all right."

"Yeah, okay," he said. "Take your time."

Antoinette Chloe Brown was indeed back from wherever she was. Her delivery van was parked on the side, windows down.

"Go around back, Ty. ACB will probably be in the kitchen with Sal's brother, Tony."

Since Antoinette Chloe's husband was doing hard time in Auburn Correctional Facility, she'd found a friend—or maybe a lover—in Sal's brother, Tony. They could often be seen riding around on Tony's motorcycle, or rather the flamboyant ACB would be in the sidecar.

I knocked on the screen door of the kitchen. "Antoinette Chloe? It's Trixie."

"Trixie? Welcome. Come in. Can I fix you something?"

"No. I'm all set. I just wanted to tell you that I fed three buses of mystery lovers at the Silver Bullet. They were booked at your place, but you weren't open."

"Trixie, I forgot all about them. Tony and I were motoring along the wine trail in the Finger Lakes."

The colorful muumuus that ACB used to wear were replaced by black leather, lots and lots of it. Chains hung from every part of her, like tinsel on a Christmas tree. She wore goth makeup and her platinum hair with black roots was parted in the middle and gathered into a ponytail, which jutted out from the back of a black leather visor.

When ACB dresses, she goes all out.

"So everything's okay, Antoinette Chloe?" Never just call her Antoinette or you'd hear about it.

"I've been having a ball with Tony on his Harley. I love riding in the sidecar next to him and roaring down the highway of life. But then he dropped me off here and said that he might be back, but maybe not. He had to find himself. I didn't think he was missing." Tears pooled in her black-painted eyes, and she changed the subject. "Did you hear that they found the body of Claire Jacobson?"

Wow, gossip traveled faster than Tony's Harley. ACB even heard the news on a sidecar on the highway of life.

"How did you know?" I asked.

"When we rolled into town, we stopped at the Grab and Go. The headlines in the *Lure* caught my eye. I've always wondered what happened to her. She was such a sweet girl."

"Someone didn't think so."

"That's true. I remember that night. We were having so much fun at the bonfire, singing and all. I remember that Marvin Cogswell brought out his guitar and yelled, 'Antoinette Chloe Switzer, sing us some songs.'"

"Any thoughts on who would want Claire dead?"

"Not at all. Everyone liked her. We'd gotten to know her since she came here every summer. She was like one of us."

"Did everyone feel the same way?"

"Naw. Laura VanPlank Tingsley didn't like her in the least."

"Wonder why."

"Probably because her Ricky asked Claire to the bonfire."

"As his date?" I asked.

"It looked like it to me. Matter of fact, Ricky looked more in love with Claire than with Laura, and he'd been going steady with Laura for years."

*I knew it! I just knew it.*

"At any point did Rick and Claire go off together?"

"Not that I can remember, but they were holding hands."

"I'll bet Laura didn't like that."

"She was sitting at the bonfire, staring at Ricky and Claire, and steam was shooting from her ears. I told her that she should cool off in the lake. She told me to shut up and sing."

ACB laughed loudly, sounding like rusty springs, and the noise bounced around the kitchen. Her laugh was so contagious, I couldn't help joining in.

I said good-bye, promised that I'd stop by for dinner with "that hunk of a cowboy cop," and left.

My head always spun after an encounter with ACB, but basically I got some good information:

Rick Tingsley definitely was with Claire Jacobson, and Laura VanPlank Tingsley hated seeing them together.

But there was no "B" still and did Laura hate enough to kill?

# Chapter 8

*I* told Ty what ACB had said.

"I should get her down to the station and get an official statement from her."

"Can you hold off for a while? Don't scare everyone off."

"Maybe it'll be good to shake everyone up, especially those who were interviewed for the *Lure* back then."

"I don't get it, Ty. Claire was two months pregnant before she even showed up at the cottages the year she died. It couldn't have been a townie. It must have been someone from her hometown!"

"It still could have been a townie. Someone with wheels who took a trip to visit her in—" He checked the file. "In Rochester. I still want to interview everyone in that senior class, but that'll take such a long time, and probably less than a third are still here. Maybe I'll just start with Rick Tingsley."

"If you law enforcement types start getting all

official with the future president of the United States, he'll suddenly take an extended vacation or lawyer up."

"It's just questioning." He shook his head, obviously frustrated. "I'll take that chance."

"If the First Ladies get wind of that, they'll be all over you like salt on french fries."

"The . . . who?"

"Laura Tingsley and her mother. They just remind me of . . . Oh, never mind. It's just me."

He was silent for a couple of miles. "You know, Trixie, I'm getting kind of tired of chauffeuring your butt around."

"Hey, wasn't it your idea to drag me around?"

"I believe that it was your idea," he said.

"Everyone was blabby today. I got some stellar gossip."

"Uh-huh. Like what?"

"Nothing much. Just gossip. If it turns into anything, I'll let you know," I said.

A misty rain started falling, just enough for Ty to turn the wipers on slow. On the right side of the SUV was a rainbow.

"Isn't that just beautiful?" I asked, pointing to the right.

Ty looked quickly, then returned his gaze to the road. "Look for a pot of gold."

"I could use a pot of gold, but I'd settle for solving these two mysteries." I sighed, suddenly feeling that I was concentrating on Claire and wasn't paying enough attention to Mr. Burrows.

"Ty, let's figure out if Mr. Burrows was in fact Claire Jacobson's brother—or even a relative of hers."

"The state police are working on that now— matching fingerprints, doing DNA, and contacting any living relatives. I expect a phone call in the next couple of days."

"I feel it in my bones that he's Phil Jacobson," I said, feeling my innate impatience boiling. I was confident I recognized his eyes.

"I suspect that you're right."

A plan formulated in my mind. "Ty, I have a scathingly brilliant idea. I was already planning to reinstitute the Saturday night Dance Fest, and all the cast of characters will probably attend. I can circulate, make small talk, gossip, snoop, whatever. Everyone will be in one place, drinking beer and wine, and liquor loosens the lips."

He shook his head. "I don't want to deal with a lot of drunks."

"Max will tend bar. He'll keep an eye on everyone's intake and won't let things get out of hand. Clyde will walk around and make sure no one has brought any liquor in. At eleven o'clock, the coffee will come out, and so will the designated drivers. Of course, you'll be in attendance. They'd have to be stupid to overdo it with you there."

"And Vern McCoy. It'll be his night off, but he's talked about the Silver Bullet's Dance Fest since I hired on. You can be sure he'll be attending. He can park cars, too."

"Let's see . . . today's Friday. I can get the word out and be ready to rock this coming Saturday."

"That fast?"

"Faster than you law enforcement types move—that's for sure."

He chuckled and pulled into the Silver Bullet's driveway. He left the car on but opened his door. "I'll go in and get our lunch. You stay somewhat dry."

It was raining harder, and the breeze had morphed into wind.

"Thanks." For once I didn't want to go into the diner. It had been a long couple of days, what with finding a body and everything. What I wanted was to have my burger and do the payroll in the kitchen of my house. Maybe I could be on time with the paychecks for once.

Ty came out with two take-out bags. "I hate to drop you off and run, but I'm going to eat at my desk downtown. I want to check on a couple of things."

"And you'll let me know if David Burrows is Phil?"

He nodded and drove me the short distance to the Big House. He'd better give me some information, or I was done giving him any information that I obtained.

As I walked up the stairs, I realized I couldn't withhold information from Ty. He was Sandy Harbor's lead investigator. No matter how trivial it might seem, I'd tell him.

Just as I opened the door, Blondie greeted me with a whine. Then she zoomed past me and ran down the steps as if she chasing a bird or a rabbit or a cat. That was unlikely as she was scared of all three, plus her own shadow.

"Blondie!"

Oh! She was watering the already-soaked lawn. I had taken too long in getting back from my travels with Ty.

I waited on the front porch as she rolled in the grass, lay on her back with her paws raking the air, sniffed several square feet of grass, and then started pacing in a line. Oh, time for Number Two.

Poor sweetie.

She decided to sniff the side yard, so I followed her onto the wraparound porch. Then she sniffed the lawn on the lake side of the house. I still followed, getting chilled, and so were my burger and fries. Then we progressed to the left side.

Then she put her paws to the metal and sniffed right along the trail of the mystery woman that I saw walking the night of Mr. Burrows's murder.

"Blondie! Come!"

Blondie had been a half-frozen, filthy, and wet stray when she showed up at the back door of my diner last winter. Every now and then, she ignored my commands whenever she got a taste of freedom. But sometimes she surprised me, like now.

Then again, she was just hoping to get a hand-out of burgers and fries.

She sat in front of me on the porch and looked

at me with those big brown eyes of hers as I opened the bag. She was already soaked.

Was it ever going to stop raining for more than five minutes? This town was starting to feel like a tropical rain forest without the humidity and the funky vegetation.

I pulled out a fry and handed it to her. She took it ever so gently from my hand. I don't know what I'd do if I ever lost Blondie. All my love was directed at that furry blond dog. Since I'd never been able to have children of my own, Blondie filled a void in my heart. The rest of the void I filled by dishing up nourishing comfort food at the diner.

I shared some of my takeout with her, then let her back into the house and toweled her off.

She shook off and got me wetter than before. Deciding that I couldn't look any worse, and Ty couldn't get madder at me, I was going to explore the field where I saw the footprints.

The cops had to be finished with the area by now, so I didn't feel as though I'd be disturbing a crime scene. If the tape was still up, I wouldn't go there.

I slipped and slid through the long weeds and grass of the meadow—the wet vegetation wrapping itself around my jeans and the wet ground seeping into my boat shoes.

Taking a deep breath of the moist air, I felt rejuvenated and my head seemed clearer. I should find the time to walk more often. I could make it a habit to walk Blondie more often. We could certainly walk the beach as far as the marina, some five miles away.

I was busy looking for something, anything, when I tripped. Like a giant redwood, I flew through the air, wincing in anticipation of feeling the impact of my pounds-per-square-inch when I hit the ground.

But my impact was negligible. The tall grass cushioned my fall and flossed my teeth at the same time. Taking a couple of deep breaths, I opened my eyes and stared into the thorns of a burdock plant. Missed it!

Clinging to the prickers was a soggy piece of white paper. I could see the dark letters of typewriting bleeding through. Wait. Typewriting! Carefully, I plucked the paper off the burdock, and opened it.

> . . . *the trail of Claire's murderer. I know that the answer lies in Cottage Eight, and I don't care if I have to take the whole building down—I will find the final clue that will put the murderer behind bars for life.*
>
> *With this book, I will make sure that the world knows that Claire—*

*That's it?*
*Oh, for Pete's sake!*
The excerpt from his book didn't give me much information other than to verify that Mr. Burrows

was writing a book, which I already had guessed. It did verify that the book was about Claire and that he'd specifically rented Cottage Eight, which I'd guessed, too.

So far I was good at guessing.

Over the falling rain and the rumbling thunder, I heard something coming toward me. Whatever it was was coming fast, like someone running toward me. Stuffing the paper into my bra, I lay still on the grass, closed my eyes, and hoped that this wasn't the murderer returning to find that the last page of his manuscript was missing.

There was nothing to defend myself with, other than a burdock plant. I gripped the roots, preparing to rip the plant out of the ground and scratch the killer to death.

The rustling stopped, and someone was breathing hard on my right side. My heart was going to pound right out of my chest.

Someone was licking my hair, then my cheek.

"Blondie!"

I scrambled to my feet and wiped off my face with the hem of my T-shirt.

"How did you get out of the house?"

The paper must have blown over here in the wind when the murderer raced away. Or maybe the murderer tripped over the same tree root that I had.

Blondie walked next to me, her tail wagging happily after her escape from the Big House.

We walked back. It was then I noticed that I

hadn't closed the back door carefully. Blondie could have easily pushed open the screen door and then the outside door with her nose.

"Bad Trixie," I said, feeling the same emptiness pre-Blondie that I'd had. I'd have to be more careful.

In the warmth of my kitchen, I gently got the paper from my bra and set it on a paper towel on the counter to dry. Then I dried Blondie off again with her big fluffy towel.

Upstairs, I shed my clothes and took a hot shower. Then I slipped into a navy blue Philadelphia Eagles sweatshirt and matching sweatpants.

On one rare occasion that Deputy Doug and I went out together, it was a Super Bowl party at another cop's house. Doug insisted that I dress for the part, even though I couldn't care less about any sport with the possible exception of the summer and winter Olympics. I am obsessed with the Olympics when they're on TV.

Then I slipped on my fuzzy pink slippers.

At the kitchen table, I reached for a pen and my favorite notebook and opened it to a clean page. On the top, I wrote DANCE FEST TO-DO LIST.

Then I started writing. I listed the buffet menu: pulled pork, three-cheese baked macaroni, chef salad with my special basil vinaigrette dressing, salt potatoes, baked beans, potato salad, hot dogs, Juanita's burgers, kielbasa, and kraut. Oh, and that fancy cottage cheese and walnut salad that

Aunt Helen always made. I'd make one with nuts, and one without.

For dessert, I'd make trays of brownies and trays of my friend Michele's Chocolate Cowboy Cake. That would take care of the chocolate lovers. Then for the others, I'd make a fruit salad, mini-cheesecakes, and trays of chocolate chip cookies.

The list would get me started. I'd make another list of all the food, condiments, paper plates, and plastic utensils that I'd have to order.

Then I'd have to find a band. I wondered if Frankie Rudinski and the Polka Dots were still around. I could still remember them after all these years. If they weren't available, Juanita would know of a good band. And I'd have to rent a huge tent because I'd wager that it would rain. Then there was the "little" stuff like a dance floor and renting tables and chairs. And I needed lots of firewood for the bonfire, a few big rolls of plastic table covering, a couple of kegs of beer, some wine and wine coolers, lots of soda, and serving stands with liquid fuel to keep everything hot. And lots of ice to keep the salads and whatnot cool.

There needed to be a bar. Clyde and Max would remember how to do that. They were working here at the first Dance Fest.

Oh, and publicity! I needed a supply of posters to put in storefronts all over town. I'd buy some radio time, too. We had a few great local stations, and some of the DJs were diner regulars. The publicity was the most important part. Flyers! I could print up some flyers that could be handed out to every customer at the Silver Bullet and slipped into grocery bags at the Grab and Go and at Super Duper Groceries on Route 13.

Aunt Stella surely had a good dozen more serving stands that the aluminum and/or metal pans fit on, but where could they be? The diner only had a handful that I used for the emergency buffet for the mystery bus people, but I definitely needed more for the Dance Fest.

There were probably some stored here in the basement.

I shuddered. Basements gave me the creeps. They were always musty and leaky, and in older houses, the furnace looked like a metal monster with dozens of arms.

In the movies and books, someone was always buried in the basement, or locked in by the villain to die a musty, damp death. And the lights never worked in the basement.

I had to go down there. Those stands were the key to a successful buffet. I didn't want to buy more if they were already here.

"Blondie, come!" I opened the basement door. There was that creepy smell.

Like a good dog, Blondie pranced into the kitchen, thinking I was going to give her a treat. She took a look at the open basement door, sniffed the air, and shook herself off, spraying me with droplets and dog hair. Then she took off for one of her favorite hiding places in the house.

She wasn't going down there with me, the big chicken.

I flipped the switch to the basement and then decided to get three flashlights. Stuffing two into my underwear, I turned one on and held it in front of me.

But wait.

The basement had been remodeled and covered in bright white paneling. Dozens of big white storage cabinets lined every wall, and black-and-white commercial tile shone on the floor. I could hold a dance right here!

I opened several cabinets full of glasses, silverware, serving bowls, old menus, china platters, rolls and rolls of plastic table covering, stacks of dishes, and lots of huge pots and pans. Then I found the stands I was looking for. Perfect.

Climbing the stairs, I looked back at the delightful basement. I'd scared myself half to death, all for nothing.

Lesson learned.

I made several phone calls over the next couple of hours, making a lot of progress on Dance Fest.

I would be able to circulate and pump the locals for information about Claire. They'd all be together, and it'd be easy to do.

The Dance Fest would be great for the Silver Bullet, too. I was all about keeping old traditions and memories alive and making new traditions and memories. The old Dance Fests were part of that tradition—my family's tradition.

I hoped that there would be a good turnout. Maybe the townsfolk would stay away because of Mr. Burrows's murder, or maybe Cabin Eight would draw them like magnets.

I'd have to talk it up and get my staff to do the same.

There was a knock on the door. I peeked out the window.

Ty and a kid.

"Sorry to bother you, Trixie," Ty said when I opened the door. "But do you have a moment?"

"I do." I was totally puzzled. What was going on? "Please come in and take a seat."

Ty made a point of wiping his feet on the throw rug by the door for a long time. The young man with him did the same.

Then they both sat down in the living room. I sat across from them both.

Ty smiled. "Miss Matkowski, I'd like you to meet Raymond Meyerson. He's interested in busing tables and washing dishes at the Silver Bullet."

I had forgotten about filling the job. That was because I had forgotten about carrying my trusty notebook of things I needed to do with me at all times. I lived by my lists because my brain was like a leaky faucet.

Raymond was about sixteen, tall and skinny with a bad case of acne, but he had a nice smile and pretty brown eyes that seemed magnified by his glasses. He sat with his hands in his lap, and his knuckles were white from squeezing them so hard.

This juvenile delinquent was nervous about a job interview. I decided to make his interview informal, but tough.

"Tell me a little about yourself, Raymond," I said.

"I go by Ray, not Raymond. I have working papers, and I have to find a job before I go to court again so it looks good."

I looked at Ty and he winked at me. I hoped I wasn't making a mistake, but I'd like to give Ray a chance.

"I'm Trixie Matkowski. You can call me Trixie."

"Okay."

"Can I trust you, Ray?"

He shrugged. "I guess so."

"I don't want you to guess. I want to know if I can trust you. Will you steal from me?"

"Hell no. I'm a hacker, not a robber or a burglar."

I decided to ask. "What did you hack?"

He hesitated, then looked at Ty. Ty shrugged, stating, "It's up to you what you want to disclose. You're protected by law, so you don't have to say anything."

He looked down at his hands. "Records at school. I upped the grades on some kids."

Not a biggie in the grand scheme of things, but

in a way, it was like stealing. I decided not to point this out, not now at least. "Can you get along with my other workers?"

"As long as they don't mess with me."

"They work hard and like to have fun and tease each other, but they will never intentionally hurt you. It's all in fun."

He nodded. "Okay. That's cool."

"Will you show up on time and work hard?"

"I'll try."

"Huh?" I asked, cupping an ear with my hand.

"Yeah. I'll show up on time and work hard."

"Excellent. Will you be nice to my customers?"

"I'll try . . . I mean, yeah, yeah, I will."

"You look nice, Ray. You have on a nice pair of dark jeans and a nice T-shirt. Do you dress like that all the time or just for job interviews?"

"My mother made me wear this."

I grinned. "Your mom has good taste. But, Ray, will you continue to dress like this? I mean, please wear a decent T-shirt without anything written or drawn on it. And a nice pair of jeans. I can't stand underwear showing and pants dragging. This is a family diner."

Ray unclasped his hands and put one on each knee. "That kind of shit—" Ty elbowed him. "Sorry. But that kind of stuff isn't me anyway. I'm not a gangsta or a rapper."

"Who are you, then?" I liked talking to Ray.

"A geek, a nerd, or a computer hacker." He got

another elbow from Ty. "I mean, I'm a computer expert."

"Could you make some flyers for my Dance Fest, buffet, and bonfire? I'd like a fun picture and fun fonts, lots of color, and it has to be eye-catching."

"Piece of cake." He grinned and his eyes brightened.

This kid wasn't going to be a dishwasher for long. His heart was in the computer field. I wondered how good he was at spreadsheets.

"Ray, you're hired. I'll put you on the clock if you can start right now by helping me. Flyers today, dishes tomorrow."

I leaned over and offered my hand in a handshake. I was rewarded with a nice, strong handshake from Ray and an uneasy smile.

"Officer Ty gave me a ride here. I'm going to have to call my mom and let her know I'm staying for a while so she can pick me up."

I looked at Ty. He turned to Ray and said, "I'm going to grab some chow at the diner. I'll give your mom a call and tell her that you're helping Trixie and that you got the job. I can still drive you home."

Ray whispered not too quietly to Ty that he'd like to tell his mother that he got the job himself, but that he'd appreciate a ride home because his father was out of town and his mother didn't like to drive in the dark.

Ty clasped the boy's shoulder. "Yeah, Ray, you're right. You should tell your mom yourself. This is your first job. It's a big deal."

Ray pulled a cell phone out of a pocket, and he looked around the sitting room.

I stood. "Officer Ty, please join me in the kitchen. I have something to show you. Ray, talk to your mother as long as you like, then come into the kitchen when you're done."

"Cool," Ray said.

Ty and I walked into the kitchen. "Sorry to surprise you, and to bring Ray here, but he has to go to court. I forgot all about it because of everything that's been happening. And normally, I wouldn't bring anyone to your house, but—"

"Don't worry about it. It's fine. Ray's a computer hacker, not a burglar, anyway." I pointed to the partially dried paper on the table. "I found this in the meadow. I'm sure that Mr. Burrows typed it, and I found it clinging to a burdock plant when I went looking for Blondie."

At the mention of her name, Blondie came down the stairs and nuzzled Ty's leg. He absentmindedly petted her as he read the document.

"I have to read this again," he said, leaning over the table to get closer.

I pulled out a chair and sat down and took over petting Blondie.

He whistled, long and low. "This is interesting. Where did you say you found it?"

He sat down and returned to petting Blondie, only he was petting my hand instead. I pulled it away after a while. If he couldn't tell the difference between my hand and a dog's head, I had some serious electrolysis to do.

"I found the paper about equal distance between Cottage Eight and where the ruts are from when the murderer drove away. He or she dropped page eighty-six."

"After the murderer reads the manuscript, he or she will realize that page eighty-six starts in the middle of a sentence."

"Oh! And the murderer always returns to the scene of the crime!" I said.

"That's an old wives' tale, but yeah, they sometimes do."

"But there was nothing exciting on page eighty-six."

"True. But he or she wouldn't know that."

I groaned. "Terrific."

"Don't worry. They don't know that you found it."

"That's a good thing."

He chuckled. "Can I bother you for a plastic bag that'll fit this paper?" He lifted the paper and the paper towel. "It's still wet. Maybe a plastic bag will ruin it. How about a paper bag?"

I turned around, opened a cabinet, and handed him a paper grocery bag.

"That'll do," Ty said, slipping everything into

the large bag. Then he snapped his fingers. "I also came by to tell you that David Burrows is indeed Phil Jacobson, Claire's younger brother."

"I knew it!" I continued with my theory. "And Phil was here to write an exposé about his sister's murder. He hoped to find secrets in Cottage Eight. Matter of fact, Phil was ready to tear the walls right off the place. No wonder he didn't want to be disturbed."

"And page eighty-six said that he didn't care if he had to tear the whole building down," Ty said.

"I'm going to tear the walls down, Ty. I want to know what Phil was looking for. Maybe there's more than just that sonogram if it was Claire's hiding place."

"Tear the walls down?" Ty asked. "I wouldn't do that if I were you. It's a crime scene. Let the state troopers—"

"Can't the Sandy Harbor Sheriff's Department do it?"

"We called the state in. They have the lead. They have a bright and shiny crime lab with a gaggle of lab people in white coats."

"Can't you call Trooper Whomever, Deputy Brisco, and get the green light? Tell them you have my full cooperation."

"I'll call Captain Drennan and see if they'll release the cottage. However, until I get back to you, don't touch anything, Trixie. I mean it. I'll lock you up quicker than you can cut up a tomato."

"Sliced or diced?"

He didn't say a word but glared at me.

"And we might not release the fact that Phillip was Claire's brother for a while. Let's keep this between us for now."

"Would Hal Manning know?" I asked.

"No. Not yet. The information is straight from the state police. Only you and I know this, Trixie, and I'm trusting you."

"My lips are sealed, Sheriff Brisco, but . . . wow! This is incredible information. David Burrows is Phil Jacobson, and Phil Jacobson is Claire's brother."

"You pretty much guessed it before."

"Pale, pale blue eyes."

"Not a word, Trixie."

I believed he'd lock me up, but he'd better hurry with the green light to release the information.

# Chapter 9

"I'm heading to the Silver Bullet for the daily special," Ty said.

"Spaghetti and meatballs, chef salad, garlic bread," I said.

"Yeah. I know." He took page eighty-six with him and headed out the back porch door. "I'll be back in a while to take Ray home."

"Okay."

I began to angst over all the stuff I needed to do. Lists? Where were all my lists?

Combing through them, I decided that the only thing I needed to concentrate on now was the flyers. I found a clean sheet of paper and did a mock-up by hand of what I wanted it to look like.

Ray cleared his throat as he walked into the kitchen so as not to scare me. Thoughtful kid.

I showed him my scribbles and my stick art. "This is what I had in mind."

He studied it, rubbing his chin like a professor I once had in community college.

"What's this in the middle?" Ray asked.

"People dancing." Okay, my drawing was a little too abstract.

"Looks like barf on the floor. But okay. I know what you want. Let me find some free art for you. I'll design a border with the food you are going to have, too."

"Brilliant, Ray." This kid was going to be invaluable. "Here's my laptop. Have at it." As I was pushing it toward him and pulling out a chair for him, I realized that my whole life was in that laptop—my banking, my spreadsheets for the diner, payroll for my staff—everything.

And Raymond Myerson was a hacker.

"Remember our conversation about trust, Ray?"

"Yeah, I know. I won't hack into your private stuff."

"Sorry. I just had to mention it. It made me feel better."

"Cool." Ray started typing a zillion letters per minute. Sister Marianne James, my high school typing teacher, would be blown away. He was using all his fingers, too.

"Do you need me, Ray?"

"Nah."

There was nothing more boring than watching someone type unless it was watching golf.

"Just yell if you do," I said. "I have to take care of a couple of things."

And one of those things was to listen to my messages on my blinking answering machine.

*Beep.*

"This is Janice Eggleston. I am calling to cancel my reservation for Cottage Two. I am very sorry, but I don't want my children around . . . well, you know. I'd like my deposit back, please."

*Beep.*

"Carl Pangburn here. We won't be coming to the cottages this year. Sorry, but I have to cancel. Please send my deposit back. First time in thirteen years we aren't coming to the cottages. I hope that everything gets straightened out soon."

*Beep.*

There were four more cancellations. My stomach sank along with my bank account.

I went back down to the basement with a mission in mind, and without a flashlight. Finding a crowbar, a sledgehammer, and two regular hammers, I carried them all upstairs. If there was something in the walls of Cottage Eight, I was going to find it.

Just as soon as Ty Brisco gave the go-ahead.

Or even if he didn't.

Ray jumped up to help me just as the two hammers slid out of my hands and hit the floor. Blondie tore upstairs like a frightened rabbit.

Ray picked up the hammers and handed them to me.

"Thanks."

He answered with a grunt that I deduced meant "You're welcome." Then he returned to my laptop, cracked his knuckles, and started typing.

I put all my weapons of cottage destruction on the porch that faced the lake.

Sitting on one of the white wicker rockers, I stared at the back of my cottages. They were so darn cute—all white with forest green shutters and little porches on the front facing the lake. Each porch contained two forest green Adirondack chairs. The driveways for parked cars were to the side, so there would be nothing to block their view of the lake.

Right now the lake was flat, but the moon was shining, making a glittering path. When I was a kid, I liked to believe little fairies were playing and frolicking on that bright path, making the tiny ripples that sparkled.

Twelve cottages.

Since 1952, those twelve cottages had been enjoyed by generations of families—families that vacationed together and enjoyed the lake, the boating, tubing, and fishing, or just making sand castles.

They cooked hamburgers on the grill or came up to the diner for meals. They played lawn games like badminton or volleyball.

I should rename them. Maybe I'd call them the Ghost Town Housekeeping Cottages.

Sitting down on a rocker, I hoped the Dance Fest this Saturday night would be a success. I'd love to be able to come close to the fun that everyone had when Porky and Stella ran them. And I needed it to be a success to even break even this summer without cottage rentals. I was going to give it my best shot in the little time I had to plan.

And my best shot included getting to know the pasts of the people of Sandy Harbor a little bit more, with the Sandy Harbor Class of 1989 leading the pack.

One of my first targets would have to be Rick Tingsley, the mayor. Ricky, as he was known back then, was the one who'd asked Claire to the bonfire where she was last seen. Laura might have been jealous of Claire back then, but jealous enough to kill her? She seemed more like a mean girl than a murderer.

I knew from history that Antoinette Chloe Switzer had married Sal Brownelli. They, too, were a long-term high school couple. Did Sal have an eye for Claire, too?

I could see ACB, the colorful and eccentric dresser, picking up a gun in a fit of rage should anyone poach Sal.

Who else did I suspect?

Of course, I'd eliminate Marvin Cogswell as a suspect. He'd been murdered last winter. Then again, he'd been murdered after Claire, but before Phil Jacobson.

I suppose if I discarded the theory that Claire and her brother were murdered by the same person, Marvin Cogswell could have killed Claire. But that would mean there were two murderers loose in my town. And they'd just happened to kill two members of the same family.

And what about the rest of the class? I could see all the women being jealous of Claire and all the men lusting after her. Any one of the women could have secreted a small handgun and shot her during the noisy celebration and dragged her away.

Any of the men could have shot her, too. If she was pregnant, and they didn't want anyone to know, they could have done away with her.

And killed his unborn child, too.

I shuddered. How awful! How could anyone kill someone and kill an innocent, unborn baby, too?

Unless they didn't know about the baby.

So, how would I narrow down the rest of the class? What about those who had moved away postgraduation?

I squeezed the bridge of my nose. Some TV doctor or celebrity said that doing this would get rid of a headache. I waited and rocked, thinking that there were too many suspects, and no witnesses.

Whoa!

I'd witnessed someone running away from Cottage Eight about the time that Phil Jacobson was killed. I was one hundred percent sure that the person was either a man or a woman—*HA!*—but it was dark, stormy, and pouring rain, so I couldn't pick a gender for sure. The footprints nearby were of a woman, though. Probably.

Or maybe a petite man with small feet.

I smiled at my own joke, but then my mirth dissolved and my heart sank when I remembered that I wouldn't have enough money to make another installment payment to Aunt Stella.

I wanted to keep the diner funds and the cottage funds separate, treating them as two separate businesses. This was because I wanted to make improvements and didn't want to rob the diner to improve the cottages and vice versa.

I could always combine the two accounts. There was enough money in the diner fund to make the balloon payment, but again, I didn't want to do that.

But it looked as though I didn't have a choice.

I rocked my cares away and concentrated on the moist smell of the rain on the air and the soothing swish of the lapping of waves on the shore. This was such a wonderful place to live in the spring, summer, and fall. In the winter, it was a little overwhelming with the snow and ice, but breathtaking to watch from the comfort of a heated room with big windows.

A twig snapped and I jumped. It was probably a rabbit or some other harmless creature, but I had to remember that there was a murderer running around loose, or perhaps two murderers.

But the person who walked into the light was Ty Brisco, upholder of small-town justice—a modern-day Wyatt Earp—and handsome from the top of his creased white cowboy hat to the bottom of his polished snakeskin boots.

But I didn't notice.

"How was the special, Ty?"

"Delicious."

"Glad you liked it."

"Is Ray 'don't call me Raymond' finished?" he asked, looking over my head to the lighted kitchen.

"He has to be by now. If not, I can do the rest, I hope."

Then he looked down on the porch floor. "What the hell is all this?"

"You're a detective. I think you know what it all is: a sledgehammer, a crowbar, and two regular hammers."

"You're just aching to see the inside of a jail cell, aren't you?" he snapped.

"Most definitely," I snapped back. "My hobby is checking out jail architecture."

He chuckled. "By the way, I called Major Zale over at Troop D Headquarters."

"And?" *C'mon, Ty, spill the beans!*

"And he'll call me back tomorrow with the answer as to whether or not the hold on Cottage Eight is lifted. Can you freaking wait until then?"

"I suppose I have to."

"Of course you do. If you disturb any evidence, it could blow a clue or a lead. And even then, you can't go tearing the place down like a crazy woman. Everything has to be documented. I'll be taking pictures and notes."

"Okay, okay." I tamped down my impatience. "So you're doing this with me?"

"I'm the one who's officially tearing down the walls."

"Unofficially?"

"Unofficially, you can help me, since it's your property."

"Good." I felt better. "What time will Major Zale have an answer?"

"About eight thirty in the morning, just about when you get out of work."

"You'll come to the Silver Bullet and tell me?"

"Yes."

"Thanks, Ty." I stood, and must have misjudged the distance, as I was remarkably close to him. I inhaled his aftershave of pine and musk. It fit him—outdoorsy and masculine.

My heart began pumping wildly in my chest. Hmm . . . CPR from Wyatt Earp here might be . . . just fine.

Remembering my first marriage to a cop, although Deputy Doug was a cheater first degree, I figured I just wasn't ready to get involved. I had two businesses to run.

Plus, Ty hadn't made any real overtures toward me—darn him! He was just a friend and a regular at the Silver Bullet. That's all.

But when he looked at me the way he was looking at me now . . . wow! It made me feel all warm and fuzzy, and I was not the warm-and-fuzzy type. Not anymore.

"Excuse me," I said as he stepped back.

"Sure," he said, cordially, moving around me to open the screen door.

I walked into the Big House and saw Ray hard at work. "How's it going?"

"I think I'm done. I'm just tweaking it," he said, turning the screen toward me.

The flyer had a retro look to it. It had the appearance of something that Uncle Porky and Aunt Stella would have prepared in the fifties. It was awesome.

It's amazing that a sixteen-year-old kid could come up with a design like that.

I scanned the facts—the time, date, place, cost, food that would be served, and that Frankie Rudinski and the Polka Dots would be returning after twenty-five years. Perfect. And they were confirmed and ready to get the crowd polka-ing.

"You're very talented, Ray, very talented. I just love it."

"Cool."

I held out my hand and we shook. "I'll add the hours to your paycheck and give you a little extra for the great job. Okay with you?"

"Piece of cake. I woulda done it for free."

"We had an agreement, Ray, and we still do. Remember? You start tomorrow as a dishwasher and busboy, so you'd better get some sleep tonight." I checked my watch. "I'm cooking in about two hours, and I have a couple of things to do. Just hit the print button for me, and I'll take it from there."

"Ready to go, Ray?" Ty asked.

"Yeah, I guess so." He turned to me. "Do you want me to put them up around town?"

"You'd do that?" I loved this kid!

Ray shrugged. "Sure. I don't have anything better to do."

"I'll call you when the flyers are printed."

Ty touched his hat brim to me, and my knees almost buckled. That gesture got me every time. "Good night, Trixie."

My name rolled off his Texas tongue like a rambling river.

"G'night, Deputy. I'll call you tomorrow about the flyers, Ray."

"Uh . . . um . . . thank you for the job, Miss . . . uh . . . Trixie."

"You're welcome."

The second I opened the door, Blondie came bounding down the stairs. "Stay," I ordered, not wanting her to run out the open door.

She sat down and whined until both Ty and Ray petted her.

Finally they were gone, and I e-mailed the flyer to Sandy Harbor Printing. I included a cover letter asking them to make one hundred copies of the flyer as soon as possible and that Ray Meyerson would pick them up tomorrow. Then I went upstairs to change into my tomato chef's outfit.

Then it hit me. Today was the day I had invited Laura Tingsley and her mother, Carla VanPlank, to lunch.

What had I done? I didn't particularly like their company, but I was thinking about the case, or cases.

I wasn't in the mood to listen to their accolades about Rick Tingsley, their future presidential candidate.

I found Rick Tingsley to be an arrogant worm who gave politicians a worse reputation than they already had.

At the Dance Fest, Laura might be able to tell me more about the bonfire evening, or maybe her mother would put a lid on whatever Laura said. I'd just have to separate them somehow.

And Rick Tingsley from them all.

As I walked over to the Silver Bullet, I stopped and looked up at the sky. The stars were brilliant and so close I felt I could pluck them out of the darkness and put one on each finger, like diamonds.

Speaking of diamonds, I wondered if "B" had promised to marry Claire when he found out that she was pregnant. Or maybe she hadn't even told him.

She must have. Claire was so happy, even I could see the joy on her face back then. Certainly, the father of her baby could see her happiness, too.

So who was the father of her baby?

I thought I needed to hit the library and pull out the yearbook of the class of 1989. Nothing like a yearbook to find out information about the past.

I'd bet my tomato pants that I'd find someone with a *B* name if it's the last thing I did.

Question: why hadn't I thought of that sooner?

Answer: because this chef had too much on her plate.

I should have brought my lists with me. In between orders, I could make more phone calls and do more planning for the Dance Fest.

Going in through the back door, I noticed that Juanita and Cindy were doing some cleaning. Everything was neat and tidy, and the floor was so clean, I could eat off it.

"Fabulous!" I said. "Everything looks wonderful."

"Thanks," Cindy said. "We got a little slow, so we thought we'd straighten things up."

"Well, things aren't going to be slow for long. I've decided to reinstitute the Dance Fest," I said. I could feel the excitement bubbling through my veins. This was going to be fun!

"Really, Trixie? My parents have told me about them and how much fun they were. Bonfires, dancing, food, men!" Cindy giggled.

Juanita clapped. "Perfect. It's about time this stretch of beach heard laughter again!" She suddenly sobered. "Too much death. Time for fun."

"That's what I think, too," I said, still hoping that I could get good tidbits of information from those attending.

"Trixie, I almost forgot . . . you have a message," Juanita said. "Laura Tingsley can't make lunch with you, but her mother will be here at one o'clock."

"Carla?" It was strange that she'd come alone. I didn't really know her mother from the latest boy band, but what the heck? "Okay. Lunch with Laura's mom."

I told Juanita and Cindy to go home, that I'd start my shift early, and thanked them again.

"I want to tell you that I hired a busboy. His name is Ray Myerson. He starts tomorrow at noon."

"I know him," Cindy said. "He's in my sister Maria's class. She told me how he got into trouble for hacking into the school's computer and giving everyone A's and B's."

"We're going to give him a chance," I said.

Cindy nodded. "I won't bring it up."

"Yeah, there's no need," I said.

"About the Dance Fest, Trixie," Juanita said. "You know I'll do anything to help."

"Me, too!" Cindy said.

"I knew I could count on you both." Tears stung my eyes. I was blessed to have such a great staff. There weren't any problems that we couldn't handle together.

I rolled up my sleeves and got to work.

My waitresses tonight were Judy Daniels and Laurie Lanco, two veterans who had worked for Uncle Porky and Aunt Stella, so it should be an easy evening. I told them about the Dance Fest also, and like Juanita and Cindy, they volunteered to do whatever I needed.

I didn't expect a big evening crowd tonight, so I'd have some time to work on my lists. I was going to inventory the meat and veggies that I had on hand, and then I'd make a list of veggies and meat that I'd need. Then tomorrow I'd place a big order at the local organic farm and the rest at the local food supplier, Sunshine Foods.

I also had to watch for Sarah Stolfus the next time she dropped off an order. I wanted to ask her to make several dozen biscuits for strawberry shortcake and a buggy load of chocolate chip cookies for the kids.

And I was going to make Michele's Chocolate Cowboy Cake. Michele was a pal of mine from the old neighborhood who was noted for this cake. The best thing about it was that the cake could be frosted when hot—a wonderful timesaver.

Oh, I had to call my liquor distributor, too. I'd need a couple of kegs of beer, a few boxes of wine, and several cases of soda.

Laurie greeted me and gave me seven orders for the Friday night special: fried haddock with coleslaw and fries and a side of either macaroni salad, potato salad, or mac and cheese.

The Silver Bullet's coleslaw was just fabulous. It was all in the dressing—Uncle Porky's special recipe that was passed to him from a good neighbor, Grandma Wojcieson.

And he always put a "secret ingredient" in his macaroni and potato salad—dill weed. I've told a few people, but I've always made them promise not to tell anyone else.

A fistful of orders came in from Judy. She was tall and slender with brownish red hair that was always up in a twist. She reminded me of a very professional waitress. She never took a wasted step or forgot a thing that the customer wanted. Laurie, the other waitress on duty, was a people person and could talk the ears off an elephant.

Laurie was a librarian by trade, but her library was downsized, and she was cut. She was as short as Judy was tall, and she was always on a diet. Laurie seemed scattered, but she did a wonderful job and the customers loved her wit and happy-go-lucky attitude.

It was fun bantering with both of them, and I still managed to make some progress on the Dance Fest.

Soon my shift was over and Darlene Wilson came in to cook. Dar worked on the weekends and was on call to fill in. She was an English-as-a-second-language teacher who did a lot of work with the migrant workers in the area. Dar seemed to always run in fourth gear. Just five minutes with Dar and her energy made me feel like a slug.

Ty Brisco walked into the diner with his cowboy boots and hat, perfectly faded jeans, and a white long-sleeved shirt. You could cut your hand on his creased sleeves.

But I wasn't looking.

Laurie immediately reached for the coffeepot, pouring him a cup of coffee.

Ty took the coffee with a "Well, thank you very much, darlin'," looked at me, and slanted his head toward a back booth.

I got the message. Hopefully it was good news! I poured myself a cup and joined him.

"Cottage Eight has been released on the condition that I take pictures and document everything we do."

I was thrilled. I just knew that we'd find something related to Claire. "That's just what you said would happen."

He grinned. "When do you want to start tearing down the walls?"

"Is now too soon?"

# Chapter 10

*I* hurried to the Big House, excited to start the search for clues.

"Is this your morning jog?" Ty asked.

"Jog? In my dreams."

His long legs made short work of keeping up with me.

"I left the tools on the porch, but I want to change into some old clothes. I don't want to ruin my tomatoes."

He chuckled. "That would be a shame."

Ty sat down on a rocker as I ran upstairs. The answering machine was blinking, but I didn't want to answer it. It'd probably just be more cancellations.

After I destroyed Cottage Eight, I needed to go to the library and find *B* names from the 1989 graduating class. I shuddered to think that the baby daddy might not be a local male. Then how on earth would we find him?

Unless there was a clue in the walls of Cottage

Eight, it would be next to impossible to find the guy. Obviously, the father hadn't come forward in twenty-five years.

I slipped into a pair of jean shorts and an old T-shirt and went to meet Ty on the porch.

Then I remembered something important. "Ty, where's the folder that I borrowed from Dr. Francis's office? I want to go through it."

"I already did. There's nothing exciting in it."

"I want to read it anyway. Maybe something will click with me that didn't click with you."

"If such a folder did exist, it'd be in my office under lock and key," he said. "And, you know, you probably should put it back."

"That'll be fun. And if I get caught?"

"You'd better hope that Miss Shannon Shannon calls me so I can get you off," he said as we walked down the stairs with our tools.

"Don't you love her name? At least it's easy to remember," I said. "And she certainly will remember your name. You charmed her."

Ty grinned. He was pretty proud of himself, the cowboy flirt that he was.

I had to admit that Ty wasn't like my ex, Deputy Doug. Sure, Ty powered up his Texas drawl to get information when he was working a case, and it worked like a charm.

Ty was a natural flirt who loved women of all shapes and ages, but he wasn't a player.

Deputy Doug, on the other hand, used his uniform to pick up women—younger women—who were obviously impressed by his blues, badge, and gun.

He thought he was a player.

I shook my head to clear out the Deputy Doug cobwebs and concentrated on the task at hand.

Ty pulled the yellow crime scene tape away from the door of Eight. It felt good to see some of that go, but the cottage was still tightly wrapped. I opened the door with my extra key.

"Nothing has changed, huh?" I asked Ty.

"The typewriter is still on the floor," he said.

"I'm going to pick it up, Ty. Okay with you?"

He hesitated. "Yeah, go ahead. It's been photographed enough."

I lifted the typewriter with a grunt and put it on the table, just where Phil Jacobson had placed it. I wished that I had the scrapbook that I'd seen on the table.

The murderer had taken it.

"Ready?" Ty asked, handing me the sledgehammer.

"You know, I thought I was ready for this, but it seems like I'm ruining the history of the place. Look at all these names of people who stayed here. Look at the dates: 1952, 1954, 1961 . . . It's just so cool."

"I'll take pictures before we start. Would that make you feel better?"

"I guess so."

He had an official-looking cop camera, so the pictures should come out good.

"Go for it, Trixie. Let's start by the door and work around the main room first."

I took a deep breath and then swung the hammer— *whack!*

I dented a big chunk of the wainscoting. Ty worked the crowbar and the sledgehammer. We traded tools and kept ripping, making a big pile of wood. It became so high that we started tossing additional paneling out the door.

I hated to see the cottage being destroyed like this, but there was a black cloud that hovered over this cottage. Maybe with renovations, it'd become the fresh, new cottage that Uncle Porky had built in the 1950s.

It was exhausting and dirty work. I used muscles that I didn't know I had.

Ty swung the sledgehammer as if it were as light as a badminton racquet.

Finally it was time to wreck the bathroom.

That's where I'd wanted to start this project, where I thought Claire would hide something because of the big knothole behind the medicine cabinet that someone had made much larger, but Ty insisted that we do this methodically and in a logical pattern. Sheesh.

I just had a feeling that Claire had hidden something in the wall—something that she had to hide from her family, but something that she wanted to retrieve later.

The panel was finally free. I examined the inside of the wall. And just as I thought, there was a yellowed piece of paper folded and lying on the floor. There seemed to be a long piece of yarn attached to it with a piece of yellowed tape clinging to the yarn. Yes! This was how she'd retrieve the paper later with the yarn. Ingenious.

"Oh . . . oh . . . oh . . ." That was all I could say.

"Don't touch it! I need to take a picture." Ty snapped photos in every direction. I almost expected him to stand on his head.

"Oh . . . my . . . goodness!"

"Go ahead and read it, Trixie. You knew that something was here all along."

He gave me a pair of gloves and I could barely put them on because my hands were shaking as if I had the d.t.'s.

I carefully moved the blue yarn aside. "Ty, do you see this dried-up, yellowed piece of tape on the yarn? I can see a yellowed tape mark on the letter."

He took more pictures. I looked where I found the letter and pointed to another strip of old tape that lay on a board. Ty took more pictures.

"It looks like Claire taped the yarn to the letter and then taped the yarn to the inside of the wall. She wanted to retrieve it, wanted to keep it," Ty said. "Probably when her stay at the cottage was over."

"Just what I thought. Just what I'd do."

I unfolded the letter and read it out loud:

*Dear Claire,*
    *I don't know when I'll be able to visit you*

*again, if ever. I guess I'll have to wait until you are back in Sandy Harbor.*

   *I know that we probably shouldn't have made love last night. I should have been strong. After all, I'm older, but I couldn't help myself. I just had to. It was beautiful and being that it was the first time for you, it was extra special.*

   *I love you and want to spend my life with you. You're the only girl—*

"Ty, he crossed out 'girl' and put 'woman,'" I said, then continued:

   *You're the only woman that I've ever loved. As soon as I can, I'll ask you to marry me. Until then, we'll have to be satisfied by writing letters. I don't dare to call you because of your parents.*

   *Think of me. I'll be thinking of you.*

                 *All my love,*
                     *B*
               *XOXOX*

"Oh, for Pete's sake. Why the hell didn't he sign his damn name?"

I handed Ty the letter, and he read it. "I can see why Claire hid this from her family and why she wanted to keep it."

"Exactly! I'm sure she didn't want her parents to find out that she lost her virginity to 'B' when he surprised her by visiting her at home. Yet it was a romantic letter full of promises for the future. Claire was the type who would fall for that. And obviously he drove to Rochester, where she lived."

Ty grimaced. "I'm wondering if Claire got pregnant the first time she had sex with 'B.'"

"That's my guess. Was there anything in her record? Anything that Dr. Francis wrote down? Anything that Claire might have said?"

"Not that I found, but since you're going to go through her file again, maybe you can find something."

"You know, Ty, I don't think that this letter is the key to Claire's death. It's just a love letter with a pseudoapology and promises for the future. There must be something else, something more." I looked around at our mess. "I think we have to finish tearing up the place."

"Might as well. We have the bedroom to do. Maybe she hid something in the wall there, too."

But there was nothing. Nothing.

"Okay. Let's call it a day," Ty said. "It's almost one fifteen."

"One fifteen?" I was late for my lunch with Carla VanPlank. I looked like a construction worker, but I didn't have time to change. "Ty, I have to fly. I have a lunch date with Carla VanPlank that I'm late for, and she isn't the type of person that would tolerate lateness."

"Sounds like a wonderful time," he said sarcastically.

I took off my gloves and tossed them onto a pile

of wood. "I'd like to get to know Carla better. I'd love to find out what makes her tick, other than her loyalty to her husband and to the mayor. And, of course, she adores Laura. Maybe she'll give me some good information."

Trotting from the cottage to the back of the diner, I washed up in the back tub. Then I put a white chef's jacket over my filthy clothes. It'd do.

Carla VanPlank was sitting at a window booth toward the back of the diner. I could smell the Chanel No. 5 even from halfway there.

She rolled her eyes as I slid into the red vinyl booth. "I thought I might have had the wrong time."

"Sorry, Mrs. VanPlank. I was busy."

Her eyes bored a hole through my chef's jacket. "I can see that you were occupied. I watched things being tossed out of one of the cottages. What on earth were you doing?"

I didn't know how much I should tell her, so I decided to lie. "I'm doing a little remodeling."

"I see," she said. "Are you remodeling all the cottages?"

"Uh . . . eventually."

"But you started in the middle?"

What did she care where I started? "Yes. To be blunt, I thought it would be a good idea to re-model it since there was a murder there."

She took a sip of coffee. "Oh yes. Of course."

"It's too bad that Laura couldn't make our little luncheon."

"Mayor Tingsley needed her. Of course, her place is with him."

What century was she living in?

"I see. Is there another Sandy Harbor crisis?" I asked.

"Obviously. The mayor depends immensely on my Laura."

"Maybe Laura should have run for mayor." I smiled, thinking that complimenting her daughter might be a way to soften her up.

"Nonsense! Women shouldn't be in office. It's a man's job, but there's always a great woman behind every powerful man."

*Oh boy. Where's she been living?*

"Didn't I hear that your husband was the senator of somewhere at one time?" I think that Clyde or Max told me that.

"The Northern District of New York," she said, tilting her head as if I should have known this information.

"And he retired instead of moving on to a higher office?"

She was about to take a sip of coffee, but she set the cup down so hard, it sloshed into the saucer.

"Grant was going to run for president, but he . . . he . . . couldn't keep it in his pants. So all my work campaigning for him was for nothing. Nothing! He withdrew in disgrace."

I motioned for Judy to come over before Mrs. VanPlank really lost it.

Judy held up her order pad. "What can I get you ladies?"

"I lost my appetite," said Mrs. VanPlank, grabbing her purse.

She couldn't go yet. There were a lot of questions I wanted to ask her about the old days in Sandy Harbor.

"Please, Mrs. VanPlank, stay and have lunch with me. I apologize for asking about Grant. I didn't know." But I was going to do a computer search and read up on Grant VanPlank just as soon as I could.

She opened her purse, took out a brown prescription bottle, and shook some white pills into her hand. She passed up the glass of water with ice that was sitting in front of her and tossed them down with her coffee.

"Are you all right?" I asked.

"I'm perfectly fine."

Judy smiled widely. "Would you like me to come back, ladies?"

"No. I've stared at the menu long enough," she said. "I'd like a BLT with mayonnaise on toasted wheat bread, but first, I'd like a bowl of your split pea soup."

"Got it," Judy said. "Trixie, how about you?"

"I'll have the same."

I loved Uncle Porky's split pea soup. After the split peas were done cooking in chicken broth, with ham chunks, carrots, and onions, he whipped it up in a blender with equal parts cream and milk until it was a lighter green and all the ingredients were melded together. Delicious. I, of course, kept his brilliant recipe the same.

We talked about the Dance Fest over soup and the "old days" when Carla's husband, Grant, was the senator of the area. They moved to Port Palm, Florida to escape the scandal.

Carla made it clear that she considered Port Palm her primary residence now, but she "just can't stay away from the mayor and my daughter, especially during campaign time when her husband is running."

"You know, I don't even know if you have any other children or grandchildren," I said.

"Laura doesn't have any children. She's my only child, so I'll never have any grandchildren." Her voice faded into her coffee cup, which she held in front of her face like a shield.

"I'm so sorry. It must be hard for Laura." I understood her pain. I took a deep breath and changed the subject to her favorite topic. "I'm sure Laura could use your help and expertise when the mayor runs for higher office."

She smiled. "I'll be here."

"Tell me, Mrs. VanPlank, did you know Claire Jacobson?"

"A little."

Our split pea soup arrived and there were the appropriate oohs and aahs over the pure deliciousness of it.

"You knew Claire just a little?" I prodded.

"Why, yes. She was just a summer visitor, so why would I know her well?"

"Did Laura know her?" I asked.

"Just a little."

She wasn't helping much at all. "But you were living here when Claire disappeared, right?"

"Yes. There was quite the search for her, and personally, I thought she ran off with someone. I thought she was that type—a little loose."

*No way!*

"But I thought you said you didn't know Claire very well."

She put down her spoon and dabbed at her mouth. "She had a . . . reputation."

"Oh?" I was adamant that if Claire had the reputation of being loose, the gossipers should be put in a room and forced to watch the channel guide for a month straight.

"If we are going to continue to talk about Claire Jacobson during this luncheon, I'll be leaving," Mrs. VanPlank said.

"I'm sorry, Mrs. VanPlank, but I'm very interested in this matter. It's a personal thing, but I'll change the subject." I gathered my thoughts and proceeded with my lame questioning. "Since you've shared so much with me, can I just ask you a personal question?"

"I don't suppose I can stop you. You're very nosy."

Ouch. But fair.

I took a deep breath. "My husband cheated on

me, and I left him quicker than the time it takes to poach an egg. Can I just ask you how could you stay with Grant when his unfaithfulness was so public?"

She closed her eyes as if it pained her to discuss it. Of course it would pain her. What kind of hostess was I?

"I'm so sorry, Mrs. VanPlank. I didn't mean to hurt you. I was just wondering how you handled Grant's cheating. I handled it very poorly when I found out that my husband was cheating on me. I called his mother and tattled. Then I donated all his clothes, his motorcycle, and his boat to the Salvation Army, so when he came home, he had nothing to wear but the clothes on his back. Our only car was registered to me."

She didn't laugh, but her eyes twinkled.

"I did give him the receipt for his income tax," I said.

Mrs. VanPlank took a sip of her water. "I will share my reason with you, since I've been interviewed about it by several media sources." She sighed. "My reason was, and still is, that I simply felt that I should continue to support him. I think that his reputation can still be salvaged and he can get back into politics. Others have done it. Besides, I've worked hard for him. I deserve a reward. I couldn't let his dalliance with a young hussy ruin my life."

"I see."

I didn't see at all, but her statement confirmed

my opinion that she believed that a woman shouldn't hold office herself but could shine in the limelight through her husband.

Just what Laura Tingsley seemed to believe! Nothing like brainwashing.

I dropped my spoon into my pea soup and it splattered on the table.

Oh my! Could Grant VanPlank be the older man who'd fathered Claire's baby?

"Excuse me," I said. "I'm so clumsy. My hand seems to be weak from all the work I did on Cottage Eight." That was true. My wrist *was* killing me.

She nodded and took a drink of water.

"Mrs. VanPlank, I can't believe that I'm asking you this, but if you don't want to answer, I completely understand. Here goes: I knew who my ex-husband was fooling around with. Did you know who your husband was . . . uh . . . with?"

She hesitated and stared me down like a gunslinger at high noon. Then surprisingly, she answered, "No. I didn't want to know. All I know was that she must have been very . . . young. He said that she made him feel like a teenager again."

Claire! Oh no!

Grant VanPlank would have been old enough to be her father. Could he have written that sappy love letter to her?

She looked out the window, and I realized that this had to be a painful conversation for her. I didn't want that, but I continued to be surprised as to what she'd shared with me.

Time to change the subject.

"Mrs. VanPlank, I hope you, Grant, Laura, and the mayor will come to the Dance Fest. It should be a fun time. Just like the old days when Uncle Porky and Aunt Stella ran the Silver Bullet."

"I'll be attending. I'm hoping that some of my old friends will be there, and, of course, I'll be campaigning for the mayor's election as senator."

"Of course."

That was just what I needed at the Dance Fest, a side campaign for Rick Tingsley.

I wanted to ask her whether or not her husband had a nickname, but I couldn't figure how to broach that subject. Oh, I just got an idea!

"Carla. May I call you Carla?" I didn't wait for her to answer. "Carla, I wanted to ask you if you know my aunt Beatrix. I'm hoping that I can get her and my aunt Stella to fly up for the Dance Fest. It'll be so good to see them. You know I was named after my aunt Beatrix. It's funny, she hates to be called Trixie and I hate to be called Beatrix. Did you ever have a nickname?"

"No."

"What about Mr. VanPlank?"

"Never."

Darn it. I was hoping that he'd be "B."

But then who wrote that letter to Claire?

Grant VanPlank had a motive. It wouldn't look good in the media for him to have a seventeen-year-old pregnant mistress, would it? He killed her so the scandal wouldn't be hanging over his head when he ran for president of the United States.

Was Phil Jacobson onto him? Was that why he had to go?

I looked forward to meeting Grant VanPlank at the Dance Fest. I had a couple of questions for him.

The rest of the lunch was mired in small talk. I couldn't wait to see Ty and tell him what I'd found out.

Did Grant VanPlank kill both Phil and Claire? Maybe, maybe not, but he was certainly number one on my leader board of suspects.

But I had more investigating to do.

# Chapter 11

"I'd like that tour that you promised me, Trixie," Carla said, but more like a command than a request.

I told her that the meal was on me, but the least Carla could have done was to leave a tip for Judy. She didn't even make an effort to reach for her purse. Maybe it was too much of a strain with all the diamonds that she was wearing.

We walked by the lake. I ran out of small talk, but she rattled on about campaign advertising, Republicans vs. Democrats, the current president, and her recipe for sauerbraten.

And don't even get her started on insurance companies!

Soon I realized that she was walking toward Cottage Eight. In her heels, she sank into the grass, a little less than the sand, but it was still a struggle for her to walk.

She surveyed the mess of wainscoting in the yard. "Remodeling, you say?"

"Yes. I'm going to either remodel it or tear it down."

"Oh!" Her lips pinched tight until they lost their color. You'd think that the place held some importance to her.

"Carla, does Cottage Eight mean something to you? I mean, did you ever stay in it?"

"Never. But I do remember visiting Jean and Mel Jacobson on occasion. Jean and I were in the Daughters of the American Revolution together. We both had ancestors who participated in the Boston Tea Party."

"That's pretty cool."

"I wouldn't call it cool. I'd say it was historic, patriotic, and radical."

"Oh, sure. All of that, but pretty cool, too."

She sniffed. "How far can you trace your ancestors?"

"On my father's side, I can trace them all the way from Warsaw, Poland. On my mother's side, to Russia."

"So they were immigrants."

"Yes. Just like your ancestors."

She didn't like that. I've never known such a snob.

"So you visited the Jacobsons?" I asked.

"Yes. They were very nice people."

"I wonder whatever happened to their son. I can't remember his name," I said.

"I'm sure I don't know."

We were standing in front of Cottage Eight.

"I was hoping that we'd get a chance to go inside," she said.

"As you can see, it's wrapped in police tape."

"But surely we can go in. You're the owner."

That was curious. "Why on earth do you want to go in there?"

"I—I thought it would help me remember Jean and Mel."

Carla didn't strike me as the sentimental type.

"Sorry, Carla. I don't dare go in. Deputy Brisco has taped up the place for a reason."

"But you two were just in there, taking down the walls. Are you looking for something? Something that has to do with the murder?"

"No. Not at all," I lied. "Why do you ask?"

"Because you wouldn't tear down paneling with crime scene tape around it. You'd wait to remodel until the tape was gone."

She had me there. Time to shift gears.

"Well, I think that this is the end of the tour, Carla. Is there anything else you'd like to see?"

"Not particularly," she snapped.

I wondered if the reason she came to lunch alone was to see Cottage Eight. Why the fascination?

I chalked it up to just plain curiosity. Something she could talk about during cocktail parties. Something out of the ordinary for an upper-middle-class matron.

Whatever it was, I didn't care about it now. I was ready to walk her to her car.

"Well, thanks for visiting, Carla. I'm sure you want to head back. Maybe the mayor needs you. Or Mr. VanPlank." I slapped my forehead. What kind of detective was I? I could have asked him some questions, also. "I'm so sorry. I should have invited your husband, too. I didn't think of it."

"No. That's not necessary." She shook her head. "I like the time away from him. I think it's very important for a married couple to live their own lives."

That was just what Deputy Doug had been doing while married to me—only he was living his own life way too much.

"Let me walk you to your car," I volunteered. "Or do you want me to drive it closer? Those shoes aren't very good for walking outside."

"I have casual shoes in my car. I should have worn them on our little walk."

I nodded. "So, should I get your car?"

"I'm fine, dear."

She was doing a fabulous job of aerating my grass, but it was taking forever to cross the lawn. It'd be faster if I carried her on my back.

Finally we made it to her car, a candy apple red Chevy Malibu.

"Thank you for coming, Carla. It's been a lovely afternoon."

And interesting. *But please start the car up!*

Finally, finally, finally the Chevy's motor started and Carla VanPlank moseyed through the parking lot, up the road to the highway, and turned right onto Route 3.

It felt as if I'd lost ten pounds.


"Will Beatrix Matkowski please approach the bench."

Ugh. Could I tell the judge of Sandy Harbor Justice Court that only my auntie goes by that name?

I walked on the marble floor shined within an inch of its life. My new flats, which were half sneaker and half-dressy, if that can possibly be, were squeaking like crows on a rampage.

Finally I was in front of the bench, which was a folding table set up in a huge hall often used for wedding receptions. It became the justice court on Wednesday nights.

"Thank you for coming, Miss Matkowski."

"No problem, Your Honor."

His Honor was Joe Newell, the owner of the Sandy Harbor Movie Theater and Arcade on the north side of downtown. Everyone was buzzing about the renovations he did to restore the theater to its original state, somewhere around the 1940s.

Joe frequented the Silver Bullet regularly, and I knew him. He was a great kidder, mercilessly funny, and he often butted heads with Mayor Tingsley.

Rick Tingsley couldn't keep up with the sharp brain of Joe Newell.

"Please take a seat. This is an informal hearing," he said.

"Then please call me Trixie, Your Honor."

"All right."

I took a seat in the folding chair in front of the table. Also seated were Ty and Ray Meyerson. Ty winked at me. Ray lifted his hand in a slight wave. I nodded back. I didn't know Ray's parents, but I assumed the couple holding hands were them.

Ray's lawyer was there with a floppy black briefcase and a stack of manila folders. A striking red-haired woman that I assumed was the district attorney smiled at me. She had more folders than Ray's lawyer. Hers were stacked in a bright blue plastic milk crate.

If this wasn't a Wednesday night in a makeshift courtroom, I'd swear that we were all here for a bowling banquet.

"Miss Matkowski, I understand that you have employed the defendant, Ray Meyerson," stated Joe the judge.

"I have, Your Honor."

"And how is that working out?"

"Fabulously." Was that even a word? And please don't ask me to spell it for the court stenographer.

Oh, she was also in the room. She was at least a hundred years old and wore two sweaters and a red shawl wrapped around her shoulders.

I thought it was hot in here.

"That's good. Can you tell the court what Mr. Meyerson has been doing for you?"

"Computer work. And also, Ray is the head busboy at my diner."

Ray was the *only* busboy at my diner.

Both Ty and Ray grinned. Judge Joe stifled a smile.

Then the smile left his face. "Did you say computer work, Miss Matkowski?"

"Yes. Yes, I did. Ray did some wonderful pamphlets for me for the Dance Fest. I hope you're coming, Your Honor."

He nodded. "Of course I'll be there. Wouldn't miss it. But, Miss Matkowski, are you aware of the incident that Mr. Meyers is accused of committing?"

"Yes. Ray has shared the incident with me."

"And you still let him use your computer?"

"Absolutely. I trust him implicitly." And don't ask me to spell that. "Or else I wouldn't trust him with my computer."

"Good."

"You should see him, Joe." Oops. "I mean, Your Honor. He is a typing whiz. Very artistic. He should be working for a computer place, not the Silver Bullet. However, he's the best busboy that I've ever employed. He's a real self-starter. He knows exactly what needs to be done, and then he does it. And I just love him."

His mother sniffed and blew her nose.

"Well, that's good enough for me," said Judge Joe. "Is there a motion from the district attorney's office?"

The redhead stood. "Yes, Your Honor. I'd like to make a motion that the defendant's conviction be vacated, that he be adjudicated a Youthful Offender, and that his record be sealed."

"Mr. Udder?"

His name was really Udder? The poor man must have been teased unmercifully at school.

"The defense agrees, Your Honor."

"Mr. Meyerson, will you and Mr. Udder please approach the bench."

Ray, swimming in a three-piece suit that must have belonged to his father, stumbled getting to the appropriate area of the banquet table.

I looked at his feet. His shoes were so big he might as well be wearing the box that they came in. His father's shoes?

"Ray Meyerson, I am vacating your conviction. I am adjudicating you a Youthful Offender, and after reading the report from the county probation department, I am sentencing you to a one-year conditional discharge with the conditions that you maintain employment at Miss Matkowski's Silver Bullet Diner for a year and that you remain out of all further trouble. If you get in trouble again, heaven help you. Do you have anything to say, Mr. Meyerson?"

"Only that I won't get in trouble anymore. My hacking days are over. And I'd like to thank Deputy Brisco for getting me the job. And I'd like to thank Trixie . . . um . . . Miss Matkowski. She's a blast to work for. It's not really like a job."

"Good." The judge pounded his gavel. "Court's dismissed."

He motioned for me to come closer.

"Yeah, Joe?"

"What's the special today?"

"Chicken and biscuits with your choice of soup— split pea, French onion, or bean. A chef salad, rolls fresh from the oven, and your choice of dessert. You should see the pies that Sarah Stolfus brought over."

A piece of coconut cream was waiting for me.

Mr. and Mrs. Meyerson came over and introduced themselves. Donna and Ed. Ed couldn't stop pumping my hand, and Donna wrapped her arms around me and clung to me like a piece of lint.

Finally Ty suggested that we all head down to the Silver Bullet and have something to eat.

"Trixie must get tired of always eating there. I made a little spread," said Mrs. Meyerson. "Please come. I have a lot to eat. I always cook when I'm stressed. I thought my little Ray—" She dabbed at her nose. "Was going to jail."

"Oh, Mom. It's okay," Ray said, looking helpless, as did Ed.

"Don't cry, Donna. It's all over, and Ray made out fine," I said.

"It's all due to you."

"I don't think so, Donna. It's Ray who worked hard."

Ray's girlfriend, Liz, was hugging the stuffing out of him. Liz looked like a nerd herself. She wore a T-shirt with a picture of Albert Einstein and had on red polyester pants and black sneakers with lime green shoelaces. She could stand to lose twenty pounds—not that I'm pointing any fingers—and she had a nice smile. I could tell that she was head over heels in love with Ray.

After we were all shuffling out, I saw that Liz was carrying a white plastic container. It looked as though she had made a cake.

How sweet!

I was just about to make some excuse to get out of going to the Meyersons' for the "spread" when Ty whispered in my ear. Honestly, when he did that, it gave me the shivers.

Yum!

"Let's go," he said. "It'd mean a lot to the Meyersons."

I nodded. "Just for a short time."

"You got it."

Ty had taken me to court, so I really had no choice but to go.

As we drove to the Meyersons' house, I realized that by the twists and turns and the smell of cows, we were going deep into the Sandy Harbor countryside. The roller-coaster roads made amusement park coasters seem like anthills.

Ray rode this on his bike to and from work?

I was impressed, but I wondered if Ray would continue to work at the Silver Bullet after his sentence. Oh, wait. He was chained to me for a year!

That was a long time. If Ray wanted to move on, I'd talk to Joe Newell myself.

But I hoped he wouldn't. Boy, did I have spread-sheets and some other things that Ray could set up for me on the computer!

It was interesting being in Ty's cop car. He had a laptop on a swivel stand somehow screwed to the floor. There was his radio and a bunch of other cop buttons that I had no clue as to what they were for.

I stole a look at him. He had a strong jaw and the hint of a five o'clock shadow. It was seven thirty, so his shadow would catch up soon. He smelled of leather and pine trees and maybe a trace of vanilla.

"You did a great job in court," he said.

"I didn't do anything. Ray is the one who's work-ing hard. He has a good mind. I think he just did the hacking at school to be accepted by his peers. Kids do dumb things like that. I know, I always did dumb stuff."

"Oh yeah? Like what?"

"Like taking dares. Not dangerous things, but things like singing Barry Manilow songs on the street corner. Or tap-dancing at a school dance. Oh, and one of my biggest blunders was rolling a grapefruit like a bowling ball down the school hall during change of class and watching everyone trying to avoid it or actually kicking it around."

He chuckled.

"I got detention for that one. Five days. Sister Mary Mary said that I could have really hurt someone if they tripped over the grapefruit or something. Mostly, the grapefruit just turned to mush. Oh, I had to clean up the remains, too, under the supervision of Mr. O'Neill, the janitor."

"Such a juvenile delinquent."

"Ah . . . the good old days—high school. But no one got murdered. No one got hurt. If anyone carried knives or guns to school, no one knew about it and no one used them. I don't want to preach, but I feel sorry for kids these days."

"Me, too." He put on his blinker to turn right. "In my high school days, there weren't any armed police officers or security guards in the school."

"Maybe there should have been a couple for the Sandy Harbor class of 1989. But, Ty . . . I just can't get over the feeling that no kid in Sandy Harbor would have killed Claire."

"You never know. I've seen some awful stuff as to what kids do to other kids."

"Sad."

"Yeah."

Finally we were at the Meyersons' house. It was getting to be sunset, and Ed hurried inside and turned on a passel of lights even though we could still see.

The house, a creamy yellow, was mostly a ranch with interesting windows and a fancy roofline. It had a huge front porch and looked warm and inviting.

Just like the Big House.

Ed escorted us into a foyer where we dispensed with our Windbreakers and sweaters. Donna scooted away, muttering something about "getting the spread out."

"I'll help Donna," I said, hurrying after her.

The kitchen made me gasp. If I ever died and went to heaven, I'd want a kitchen like Donna Meyerson's. There was a big island, blue granite countertops, pale oak cabinets, and stainless steel appliances. Huge windows looked out over grasslands with long-legged horses in a white fenced-in area away from the house, and cows dotted the fields in the distance.

"I don't know horses, Donna, but those look extra fine to me. Like racehorses."

"It's a hobby of Ed's. He's been known to ship them to a trainer and race them at Saratoga or Meadowlands or the like. I think they're mostly a money pit, but I have to admit that a couple of them have done well. And I like looking at them, especially when they have a little one. The babies are just darling."

Donna had the oak table in the kitchen set already. She had a lace tablecloth and it was set for what looked like twelve people.

She stuck her head into the commercial fridge and started pulling out plastic-wrap-covered dishes.

"Let me help you," I said.

"No. You're a guest."

"I want to help."

"Okay."

Bowls full of salads and fancy plates with rolled ham, turkey, roast beef, and cheeses came out. I took them from her and put them on the island as she handed them to me.

"We'll put everything here and eat at the table. That's what I often do because everything won't fit on the table."

"Are you expecting the army from Fort Drum to stop in?"

I shouldn't talk! I always cooked way too much food myself. I still hadn't mastered the art of toning it down.

Everything was out of the fridge, and Donna and I fussed with positioning everything on the island. She had a good eye.

"Ty Brisco is just fabulous, don't you think, Trixie?" Donna asked.

"Uh, yes. Just fabulous." What did she want me to say?

"I owe him so much for all that he's done for Ray. You, too, Trixie."

I held up a hand like a traffic cop. "Enough said. Ray was the one who did it."

"He's a good kid."

"He is. And smart. I enjoy him a lot."

"Good. Did he tell you that he's saving up his diner money for a new bike?"

I smiled. "Don't tell him, but his new bike is on me. I owe him for some computer work, and there's more that I'd like for him to do. I know what I want, but I don't have the skill that he does. And I don't have time to learn it."

She sniffed. "You're so good to Ray."

I was afraid that there would be a flood of tears soon. "Donna, be happy. He just made a stupid kid mistake to be liked. I don't know about you, but I can understand it."

But what I couldn't understand was murder. Again, I thought of Claire and her brother. I would be front row and center, eating popcorn and sipping soda, if the person or persons who killed them were in court, answering for their crime.

But my popcorn was going to be stale and my soda was going to lose its fizz, because I wasn't close to finding out who killed them.

"Donna, is that dill weed I see in the potato salad? Oh, it's in the mac salad, too."

"Shh. I'm not supposed to tell."

"Said who? Porky Matkowski?"

"Yes!"

I laughed. "It's the worst-kept secret in the world."

She grinned, and it was the first time I saw her eyes light up all evening. "I've never told a soul."

"You're a good friend of Porky's, Donna, but I think that the secret is out."

"Not from me."

We both laughed.

"I wish I knew you were putting out a spread." I thought I'd use her words, but they sounded so foreign to me. "I would have brought something."

"Not necessary."

"Hey, wait a minute. Is that my aunt Helen's lime, cottage cheese, and nut dessert?"

"Guilty," Donna said.

"Sheesh."

The coffee started perking, and the scent permeated the room. I just loved the smell of brewing coffee.

"Donna, can I ask you something?"

"Sure."

"You knew Claire Jacobson, didn't you?"

"Absolutely. I worked for Porky and Stella as a room attendant through my four years of high school. I was a year behind her."

"So you didn't go to the bonfire for the class of 1989?"

"No, thank goodness, but I helped them search for her. I liked Claire a lot."

"I don't remember you. I was there every summer, too."

"They used to call me Peaches."

"Peaches? Oh yes! I remember a girl named Peaches. You?"

"I was quite a bit heavier back then. Even recently. I had a gastric bypass four years ago."

"Oh! Tell me something about Claire that you remember, Donna."

"I remember how she was always nice to everyone, no matter who."

"Yeah."

"Oh! Speaking of Judge Newell—"

"Were we speaking of him?" I asked.

"We are now. But speaking of Judge Newell, he had a major crush on her. They dated a couple of times."

"Really?"

"Oh, absolutely."

"And what happened?" I asked, unwrapping the meat tray, ready to pluck off one of the rolls of roast beef.

"Well, I guess it was pretty ugly. Claire asked him not to stalk her."

"Stalk?"

"I guess he was a bit too overbearing."

Ty never said anything about this. "Was Joe arrested?"

"No. Claire didn't want to do that to him because she knew he wanted to become a lawyer."

"So, what happened?"

"Apparently, her boyfriend beat the snot out of Joe, and Joe packed up and headed off to Boston somewhere. We never saw him again until he surfaced here as a lawyer, but that was well after Claire's death."

So Claire had both a stalker and a semiviolent boyfriend. Both would make good suspects.

"Donna, who was her boyfriend?"

She shrugged. "I don't have a clue, but the man was legendary after he beat up Joe. No one would even smile at Claire unless they were looking for a beating. He got a nickname as the Phantom because no one ever saw him."

"Did he beat up a lot of high schoolers?"

"I hear he did. And he beat up one old guy who was hanging around Claire."

"Really? An old guy? How old?"

"I don't know the answer to that either, but rumor had it that he was Laura VanPlank's father."

Before I could react, Donna was immediately penitent. "Oh, I shouldn't spread gossip like that. I know how it feels with Ray and all. The gossips accused him of everything from hacking into the IRS to change our taxes to siphoning off money from the Sandy Harbor Federal Credit Union so we can buy a motor home."

"My lips are sealed. I won't say anything."

After that tidbit of information, I pulled out a piece of roast beef and took a small bite. I was famished, but that warred with my investigative instincts. "Too bad that his nickname didn't start with a *B*."

"Huh?"

"Nothing. It's not important."

Donna asked everyone to come and eat. More neighbors stopped in whom I hadn't met, but I liked them immediately. Ty seemed to know them.

Liz's cake was cut, and it wasn't bad for a lemon box cake.

It was a nice time, and I was glad we went.

One of the neighbors, Mrs. Gillman, turned to me. "Are you and Sheriff Brisco dating?"

Ty heard the question. I could tell by the sparkle of amusement in his turquoise eyes.

"Uh, no," I said, although my heart skipped a beat at the thought. "Ty and I are like brother and sister."

He raised an eyebrow at that statement.

My heart started pounding. I really should get myself checked out.

Mrs. Gillman smiled. "But the two of you seem so close, you really seem like lovers to me."

Why did she think that? Because we were sitting on the couch together? Or maybe she was just baiting us.

Still, I almost choked on Donna's macaroni salad with the dill weed. The word *lovers* seemed to be such an intimate word to me. And the way that Mrs. Gillman said it, "lahv-ahs," so breathy, slow, and low, I wanted to open a door on the center island and crawl in there. At least I'd be hidden, but closer to the food.

Ty, however, was totally amused. Maybe it was the way he held up his mug of coffee in the air like a toast to me. It was his way of saying, "Try and get out of this one."

*I'll show him.*

"Mrs. Gillman, we can't be lahv-ahs," I said in a loud whisper. "Deputy Brisco told me that he had a training accident at the shooting range, and he, well . . . he was shot in a very, very private place."

"Oh!" she said.

"Oh!" said Donna.

"Oy," said Ed and Mr. Gillman in unison.

"T-Trixie, wh-what the hell . . . ?" sputtered Ty.

Ray and Liz laughed. They knew that I was joking, but they were the only ones.

"Oops! I forgot that I had to ride home with Ty!"

# Chapter 12

*T*here's nothing like a yearbook to find out information about people when they were younger.

That was why I was inhaling nonfiction book dust at the Sandy Harbor Library. I scratched my nose as I leafed through the muddy brown hardcover yearbook of the class of 1989.

*Go, Trout!*

I ran my finger down the list of graduates looking for male *B*'s. There were two Roberts/Bobbys, one William/Billy, and one Buddy, but that was about it. I wrote down their names to check them out. Or maybe Ty could check them out much quicker.

There was Robert Godfrey and Robert Lawless, Billy Swenti, and Buddy Wilder.

I'd never heard of any of them, but that didn't mean anything. I studied their pictures. All of the five were fairly good-looking, and I could see how Claire could fall for any of them.

"Trixie! So good to see you."

That scratchy voice belonged to Mrs. Leddy, my former college professor, now retired, who was now president of the historical association. She was leafing through a magazine and sitting in a flowered Queen Anne chair that had a pattern almost identical to her dress. No wonder I didn't see her.

"Mrs. Leddy, I'm glad that I ran into you."

"Before I forget, my dear Trixie, I wanted to let you know that I'm coming to the Dance Fest. I wouldn't miss it for the world. I'm going to kick up my heels. And if my husband doesn't dance with me—he can be such a poop, you know—I'll just have to find someone else. Maybe I'll dance with that handsome cowboy sheriff, unless you've already spoken for him."

My mouth suddenly went dry. What I wouldn't give for a tall glass of sweet tea with a ton of ice, but instead of tea, I wanted vodka. Instead of sugar, I wanted tonic. I'd keep the ice.

I could easily fall for Ty Brisco like a cut Christmas tree. He was the epitome of a hunk. He had that Texas drawl, which was my most favorite accent, tied with Aussie. He was smart, polite, and loved Blondie as much as I did.

But I hadn't spoken for him. Had I? Why was everyone so sure we were an item these days?

"Trixie?"

"Huh?"

"We were talking about Deputy Ty, and you drifted away."

"Oh. Sorry, Mrs. Leddy." I swallowed hard.

"I'm sure that Deputy Brisco would love to dance with you. He keeps telling me that he does a mean two-step."

She giggled like a schoolgirl.

"Mrs. Leddy, you said that you taught at Sandy Harbor High School before you taught college."

"That's right, my dear."

"I'm hoping that you know what happened to some of the old graduates from the class of 1989."

Mrs. Leddy tilted her head. "Does this have anything to do with Claire Jacobson?"

"Yes."

"What do you want to know?"

I handed her my list. "Do you know what happened to Robert Godfrey, Robert Lawless, Billy Swenti, or Buddy Wilder?"

May and June Burke, who were sisters and former teachers and who now volunteered at the library, came over to where I sat with Mrs. Leddy. They both had bluish hair done up in an elaborate style and sprayed with a can or two of hair spray. They were dressed in jersey shirtwaist dresses with tiny flowers. May's mostly violets, and June's was lilacs. They were probably in their mideighties. I should look so good at that age.

They were both very welcoming to me when I first moved to Sandy Harbor, and I'd always appreciated that.

"You girls are making way too much noise," May said, taking a seat next to me.

"We're going to have to ask you to leave," June

added, leaning an elbow on her sister's Queen Anne chair.

They both giggled, and I knew that they were only joking and really wanted to participate in the conversation. Why not? The more the merrier.

"Mrs. Leddy and I were talking about some of the graduates of the high school: Robert Godfrey, Robert Lawless, Billy Swenti, and Buddy Wilder."

Mrs. Leddy studied the list I handed her. "Robert Godfrey got a scholarship to Harvard Med. He's a plastic surgeon in Los Angeles. I hear that he's Botoxed or operated on half of Hollywood, but not my Harrison Ford, I'm sure. Even though Harrison is with that skinny actress, I haven't given up on him."

"Did he go to the bonfire that night?"

"Who? Harrison Ford?"

"Robert Godfrey."

"No. Bobby's your basic loner."

I pretty much ruled him out as a suspect since he didn't go to the bonfire, but I kept his name on the list.

She squinted at the next name. "May and June, do you remember Robert Lawless?"

"Oh, absolutely," said May. "He was a terrible student. I wouldn't be surprised if he turned out to be a criminal. He tried to live up to his last name, but I lost track of him."

Mr. Lawless moved to second on my list of suspects, just under the man with the severe case of zipperitis: Mr. Grant VanPlank.

Mrs. Leddy continued. "Billy Swenti was at a wedding I attended. He was always such a good-natured boy with an easy smile and a handshake for everyone. He wasn't a bad student either. He lives out on Route 237 with his partner—isn't that an interesting term? His partner is Ronnie Owens. They both are organic farmers, and they adopted a passel of children with special needs, God bless them all. Billy is a disk jockey, too. That's what he was doing at the wedding. Oh, what horrible music he played—thump, thump, thump! And the tattoos he had, oh my! Even on his neck. And he had earrings in his ears and his nose and eyebrows. Can you imagine? I said, 'Billy, you were always such a good-looking boy. Why did you do that to yourself?' But he just laughed, and he played 'My Way' by Frank Sinatra for me."

"I really liked him," June said. "He was such a lonely boy, wasn't he, May? None of the other boys wanted to play with him."

Then I remembered. "Oh, wait! I order vegetables from them. Is their farm called Various Veggies and Fruits?"

"Yep, that's them. Billy used to be such a handsome boy. He needs those tattoos and jewelry on his face like I need another boob," June said.

I burst out laughing, and got a "shush" or six from the library patrons and one volunteer librarian.

Billy Swenti didn't seem like a good suspect, and the fact that he and his partner had adopted a "passel of children" made me think that if Billy got Claire pregnant, he'd welcome his child.

But I kept him on the list anyway.

"What about Buddy Wilder?" I asked, wiping away tears of laughter.

"The last I knew he was a priest in Brooklyn and was working with drug addicts," Mrs. Leddy said. "We took up a collection for his program in church."

Buddy was a shaky suspect, but I kept him on the list, too.

I'd turn over my "B List" to Ty. Maybe he could run their raps and see what shook out.

Did I just think "raps"? Yikes! I sounded like Deputy Doug before he screwed up and was demoted to traffic.

Soon they were off on a tangent about recipes, their volunteer schedule at the library, and a tirade about how department stores don't sell slips anymore.

I wondered if I could corral them back for more information. Maybe they hadn't told me everything that they might know, but May saved me the trouble.

"How come you're asking us about those four boys?" she asked.

"I don't really want to say. I'm just checking out a letter that I found in one of the cottages," I said. "Do you ladies have any more thoughts on any of them?"

"I hear that Bobby Lawless continues to get into

trouble," June said. "And I heard that he was in San Quentin in California. Isn't that just awful? And he was the cutest boy with freckles and a big smile. He loved to hot-wire cars and drive them around. Remember when he stole Antoinette Chloe's car, sister?"

"I do. He wanted to be an auto mechanic, and we always thought that he just stole cars to fix them," Mrs. Leddy answered instead. "And Antoinette Chloe said that when Bobby Lawless stole her car, he brought it back in better shape."

They all nodded, laughing.

"I kept hoping that he'd steal my Olds," May said. "It needed a tune-up!"

I wondered if Bobby Lawless had graduated from stealing cars to murder.

"Ladies, anything more about Billy Swenti?"

Mrs. Leddy raised a hand. "You should see them all come to church—wheelchairs, walkers, crutches— the whole congregation helps out Billy and his gang."

I thought I would rule out Swenti. He was too good to be true, but maybe that was his cover.

I ruled him back in.

There were too many suspects. Aspirin. I needed aspirin.

They were all talking at once about Saint Billy Swenti.

I interrupted. "Buddy Wilder? Anything more about him?"

"He was wonderful when he was in school,"

June said, "but he always reminded me of Eddie Haskell, you know, that kid on *Leave It to Beaver*."

"I agree, sister," May said.

Mrs. Leddy clapped. "Yes! Eddie Haskell!"

May smoothed her skirt and made sure that it was almost to her ankles. "He's a priest now. Who would ever have guessed that?"

"And I won the fifty-fifty raffle that we held to support his drug addicts. Of course, I donated the money back. It was the right thing to do," said June.

"That was nice of you." Mrs. Leddy patted her on the knee.

May checked her watch, then grunted as she got up from her chair. "Who's left, dear? I have to get back to work. I'm reading *The Ugly Duckling* for children's story time."

I checked my list. "Got anything more about Robert Godfrey?"

"No. Just that he always was a brainiac and very shy," June said. "And he had a bad case of shyness all four years of high school, poor boy. He threw himself into his books."

The conversation broke up with the ladies planning to meet at the Dance Fest, what they were going to wear, and promises of partnering up to polka.

I said my good-byes and while sitting in my car, I made notes on each of the *B*'s before I forgot.

A surgeon, a criminal, a priest, and a disk jockey

who was gay and who adopted handicapped children.

None of them really seemed like Claire's type, but what did I know? Maybe one of them was the boyfriend I'd heard about.

Maybe the *B*'s were interviewed twenty-five years ago by law enforcement. I think Ty had told me that the whole class was interviewed, whether or not they attended the bonfire.

But really, back then, the Sandy Harbor Sheriff's Department thought it was a missing person's case, so how much did they really question everyone?

I was going to turn over this information to Ty and let him further investigate the B List.

But right now I was going to go to Brown's Family Restaurant and speak to Antoinette Chloe Brown.

I couldn't really call ACB a friend, as we didn't know each other very well, but she was a definite character. She always dressed in flowery muumuus, flip-flops and clunky rhinestone jewelry until she ran off with her husband's brother, Tony Brownelli. Then she turned biker chick with black leather, chains, and white hair with a black streak down the part.

As I pulled up to her restaurant, Antoinette Chloe was back in muumuu mode, her hair was a fluorescent orange, and she was sitting on the middle step of her restaurant's entrance.

I swung into a parking space and hurried out. "Antoinette Chloe, are you okay?"

She sniffed. "Tony took off on me. Said that he had to ride off into the sunset and be free. Said I was stifling him."

"I'm so sorry."

"With Sal doing life in Auburn and with Tony gone, I feel so lonely. Like no one wants me."

Fresh tears pooled in her eyes, and I prayed that they'd evaporate and wouldn't trail down the orange tanner on her face or it was going to be striped.

I sat down next to her. "I found that it's best to keep busy. Throw yourself into your restaurant. Get that CLOSED sign down, for heaven's sake. First you're open, then closed. That's not good for business."

"I know."

She unfolded a tissue and blotted her caked mascara, black glitter eyeliner, and thick turquoise eye shadow. The tissue reflected a perfect copy.

"How can I help you?" I asked.

"I'm going to close for a couple of weeks and get my restaurant all spiffed up—new paint, new wallpaper, new fixtures, new flooring, and a clean kitchen. I'll hire it all out. Support the local economy."

"That'll be nice." Brown's definitely needed some cleaning and updating. Antoinette Chloe had very flamboyant taste, and I'd love to bland down her cabbage rose wallpaper, but it was her place, and she could do what she wanted.

"Trixie, you said you'd help me. Did you mean it?"

"Sure. What can I do?" *Please, let me help you pick out wallpaper.*

She tented her fingers. Each finger and thumb had at least three rings.

"Teach me to cook, Trixie. I mean, I know how to cook, but I can't get the hang of short-order cooking. I want to see how you can handle everything all at once. Let me work at the Silver Bullet for a couple of weeks."

Her mascara left raccoon rings around her eyes.

"Uh . . . sure. Sure, Antoinette Chloe. You can learn from Juanita and Cindy during the day and me on graveyard. Whatever you'd like."

Her makeup would melt right off her face over the fryer, and she might lose a few dozen rings in the process.

"I'd like to experience everything," she said, adjusting her multicolored silk lei. "Although I'm the perfect hostess, I'd like to learn to cook. Let's face it, my husband won't be returning, not that I'd take him back, and I don't know about Tony. Brown's is my place now, but I think I'm going to rename it. I'm going to call it Antoinette Chloe's Piccolo Bistro and Ice-Cream Parlor."

"That's going to be one major sign!" I brushed off some kind of bug from my shoulder. "But you don't even have an ice-cream parlor."

"I'm going to add one."

"I see. Do you know anything about an ice-cream parlor?"

"No, but I like ice cream."

"Works for me, Antoinette Chloe."

I stood and brushed off my shorts. "Drop in to the Silver Bullet and learn how to cook whenever you like."

"I'll be there tonight. Six o'clock."

I'd make sure to warn Cindy. She was working three to midnight.

"Uh . . . Antoinette Chloe, you'd better leave off your jewelry. I don't want you to lose it in the fryer. And maybe jeans and a blouse would be better, even though your muumuu is very . . . floral. And perhaps a good pair of shoes or sneaks would be better than your flip-flops. You'll be standing on your feet a lot and you'll need support."

"I understand, and I'll even put my hair up."

"Uh . . . you have to wear a hairnet, a ball cap, or a chef's hat—something that'll keep your hair out of the food."

"Merciful heavens! A hairnet? Not Antoinette Chloe Brown! I have a pretty hat with flowers and the cutest robin perched on top. The robin is sitting on a nest with blue eggs. It's exquisite."

"I'm sure it is, Antoinette Chloe . . . but there're health codes and all that."

I could picture the robin falling off her hat, landing in the fryer, and ACB plating it for a customer, thinking that she was preparing the fried chicken and mashed potato special.

Oh, I had almost forgotten the reason why I came to Brown's. Sure, I wanted to eat, but ACB was always a wealth of information. I had spoken to her before, but now I had a list of men who might be Claire's "B."

"Antoinette Chloe, before I leave, I'd like to ask you a couple of questions about some of your senior classmates."

"That again? Well, fire away."

"Do you remember Robert Godfrey, Robert Lawless, Billy Swenti, and Buddy Wilder?"

"Sure. I went to twelve years of school with them."

"Did you see any of them with Claire Jacobson?"

"No. Never. I only saw her with Ricky Tingsley, and that was only one time, at the bonfire."

"So you never saw Claire with any of the other guys?"

"Nope."

"Okay. Thanks," I said. "But could you keep thinking of that bonfire night? I know that it was a long time ago, but see if you can remember any other detail, no matter how small."

She pulled off the platter-sized silk daisy that was dangling over one ear and reclipped it. "I will."

She stood, muumuu billowing in the breeze, and pulled me into a hug that squeezed the stuffing right out of me.

I was not aware that we were that close.

I breathed in a mix of talcum powder, perfume, cologne, body mist, laundry detergent, fabric softener, dryer sheets, body oil, deodorant, and antiperspirant, all in a potpourri of different scents.

I almost poked my eye out on her earring.

Sneezing, I gave her a squeeze, then stepped back for some oxygen.

"You know, Trixie, there is one thing about Claire that, upon consideration . . . I mean, I thought it was something else back then, but knowing what I know now and thinking back, I might have been wrong then—"

"Antoinette Chloe, what on earth are you talking about?"

"I don't have any children. I had a couple of miscarriages, and tried like hell, but I've never been able to have children."

"I'm so sorry. I know how you feel. I've never been blessed with children either. That's one of the reasons my ex-husband, well, found a fertile younger woman."

Did I just spill my guts to ACB? What the hell got into me? I'd only told that to a handful of my closest friends and stand-by-your-man Carla Van-Plank.

"I'm sorry, Trixie. So very sorry."

She took my hands and squeezed and when I looked into her eyes, I didn't see globs of makeup. I saw a very sincere friend with sapphire eyes. And good friends were hard to find.

"And Laura VanPlank is just like us, too," ACB

said. "She was in a horrible car accident in Port Palm, Florida. She was on vacation with her parents. Terrible accident. The result was that she can't have any children."

"Accident? Oh no. How old was she?"

"Fourteen."

I took a deep breath and held it for a while. My heart went out to Laura, and I resolved to enter her name on my list with the heading Be Nicer to These People. Aside from her accident, she had to put up with a pill of a mother and husband. She probably needed friends more than anyone.

"But, Trixie, when I think back, I remember that Claire was glowing, and Rick Tingsley wouldn't let go of her hand."

"And Laura noticed?"

"She sure did!"

# Chapter 13

*T*he Dance Fest was two days away, and all of us chefs—and that now included ACB—were busy making salads.

Potato salad and macaroni salad were my specialty, because of Uncle Porky's secret ingredient—a healthy dose of dried dill weed. I also used real mayonnaise and squirted some mustard or horseradish mustard into the mayonnaise. Then the usual: salt and pepper, diced celery, and lots of diced, hard-boiled eggs.

Right now huge pots of potatoes and elbow macaroni were boiling on the stove. ACB was stirring both pots with a big wooden paddle.

Cindy was putting three dozen eggs in another pot. Those had to be boiled, too.

When that batch was done, we'd do it all over again, and then we'd move on to getting the ziti ready and the meatballs and sausage.

I loved cooking for a huge crowd. At least I hoped we'd have a huge crowd. Judging by the buzz in the diner, the whole town would be there.

I just hoped that the rainy weather was behind us and it'd be a beautiful evening.

Everything was ready. The rental company had arrived and was putting up a gigantic tent. When I looked out the window, I saw them laying boards for the dance floor. Then they'd move on to putting up an elevated stage for the band.

I also ordered extra chairs and tables. Just as soon as the tent was up, Max, Clyde, and Ray would set up tables in the tent and cover them with white paper tablecloths. I also had them setting up six tables for the buffet in front of the tent. In the meantime, my brain was twirling with *B*'s as well as Grant VanPlank, Rick Tingsley, and Laura Tingsley.

Old Grant VanPlank had the most to lose. However, since he had terminal zipperitis, he probably just wanted to enjoy a fling with young Claire and then move on to less fertile territory.

His political aspirations would come to a dead end if anyone found out about Claire, so he had to kill her. Right?

But had anyone actually linked Claire to Grant? Carla VanPlank spewed something about Claire being a loose woman. Was Carla referring to Grant having an affair with Claire?

Grant VanPlank was still my lead suspect.

As for Rick Tingsley, maybe Claire was just someone different from Laura. Rick didn't really know Claire all that much from what I found out.

Granted, my source ACB felt differently, so did she really know for sure?

I snapped my fingers and walked over to ACB. I'd told her that she couldn't decorate her chef's hat with sequins because they might fall off into the food. Instead she bought a ton of fabric paint and painted flowers, bugs, and either seagulls or vultures onto it.

"Antoinette Chloe, did Rick Tingsley seem really happy on the night of the bonfire or not?"

"He seemed happy, but he'd had a few beers in him. Everyone seemed happy, not just Ricky. It was a party after all, and we'd just graduated at the end of June. We'd been waiting for this party."

"Okay." I was getting nowhere.

Through the pass-through window, I saw Ty walk into the diner. He was off duty as he was in his cowboy duds. Yum.

He tilted his head, and I knew immediately that he had information for me.

Wiping my hands on a towel, I told the ladies that I needed a cup of coffee—which wasn't a lie—and a short break. I pushed open the double doors, excited with anticipation.

Maybe we were making progress on the case.

Pouring myself a cup of coffee, I found that Ty had moved to a back booth for privacy. I slid in opposite him. I always found comfort in the well-worn vinyl. I was glad to be continuing the legacy started by my aunt and uncle when they first had the Silver Bullet transported here from the factory by eighteen-wheelers in 1952.

However, the cottages that Uncle Porky had

lovingly built one by one in his spare time were dying one at a time.

Until there were families here to enjoy them, what good were they?

Even if the two murders were solved, would that bring everyone back to the cottages? Or would they be tainted forever?

I took a sip of coffee and waited for Ty to speak.

"The *B*'s are all out as suspects with the exception of one."

"Billy Lawless? The one with the criminal record?" I guessed.

"Actually, no. The night that Claire died, Mr. Lawless was warming a cell at the Sandy Harbor lockup. He celebrated his graduation by stealing the principal's car."

"Shoot, he was a good suspect. Where was he when Phil Jacobson was murdered?"

"Attica. He's doing a nickel stretch for burglary."

"That's the real Big House," I said. "Ty, don't keep me in suspense. Who's the suspect?"

"It's the guy who works with addicts. Only your friends have it wrong. He's not a real priest—never was. He's a social worker."

"That'd be Buddy Wilder." I could recite those names in my sleep. "But, Ty, the local churches, they pass the basket and send him money. Everyone thinks he's a priest."

"The New York City Police Department will be checking him out fully. They'll get back to me with their results, but I'm guessing that he's a big fraud or the parishioners are just mistaken."

"Could you connect him to Claire Jacobson?"

"Not yet."

"Claire could never love a fraud," I declared.

"Maybe he wasn't a fraud back then. Maybe he was a good-looking, sweet-talking guy."

"Yeah. Now, *that* I could believe. He could have swept Claire off her feet. He writes a good love letter.

"Ty, would you mind checking out Grant Van-Plank, too?"

"VanPlank? Why him?"

"He has zipperitis."

Ty raised an eyebrow, and I explained, "He can't keep it in his pants, and he ruined his political career because of his fooling around." I shrugged. "I just have a suspicion that he might have fooled around with Claire."

"He doesn't have a *B* name," Ty said.

"And his wife said that he'd never had a nickname, but I'm thinking that Claire might have given him one of those goofy names that lovers sometimes do. Maybe she called him 'Beau' or 'Boo-Boo' or 'Bubbles' or 'Bumblebee'—who knows?"

"Bubbles? Bumblebee? Darlin', I'd have to shoot myself if anyone ever called me something like that."

"Well, Bubbles, the Dance Fest is in two days, and I plan on pumping all my guests for information, particularly Grant VanPlank and Rick Tingsley. And maybe Billy Swenti might come because he's local and was in that class, my dear Bubbles. I could talk to him." I snapped my fingers. "You know, I'll give Various Veggies and Fruits a call and make sure I invite the whole family."

"It wouldn't hurt. Just be careful. And don't call me Bubbles!"

"Okay, Bumblebee."

"Ouch."

We made small talk, mostly about Blondie, and then he had to leave to change into "his fishing duds" because he was going fishing with Deputy Vern McCoy.

Fishing?

Why wasn't he working on the murders?

I supposed he was entitled to some time off to have some fun, but not when I had a balloon payment to make to Aunt Stella.

Aunt Stella!

I don't know why I didn't think of her sooner. I went outside, sat down at a picnic table, and dialed her number on my cell phone.

"Hello?"

"Aunt Stella. It's Trixie."

"Hello, sweetie. I am so sorry about the man who was murdered in Cottage Eight, David Burrows. Should I know him, Claire?"

I promised Ty that I wouldn't spill the beans that David was really Phil, so I couldn't even tell Aunt Stella. "I don't think you know him."

"It's just so horrible."

"I know, Aunt Stella. It's awful. And I was the one who found David in Cottage Eight."

"You poor dear. Are his parents alive? Have they been notified?"

"No. They aren't alive. Ty told me that."

"Trixie, I meant to call you, but I've been on a bus trip with my friends to the casinos in Biloxi, and—"

"That's okay. Enjoy yourself, and don't worry." Actually Aunt Stella wasn't worrying at all. I was so happy she was able to live up her golden years with her friends. "I just wanted to tell you that I'm bringing back the Dance Fest. My first one is Saturday."

"Oh, how I wish I could be there!"

"I wish you could be, too. It won't be the same without Uncle Porky and you."

"Oh, Trixie! I miss him so much." She sniffed, and I could picture her with a real cloth handkerchief with flowers on it clenched in her fist.

"I didn't mean for you to cry."

"I'll be okay. Hang on." I could hear her blowing her nose. Then she sniffed and came back. "So, tell me. What else is going on at the point?"

"This is going to sound strange, but around the last time that Claire and her family were renting Eight, did you know anyone whose first name, last name, or a nickname started with a letter *B*? I think that Claire was in love with him."

There was silence for a while.

"I can't think of anyone off the top of my head. Let me think about it, and I'll call you back."

"Deal."

We chatted about her past and upcoming trips and at length about how she had attended a performance of the Thunder from Down Under when she was in Vegas.

My sweet aunt Stella and her gal pals at a male stripper show? You go, Aunt Stella Matkowski!

"I'll think about a *B* name around the time that Claire . . . um . . . passed away, but I have to go now. I have my Pilates class."

"See you, Aunt Stella."

"Bye, Trixie dear."

I hung up feeling as though I had done something positive. Aunt Stella had a memory like a computer. She'd come up with a name. And I hoped she'd call me soon.

Speaking of computers, Ray Myerson, the new busboy, dishwasher, and computer genius, arrived looking smart, wearing dark jeans and a green golf shirt. I was sure that the golf shirt wasn't his thing, but I appreciated that he listened to me.

He gave me a quick salute, found a laundered apron in the box behind the counter, got a gray plastic tub, and started busing the tables.

Nice.

Out of nowhere, a party of twenty-four filed into the diner. It seemed that they were in a heated discussion, because they were very loud and very animated. The other diner patrons looked at them as they noisily moved tables around and dragged chairs.

Without any prompting from me, Ray hurried over to help them. I congratulated myself on hiring the young man as I walked over to help.

"Hi, I'm the owner of the Silver Bullet, Trixie Matkowski."

"Well, little Trixie, you're all grown-up."

I just stared. He did look familiar, but not quite.

He stood and extended his hand. "Buddy. Buddy Wilder. I used to live here in Sandy Harbor."

It couldn't be! I was just questioning some of the town elders about the B List and now the faux priest/social worker was here—in person, in the flesh, in my diner.

"Buddy, what brings you back to Sandy Harbor?" I asked, not taken in by his artificial tan, his black ensemble, and his piercing black eyes. His blacker-than-black hair was slicked back with something greasy, and I could see the comb marks.

On him, it seemed to work.

Buddy grinned and his pearly white teeth nearly blinded me. Diamond studs twinkled in both earlobes.

"We're here for the Dance Fest," he said. "I told my friends that it's an event not to be missed, so we all decided to take a ride up here for a little R and R."

"Where are you all staying?"

Laurie, who must have drawn the short straw and gotten the noisy party, appeared and passed out menus.

"I was hoping we could stay here at the cottages, if there's room."

"There's room," I quickly said. "But I should tell you that we've had a problem here. A person died—actually he was murdered—in Cottage Eight."

"I heard. We can handle it. We live in New York City," one of Buddy's friends said.

Buddy nodded, and I snapped to attention. "How many cottages would you like?"

"Ten," Buddy said. "If you don't have the room, we can stay at Singing Waters. I called from the road, and we have reservations there. You didn't answer your phone, Trixie."

I remember walking by the blinking light a hundred times, thinking that there were more cancellations. I never dreamed that people would actually be calling for reservations.

"I've been having trouble with my landline," I lied. "But I'll get you all keys and you can figure out who wants to stay in what cottage."

"You can bill me," Buddy said, handing me a credit card. "I'll collect from my friends later."

"Will do," I said, slipping his credit card into my pocket. Maybe Ty could run a check on it. "I hope you brought your bathing suits. It should be a beautiful day for swimming."

"You know, it's so green here," said a woman with flaming red hair and a pronounced Brooklyn accent. "And I've never seen so many cows. They're, like, huge and roaming free."

I chuckled. "Dairy cows are definitely a wild, carefree bunch, but I think we still fence them in."

That got a round of chuckles.

Then I wondered how the not-reverend Buddy had heard about the Dance Fest way over in New York City. The ink hadn't yet dried on the posters.

"Buddy, how on earth did you hear about the Dance Fest and manage to get such a large group together in such a short time, then drive the sevenish hours to get here?"

"I received an e-mail announcement. And we were altogether at a party in Soho and just decided to hop on a limo bus—it's Andre's company—"

A man with spiked white hair and black roots raised two fingers in a salute, and I smiled at him. He had nice brown eyes.

"The Gadabout Limo Company," he said, dipping into his pocket and handing me a business card.

"So Andre drove us here, and here we are," Buddy finished. "I just had to take them to the Silver Bullet as soon as we arrived. They are going to love the cottages. They are so . . . rustic."

"They are just the cutest little houses!" said the woman sitting next to Andre with the same hairstyle.

"Just like a SoHo loft," I said.

I motioned for Buddy to take his seat, and he nodded to me as he sat.

"Trixie, do you know that I used to work here in my teens?"

Oh! My cheeks heated. "I remember you now! Weren't you the lifeguard at the beach? And didn't you always wear a red bathing suit with white flowers?"

That resulted in some comments from his friends: "Lifeguard?" "Red bathing suit with flowers?" "I'll bet you were hot!"

But I wasn't finished yet.

"But you weren't called Buddy." I snapped my fingers as his real name came to me. "Isn't your real name Donald?"

I hadn't put the two names together and his teachers—Mrs. Leddy, May, and June—and the Sandy Harbor Class of 1989 yearbook never mentioned that his real name was Donald.

Buddy's eyes flashed as his friends teased him even more.

"No one ever—never—called me Donald, Donnie, Don, or any other variation," he said loudly.

His friends were unmerciful.

"Donald Duck!"

"Donnie with the red bathing suit."

"Sandy Harbor Donnie."

"Donnie the lifeguard."

A vein pumped in his neck. "See what you started?"

"Sorry. I didn't know that you didn't like your name. But, D, uh, Buddy, weren't you friends with Claire Jacobson?"

My memory was working overtime. Thoughts of making sand castles and mud pies and diving underwater for quarters with Phil and Claire came rushing back. And Buddy in that red bathing suit with the white flowers. I remembered him talking to Claire all the time on the beach and from his perch on the lifeguard chair.

"I swear that Claire Jacobson called you Donnie," I said, thinking back.

"She was the only exception," he said softly.

Donnie "Buddy" Wilder just had to be the father of Claire's baby!

Then again, I thought that every man who'd reached puberty back in the fifties, sixties, or seventies was the father of Claire's baby.

He might have even surpassed Grant VanPlank as my number-one suspect.

The letter that "B" wrote referred to himself as an older man. Well, Buddy was a year older than Claire. The whole graduating class was. Since Claire was a year younger, maybe he'd consider himself an older man.

Grant VanPlank had much more to lose than Buddy Wilder. At the time, he had a political career that would implode when his voters discovered he had both a wife and an underage baby mama. That's why he resigned from his run for the presidency.

Buddy might have had a motive for killing Claire, too. I just didn't know it yet.

But I would!

"Buddy, you said you received an e-mail about the Dance Fest. From who?"

"I did. Very cute. The return e-mail address was interesting—Imastarhacker. One word."

"I'm a star hacker?" Ray!

I turned to look at Ray. He was resetting a table with place mats, napkins, and silverware. At that same moment, he looked over at me, and I motioned for him to join me in the kitchen.

I turned back to Buddy's party. "Well, enjoy your lunch, everyone, and I'll be back with the keys to the cottages. I'm sure you'll enjoy your stay with us, as well as the Dance Fest."

I pushed open the double doors, and Ray was standing there.

"Yes, ma'am?"

"Ray, did you e-mail the posters to people?"

"Yeah, I didn't think you'd mind."

"I appreciate that you did. It got us that party of twenty over there. They drove from New York City. But, Ray, where did you get the e-mail addresses?"

"From the *Sandy Harbor Lure*'s subscription list. I just e-mailed the out-of-towners who subscribe to the *Lure*, figuring that they wouldn't get the paper in time to see the ad about the Dance Fest in it."

"That was good thinking, but how did you get the e-mail addresses?"

"From Lizzy Ann Gladnello, my girlfriend. She works part-time in the circulation department there. It's perfectly legit, if that's what you're asking."

"I guess that's what I'm asking."

"Lizzy cleared it with her boss, Joan Paris. She said that it was for you, and that you needed the information."

That was nice of Joan. "Ray, why didn't you tell me?"

Oops, I remembered that I was going to call Joan and get together with her. Maybe she had more information from her main squeeze, Hal Manning, Sandy Harbor's only funeral director and coroner.

Hal had loose lips.

Ray's face turned redder than Santa's suit. "I only thought of it after I left the other night. I tried to call you, but you didn't call me back. Then I was going to bike over here this morning, but my wheels were flat. It took me all morning to walk to the bike shop and back home. Then I was going to tell you this morning, but then the big party walked in and you got busy."

I pulled out my cell phone from my pocket and checked it. There were several phone calls and two text messages, all from Ray.

"I never heard the phone ring." I showed him the phone, and he took it out of my hand and pushed some buttons.

"You have it on mute."

"I do?"

He nodded and pushed another button. "It's okay now."

"Uh, Ray? How many names did you e-mail?"

"About three hundred."

"Wow. I'd better make more food."

"I had them RSVP to me. So far, only about a hundred and twenty-five are coming. That was since eleven this morning."

"Only?" That was over twenty-five percent of those he e-mailed, and I didn't know math.

"Did I screw up?" he asked.

"You did not! Actually you did me a real favor, and I want to thank you."

"I thought you were going to fire me."

"Not a chance. Not when you've used your head and helped me above and beyond the call of duty. And thanks for distributing the posters all over town, too. I don't think I thanked you for that yet."

"It's okay."

"Thank you again so very much, Ray." I held my hand out because I didn't think he'd welcome a hug just yet. We shook.

He gave me a thumbs-up and went back to the main diner. I reminded myself to get him a logo golf shirt or two.

Along with that new bike.

As I walked back into the diner to get yet another cup of coffee, Ty walked in. He always had exquisite timing. Just when I needed to speak with him, he appeared.

I couldn't wait to see his face when I told him where he could find Donald "Buddy" Wilder!

# Chapter 14

Just as Ty was about to take a seat at the counter, I whispered, "Go outside. Right now." He was dressed in his sheriff's uniform, and I didn't want to scare off Buddy.

Ty didn't miss a beat. He snapped his fingers as if he forgot something, and left.

I went out the back door and was going to meet him out front, but he was waiting for me behind the diner.

"What's up, Trixie?"

I always enjoyed when Ty said my name with his full Texas twang. My two syllables lasted longer than it took to roast a fifteen-pound prime rib, done well.

"You will never, ever guess who is sitting in my diner right at this very second."

"Let's see." He scratched his forehead. "Do you want me to really guess?"

"Of course not!"

"Then why don't you just tell me?"

"Buddy Wilder."

Ty's turquoise eyes grew to the size of his cowboy belt buckles. "No way."

"Way."

"Donald Buddy Wilder. Who would have thought?"

"You know his real name?" I asked.

He made a face.

"Oh, sorry. I forgot that you ran a record check on the B List. I didn't mean to imply that you didn't know anything. Sorry."

He nodded. "Trixie, believe me when I tell you that I'm working on the cases. I have other duties, but I'm really working on them."

"It's just not moving fast enough for me. I want to hurry things along."

He looked up at the sky. "Gee, Ms. Patience, where have I heard that before?"

"Anyway, he and some pals took a limo bus from New York City, and they are renting my cottages. They heard about the Dance Fest."

"But how—"

"Did they hear about it? My newly hired computer genius, Ray Myerson. Ray decided to e-mail some out-of-town *Lure* subscribers, and guess who showed up?"

"Should I guess now?" Ty asked.

"If you can't guess this one, you aren't fit to wear that uniform."

"Buddy Wilder."

"Bingo."

"And he's having lunch inside right now?" His eyes twinkled.

"Stop it, Ty!"

He grinned, full of himself.

"Wait a minute!" I said. "Did you happen to suggest to Ray that he might want to invite the out-of-town *Lure* subscribers to the Dance Fest?"

"Nope. I can't take the credit. Ray suggested it to *me*, and I told him that it was a fabulous idea. And then I told him the right way to go about it, like asking Joan Paris, but that he should ask you first."

"He tried, but he couldn't get a hold of me. He tried to bike here, but I guess his tires were flat. He went ahead and did it anyway because time was running out."

Ty shook his head. "Damn. I'll speak to him about that."

"Don't you dare. Everything's good. He has reservations for a hundred and twenty-five out-of-towners."

"I'm glad. He's a good kid."

"And a smart one. I really like him. Today's the first day I saw him in action, and I liked what I saw. Plus, all the staff is raving about him."

"Outstanding."

"Did you have any idea that Buddy Wilder would show up?"

"I hoped he would. I love the fact that he's here on my turf. However, the New York City Police

Department will be mad that he skipped town. I'll give them a call and tell them that he's right here in little ol' Sandy Harbor."

He had a grin the size of Texas. I knew he'd love this news.

"There's more. I haven't even told you the best part."

"Do you want me to guess this?"

"For heaven's sake—"

"Tell me!"

"Donnie Wilder was a lifeguard here when he was in high school, and he paid particular interest to Claire Jacobson and her little brother, our victim number two."

"Nice job, Trixie, but that doesn't mean anything."

"But his nickname starts with a *B*. Then again, Claire called him Donnie. But he referred to himself as Buddy. Anyway, he's a better suspect as a baby daddy than Grant VanPlank, who apparently never had a nickname."

"That's according to his wife, if I remember correctly. She's not exactly a good source."

"You're wrong there. I think she knows more about him than anyone."

Ty chuckled. "I need more information on Donnie. Just because he was a lifeguard and he and Claire talked on the beach isn't enough to assume that he's our killer."

"Did the first investigation when Claire disappeared turn up anything about Donnie?"

"Just that he was distraught when Claire vanished, like everyone else, but nothing unusual. He attended the bonfire, but all his time couldn't be accounted for."

"See?"

"Trixie, no one's time could be fully accounted for that night. I think they were all in the sand dunes making out."

"Do you still think that there is only one killer?"

"That's still my theory, but I won't know for sure until I find the murder weapon and run a ballistics test."

"Ty, I really feel that we're not getting anywhere."

"We are. These little things add up. We'll get a break in the case."

"So, what's our plan now?" I asked, ready to go undercover.

"Since he's right under our noses, and because he's on the B List, and because we know he actually spoke to Claire, which is more than most of your suspects . . ." He paused for effect and grinned.

"There're a million comedians out of work, and I'm glad you're one of them." I made a face, but I really did enjoy his sense of humor.

"I think we should concentrate on Buddy Wilder for now."

"What can I do?"

"Nothing, Trixie. I can take it from here."

"Oh no, you don't."

"Pardon?"

"I'm part of this, Deputy Earp."

He took a deep breath and let it out. "You just eavesdrop on everyone at the Dance Fest and report back to me. I'll do the rest."

Oh yeah?

"Things might get dangerous," he said. "I don't want you hurt. I'm trained to do this. You're not, and I don't want a third victim on my hands. If something happened to you, where would I get a decent cup of coffee and a great meal?"

I didn't crack a smile. I was mad. Livid. I was bringing him good stuff, and he didn't seem to think that it was valuable information.

He wouldn't know a clue if it crashed on top of his cowboy hat.

"Trixie?"

"I want to find the killer, Ty, and fast. They are all going to be under our noses in a little while." Turning to leave, I said over my shoulder, "I'm going to go back to my house and read Claire's folder from Dr. Francis's office. Then I'll take it back and put it back in the file cabinet."

He knew that I was mad, but he didn't say anything that resembled "Trixie, I totally need you to help me. Let's be partners."

I kept walking, but it was easy for his long legs to catch up to me. I was ready to jog away from him, until I remembered that I don't jog because my boobs bounce around like basketballs.

"I'll go with you to Dr. Huff's office," he said.

"No, thanks. I can handle it myself."

"I can distract Shannon Shannon like I did before, and you can put the file back."

"No. You know nothing about the file. Remember? There was no court order. You could always get one and get the file legitimately."

"I could, but the file didn't say anything. Not really. Why waste the time?"

"Okay. Well . . . you just stay away. I'll handle this," I insisted.

I'd love to have Ty help me, but I needed to do this on my own and not get him involved even though when he turns on his cowboy charm, he finds out more information from people than the CIA.

"I'll head over to the Big House and change before I return the file you definitely don't know about." My tomato-covered chef's outfit was too memorable. "And then I have to get back and help with the cooking for the Dance Fest."

As I walked to the Big House, I texted Juanita that I was going to be away for a while, and that she should let the potatoes for the potato salad and the macaroni for the mac salad cool in the walk-in cooler.

I know that, she texted back.

In my kitchen, I pulled up a chair to the oak table and sighed. I felt we had so much to still investigate, but Ty wanted to concentrate on Buddy while he was here.

I could handle Buddy when I got back. Ty could just stay in his apartment over the bait shop and leave me alone.

The phone rang. No one called this number except for cancellations.

*Aw hell*, I thought.

But everyone canceled. How could there be more?

Tentatively, I answered the phone.

"Trixie, it's Ray. Buddy said to remind you about the keys."

"Oops. I totally forgot. I'll be right there."

I found the keys in the usual cabinet. At least there would be people at the cottages for a while. It was only a long weekend, but it would give the moths in my wallet a little snack.

I went back to the diner and handed out keys. Buddy had it all organized.

"I'd like Cottage Nine or Seven for myself," he said.

It was interesting that he wanted to be so close to Cottage Eight.

I handed him both keys. He chose Seven. Then he referred to the back of his place mat, all scribbled with names and arrows running in all directions along with cottage numbers.

He began calling out names and handing keys over to those people. I noticed that most of the time, there were three people in one cottage. Buddy seemed to be the only one staying by himself.

I wondered if Buddy Wilder was up to something, and if the Dance Fest was only a cover for him to drive to Sandy Harbor.

They all disbursed as soon as they received their

key. Buddy was the last to leave, and he peeled two hundred-dollar bills from a fat wad of cash.

"Keep the change," he said to Laurie.

Her eyes lit up, and she stood taller. He must have left a substantial tip for her. I'd find out later.

"That's for the excellent service here and the excellent food," he told her.

"Thank you very much, Mr. Wilder," she said.

"Please, call me Buddy."

"Thanks, Buddy."

"Did you have the special—meat loaf, mashed potatoes, and green beans?" I asked him.

"I always get the daily special."

"Always?" I asked, this being the first time in a couple of decades that Buddy had been at the Silver Bullet.

He laughed and his blinding white teeth were, well, blinding.

"I'll let you get settled in Cottage Seven," I said, making my way outside.

Five minutes later, I was in my too-small gray car with the folder, heading for Dr. Huff's office.

I pulled over into the parking lot of the drugstore and skimmed through Claire's medical folder one more time. There was nothing exciting in any of the pages and no notations that named the father of Claire's baby, just as Ty had said previously.

Matter of fact, there was a notation that read:

*Patient came alone to appointment. Says her age is 21 and she is unmarried. Pregnancy exam per-*

*formed with positive results. Estimated time is
two months. Patient refuses to indicate the puta-
tive father, but happy to be pregnant. Refused al-
ternative procedure to eliminate pregnancy or to
place child up for adoption. Follow-up appointment, two weeks.*

"So Claire really did give her age as twenty-one,"
I said to my dashboard. "Probably so her parents
wouldn't be responsible for the bill, and therefore
they'd never find out she went to the doctor."

But how could she afford a doctor's bill at the age
of seventeen? She wasn't working, unless she had
babysitting money saved.

She probably got money from the father.

Hmm . . . Grant the politician would have the
money. Buddy was working as a lifeguard back
then. I didn't know about the rest of the B List. But
I'd find out.

Some things were still tweaking me. Buddy
Wilder paid a huge bill in full for all his friends
that he brought up from New York City. And—
wait for it—he wanted either Cottage Seven or
Nine. In other words, Buddy-with-a-B wanted to
be right near Cottage Eight.

That was pretty suspicious and interesting.
Buddy was definitely worth keeping an eye on.

I turned left on Broadway Street and pulled into
Dr. Huff's parking lot. Hopefully, he'd be golfing
again. I'd brought a big purse so it'd be easier to
transport the folder downstairs to the file room.

I parked and walked across the parking lot, up the steps of the doctor's office, and into the reception area.

"I'm so sick," I said, with a sniffle. I pulled out several tissues from a box in front of her and gave a hearty sneeze. "I need to see Dr. Huff. The name is Trixie Matkowski."

Shannon rolled her chair away from me.

"I'm such a mess. I feel awful." Then I leaned over and whispered, "I have diarrhea, too."

"Yuck," said Shannon, looking through her appointment book. "But you don't have an appointment, Miss Matos—"

"Matkowski."

"Uh, yes. And the doctor is very busy. We're overbooked."

But there was no one in the waiting room. What was the dear doctor doing?

"I know," I answered. "But couldn't you make an exception for me?" I sniffed, sneezed, and blew my nose. "Can I just wait until the doctor can work me in?"

"I suppose so, but it might be a long time."

"I'll wait," I said, taking an orange plastic chair. After watching CNN for a while, I decided that it was time to go to the ladies' room.

I walked to the door. "I hope you don't mind if I use the ladies' room . . . illness and all?"

"Ick," she replied.

I hurried downstairs, but everything looked

different from before. Room was made for more file cabinets, and they were arranged differently.

I opened the cabinets—the older ones—that weren't locked. As I opened one olive green cabinet, I found a bunch of leather-bound appointment books. Wow! This would show who had appointments back then. I looked for one from 1989. There it was! I pulled out the heavy thing with the yellowed pages and knew that the huge book wouldn't fit into my purse.

I wanted to read it right there to see what I could find, if anything. I knew she was here on August third, so I leafed through the pages. I had to hurry because I didn't want to risk being seen by Shannon Shannon or Dr. Huff.

I opened the ledger.

I tabbed over to August 3, 1989, and saw that Claire's appointment was at nine a.m. Oh! Bingo. Laura VanPlank and Carla VanPlank were scheduled right after her. I wondered if Claire was so happy that she spilled her pregnancy news to them.

I quickly put everything back and hurried back upstairs.

"You know, Miss Shannon, I think I'll just stop and get some cough syrup and some cough drops and maybe a box of allergy tablets. I should be perfect in a couple of hours. I do feel a lot better. Thank Dr. Huff for me. He's just a miracle worker."

"But—" said the receptionist.

I shook my head. "He's just a great doctor. Wow! I'm going to refer everyone to him. No sense driving to Watertown or Syracuse. Right?" I said, walking backward to the door.

"Right," said Miss Shannon, looking confused.

I hurried to the car and drove away, back to the drugstore's parking lot. There I relaxed and calmed my jittery nerves.

Later, back at the Big House, I told Ty what I'd found.

"If Claire was as happy as I think she was, she might have given it away that she was pregnant. Picture this: Laura and her mama were in Dr. Huff's waiting room. Laura is my number-one suspect—well, I think there's a six-way tie."

Ty chuckled.

"Laura couldn't have children because of an accident—Antoinette Chloe told me that. Maybe Laura was totally jealous of Claire's pregnancy. She was already upset that Rick Tingsley was attracted to Claire, at least at the bonfire—although she denies it. If she thought that Ricky had fathered Claire's baby, she'd be totally jealous—maybe even jealous enough to shoot Claire."

Ty thought for a minute. "Do you want to get a bite to eat at the Crossroads?"

"Brilliant," I said. "I always get hungry when I perform on Broadway. Let's go to the Crossroads. Maybe Laura and her parents are there."

When we got to the Crossroads and went into

the rustic restaurant, only Laura and her mother were sitting at a table.

There was no sign of Grant VanPlank with the wandering eye and the slippery zipper.

Laura took one look at Ty and me and scurried off into the kitchen.

What was that about? It looked as though she was guilty to me.

I gave Ty a nudge in case he missed Laura's record-breaking exit.

I smiled sweetly. "Well, hello, Mrs. VanPlank . . . Carla. I'd like you to meet Ty Brisco. He's one of the deputy sheriffs here in Sandy Harbor."

"Oh yes, the cowboy sheriff from the wilds of Texas."

Carla casually lifted her hand with the zillion-carat diamonds and then turned her palm over, as if she expected Ty to kiss the back of her hand.

Instead Ty gave the underside of her hand a slight clap, then slid his back clawlike so only their knuckles were hooked together. Then he gave the back of her hand a tap with his fisted hand.

A hip handshake.

I tried not to laugh at the expression on Mrs. VanPlank's face. It was a cross between horror and more horror.

Without missing a beat, Ty said, "So-oo very pleased to meet y'all, ma'am." He took his hat off and put it over his heart. Then he put it back on.

Ty didn't suffer snobs lightly, but it was more

than that. If she thought that he was a hick, he'd give her hick. Maybe then she'd relax her guard around him.

"Certainly," she said, turning her nose up.

"I don't recognize your accent, ma'am. Where y'all from, ma'am?" he asked. "U-tah?"

He was pouring it on a little too thick, but I supposed he knew what he was doing.

"Utah? Certainly not! I'm from right here. And we have a home in Port Palm!" she said, uncrossing her legs, then recrossing them.

"Where's that? Wisconsin?" he asked.

"Florida!"

"That was my fourth guess, right after South Dakota, Iowa, and Kansas."

"Oh, for Pete's sake," she said. She moved both of her hands as if she were shooing away a fly. "So, this is the state of the local sheriff's department?"

"Yep. Sandy Harbor is in New York, ma'am. This is the right state," he said. "You're in the right one."

"Excuse me, Sheriff—" Carla stood.

"Brisco. Ty Brisco, ma'am." He pulled up a chair next to her, flipped it around, and straddled it. "Don't let me drive you away. Get the load off your feet." He slapped the seat of the chair she'd just vacated.

I don't know what made her sit back down, but she did.

"Ma'am, where's that other purty little filly that we scared away?"

"My daughter? Laura?"

"What a beautiful name, darlin'. Almost as beautiful as you." He took his hat off and put it over on his heart. "I'm so sorry. I didn't mean to interrupt your lunch with your big sister."

"My big sister? Oh my!"

If I didn't see First Lady VanPlank put her hand over her heart and almost swoon, I wouldn't believe it. That line was so corny, it could have been popped.

"I'll go get her," she said. "Join us, won't you?"

I started walking toward the kitchen. "You stay put, Mrs. VanPlank. I'll go ask Laura to join us."

But Laura was in the midst of a fight with her husband, the mayor.

"Richard Tingsley, I don't want to go to the Dance Fest."

It was a loud whisper, the kind you use on someone that you're mad at—through gritted teeth.

"Laura, look at my position. How would I look without you there? People will think something's wrong. It won't look good for my campaign."

"I'm sick of always campaigning. When are you going to *be* someone?"

"I'm someone now, aren't I? I'm mayor of Sandy Harbor."

She sighed. "Oh, Rick. I mean, when are you ever going to be senator?"

"Someday soon. Just stick with me. It'll be soon."

I knocked on the kitchen door, and they both spun around. "Hello, you two! Would you join us for a bite?"

"I can't," Rick said. "I have to get back to the office. I have a meeting with our tax department." He quickly turned to leave, without even kissing his wife good-bye.

The last I knew, the Sandy Harbor Tax Department consisted of Zeb Young, the part-time tax collector and full-time flea market owner.

"Mayor, tell Zeb that I have some flea market items for him," I shouted to his back.

"I will," he yelled back.

Laura was left in the kitchen, leaning against a long butcher block table. Her cheeks were pink.

"My waitress isn't here yet, and neither is my cook. They both are tied up—probably to each other. So I'll have to make up any orders," she said, tying on a white apron and ready to burst into tears. "And my feet are killing me in these damn heels."

"What size do you wear? You can wear my sneakers. They're probably more comfortable than those heels."

"I wear an eleven."

"Sorry, Laura. I wear a nine."

"That's okay. I couldn't wear sneakers anyway. My mother would carry on something awful."

Not for the first time, I felt sorry for her. Putting my hand on her shoulder, I asked, "If it's a cook you need until someone comes, I'll be glad to pitch in."

"No. I don't need your help. I don't need anyone's help," she snapped.

"Hey." I held my hands in the air. "Okay. I'll get out of your hair."

"Wait!"

I waited.

"Look, Trixie, I've been kind of stressed lately. My mother is very . . . demanding. She's always wound so tight, and she never cracks a smile. I—I just need time away from her."

"Maybe I can help, Laura. I'll invite your parents to move to my cottages. That'll give you a break."

"That'll never happen."

"You never know." I opened the kitchen door a crack. "Does that look like your mother?"

Mrs. VanPlank was laughing so hard that she was doing some unladylike snorting.

"What did that cowboy do to my mother?" Laura asked. "And where can I find me one?"

Laughing, we both pushed opened the doors to the Crossroads dining room and went to join Ty and Mrs. VanPlank.

What was Ty up to now?

# Chapter 15

*T*y stood as Laura and I returned to the table. The Crossroads was empty, very empty.

"Your place is usually crowded, Laura. Where's everyone?"

"When they found out that the cook was going to be late, they left. Apparently, they don't like my cooking. I think they all went over to Brown's with that horrible woman who wears flip-flops and muumuus. How can she even show her face with her husband in jail?"

"*She* didn't do anything," I pointed out. "And, Laura, you know very well that her name is Antoinette Chloe Brown. You went to high school with her. You even graduated with her."

"That doesn't mean I like her."

"Ladies, can I get you something to drink from the bar?" Ty asked.

The two First Ladies asked for red wine. I asked for clear water with cubes.

As soon as Ty disappeared, Laura leaned over the table toward her mother.

"What are you up to, Mother?" Laura asked.

"I'm just enjoying the deputy's company. That's all."

Laura rolled her eyes as if her mother was enjoying herself way too much.

"Laura, I've always told you to make friends, because friends are the best voters."

"Oh, for Pete's sake, Mother! He's a cop. That's not the kind of friend I need."

"He's not so bad," Carla stated. "Besides, *everyone* is a potential voter. Deputy Brisco is a fun cowboy. You just don't trust anyone. That's your problem."

Laura whirled her head around, exorcist-style. "What do you think about Deputy Brisco, Trixie? You know him the most, I hear."

"He does stay over the bait shop next door and he eats most of his meals at the Silver Bullet. He's a nice guy, but I don't really, really know him."

Laura pursed her lips. She was going to either spit at me camel-style or whistle for a cab.

I shrugged. "It's true. I don't really know him. All I know is that he came here from Houston because he needed a break from big-time crime."

"Why here in Sandy Harbor?" Laura asked.

"Because he used to fish here as a kid. He remembered how nice it was."

Laura sniffed. "I see."

I wondered what was up with her. Why did Laura have such a phobia about cops? I thought she just broke out of the six-way tie.

I didn't have much time to think about Laura, because Ty was coming back from the bar with three drinks in his hands and a bottle of beer in his front pants pocket.

"Here you go, ladies." He easily set the drinks on the table, then slid them to each one of us. He took his old seat, straddled it like before, slipped the beer out of his pocket, and held it in the air.

"A toast to long, happy lives and to two lives cut short: to Claire and David."

"To Claire and David," everyone said in unison.

Ty took a long draw on his beer, and every woman at the table watched his Adam's apple move on his somewhat shaven neck. "Thank God that I'm not on duty. This tastes good."

I chugged some water. "Yes, it does."

"What do you two ladies think of us finding Claire's body after all those years?" Ty asked.

"I don't have an opinion one way or another," said the elder First Lady. "I suppose it was a good thing."

Laura shifted on her butt cheeks. "I suppose she had to be found someday."

"Did you know she was pregnant?" I asked, turning to Laura.

"She was what?" Laura asked, clearly shocked. If she was acting, she was certainly better than me.

"Pregnant. Bun in the oven. Knocked up. With child. Preggers. Baby mama," I said.

"I didn't know that." Laura's face immediately turned red.

Carla cleared her throat. "Claire Jacobson was a loose woman—everyone knows that. And she got pregnant before those who really want a child. Like my poor Laura."

"Mother! Don't speak ill of the dead."

I touched her arm. "I'm so sorry, Laura. Believe me, I know how you feel."

Laura pulled her arm away. "I don't want your pity, Trixie."

"I'm not pitying you. I know how you feel."

"No. No, you don't."

"Yes. Yes, I do."

Laura looked away, and dabbed at her eyes.

Ty cleared his throat. "Ah . . . um . . ."

Subject change!

"Please," I said. "I want you both to come to the Dance Fest. It would mean a lot to me."

"Me, too," Ty said. "The more beautiful ladies there, the happier I'll be."

I kicked him under the table. Enough flattery already.

Then Grant VanPlank walked in. He was tall, slim, and tanned. He had a phony smile, shocking white hair cut in precision, probably in New York City. His eyes were a bright green and striking. He gave Carla a robotic kiss on the cheek and gave Ty a strange look.

Ty stood and offered his hand to Grant. They shook, gripped forearms, and grunted manly. Then Grant never took his eyes off Ty, sizing him up.

Interesting.

Ty offered to buy him a beer, and he declined, but he pulled over a chair and nudged Carla with his shoulder. She sat as still and as frozen as a marble statue.

More trouble in paradise?

I was dying to talk to him, but Ty took the lead.

"Mr. VanPlank, it's truly a pleasure to meet you. How long are you staying in Sandy Harbor?"

He pointed to his wife. "It's entirely up to Carla. She seems happy staying with Rick and Laura, but I like my privacy. If this town had a decent hotel, we'd move there."

"I have cottages on the lake," I said. "I have one available, and it's very private."

"You know, that's an excellent idea," said Carla. "I think I'll take you up on that, Trixie. Your grounds are beautiful, and I enjoy the view of the lake. How is tomorrow morning for check-in?"

"Perfect."

"Cottages? Are you sure, Carla?" Grant asked. "Anything less than five stars in Michelin, and you think it's camping."

"It'll be just like our first years of marriage— when we were poor and struggling and very happy. Remember those few days when we were happy, Grant?"

He was silent for a while. "How long are you going to punish me?"

Carla sat very still, then through her pinched lips said, "Until your dying day or mine, whichever comes first."

"Excuse me, everyone." Grant stood and nodded at everyone, like a chicken pecking at grain. "I'll see you tomorrow, Trixie. I believe that we're checking in."

I waved good-bye.

As he left, Laura appeared. "Was that Daddy I saw leave?"

"Yes. Your father graced us with his presence for at least three minutes."

Ty drained his beer. "I have to get to work, ladies. Will you all please excuse me?"

"But you haven't ordered any food, Ty. You either, Trixie." Laura shuffled the corners of the big plastic menus in her hand.

Ty tweaked his hat to her. "Sorry, ma'am. I'm going to have to take a rain check on that. Trixie?"

"Me, too, since I drove with Ty. Sorry, Laura, but I'll be back. I have a lot of last-minute things to do for the Dance Fest."

"I understand," Laura said.

"See you tomorrow," said the icy Carla. "When we check in."

"Mother? Check in to what?"

"Your father and I are checking in to a cottage. One of Trixie's cottages."

"You can't be serious."

"I'm as serious as a cheating husband."

The next morning, true to her word, Grant and Carla VanPlank checked in. Honeymooners, they were not. I could hear them sniping at each other all the way up the stairs to the Big House.

"Since Cottage Eight is being . . . uh . . . remodeled," said the First Lady, "how about Cottage One?"

"I'd like to stay in the middle," Grant said. "Near Eight."

Another person who wanted to stay near Eight, and another interesting coincidence.

"Seven is taken. I can give you Cottage Nine." I held up the key.

"That's fine," she said.

"I think that Laura is going to miss you," I said to Carla.

"She has her husband to worry about."

"Oh. Is something wrong?" I asked.

"The mayor just hasn't been himself lately," Mr. VanPlank offered.

Interesting. "I'm sorry to hear that. Anything I can do?"

"Like what?" Grant asked.

"I can certainly cook and bake, if there's anything in particular he'd like."

"Food isn't the answer to everything, Trixie," said the frosty First Lady.

"It is for me." I grinned, already wondering

what I could make for our mayor and maybe have an audience with him, even though I'd rather clean the diner with a toothbrush.

"Let's get settled, Carla. I'd like to take a swim and get my new suit wet," Grant said.

"Which one of your girlfriends gave you that?" snapped Carla.

He took a deep breath and let it out, shaking his head. "I know that this is a mistake, but let's see it through."

I almost felt sorry for him. It seemed that this was a standard fight between the two of them. Judging by his hopeless demeanor, Carla never missed a chance to remind him of his affair—or affairs.

She should have just kicked his cheating butt out.

At the Dance Fest tomorrow night, I was going to find a way to ask him about Claire Jacobson without the First Lady's presence.

"Can you find Cottage Nine or would you like me to show you?" I asked.

"Of course I can find it," Carla said, adding a sniff. "They're numbered, aren't they?"

Okay. I wasn't needed here. I thought I'd go to the kitchen and see how everyone was doing.

It was a beautiful day, and I totally enjoyed the breeze coming off the lake as I walked the short distance from the Big House to the diner.

I turned my face up to the sun and let it warm me for a while. I'm not one for sitting or lying in the sun, but once in a while, I love sitting in a chair on the beach and watching the sun sparkle on the water.

I heard laughing, and saw Buddy Wilder and his party playing volleyball on the beach. I squinted. It looked as though Buddy was wearing his old red trunks with the white flowers.

Couldn't be. The elastic had to be shot by now.

But I didn't have any time right now to relax. I had the Dance Fest on my mind. The VanPlanks were taking up space there, too. And Buddy Wilder, and Ty, who doesn't want me to help him, and Laura, and the mayor . . .

I needed a larger mind or less on it.

Going into the kitchen, I saw that it was perfectly clean and empty of people. Chelsea, Cindy, and ACB were sitting at the counter in the diner, sipping coffee. There were only four parties eating, and Judy was ringing out a fifth.

Ray was sitting next to ACB, but when he saw me walk into the diner, he jumped to attention.

"Relax, Ray. It's fine if you take a break," I assured him.

They all looked tired. One thing about being a chef and cooking is that you're constantly on your feet.

ACB's hat with her "salute to our forty-ninth state" looked as if the sled dogs at the Iditarod were ready to run off the fuchsia brim.

Juanita's eyes were at half-mast.

Cindy, the youngest of us all, had her head down on the counter and was snoring.

"How's it going?" I asked. "Anything I can do?"

"Everything on your list is done," Juanita said. "And more."

"We decided to bake hamburger and hot dog rolls instead of you buying them," ACB said, smiling. "They came out beautiful."

"And we had fun." Cindy yawned, stretching.

"The most fun I've had in months," ACB said, nodding. Her sled team hit the floor, and she bent over to pick it up with a grunt.

"And Ray was indispensable," Juanita added. "He cleaned up and washed pans as we went along and kept track of the front, too."

"You ladies, and Ray, are fabulous. What's left for me?"

"Your special Dixie chicken sauce has to be made and the chicken marinated," Juanita said. "Everything's in the cooler."

I decided to take a peek at what they'd done. Going into the walk-in cooler was always a fun time. I loved to slip on the mohair sweater that Aunt Stella kept on a hanger near the door of the cooler. It reminded me so much of her.

The cooler was loaded with aluminum pans. I saw four pans of potato salad, four of macaroni salad, baked beans, and coleslaw. There were numerous other pans of sausage, pulled pork, meatballs, macaroni and cheese, and ziti.

Tomorrow, we'd barbecue the chicken on Porky's old homemade charcoal grill, brush on this fabulous chicken sauce that had been in a friend's family for an eternity, and make up pans of crispy chef salad.

There's nothing that I hate more than a warm, droopy salad. At the Silver Bullet, I served salad in chilled bowls. Yum.

In my big binder, I found the recipe for Dixie Barbecue Sauce and Marinade and calculated it to make ten times the amount. Then I poured it all over the chicken for it to marinade in the cooler.

One more time I made the recipe, to baste the chicken with while it barbecued.

It was melt-in-your-mouth good, and it reminded me of all the neighbors getting together in someone's backyard. The parents used to take turns, and all of us kids couldn't wait until it was Mr. and Mrs. DiFantelli's turn.

Mrs. D was from one of the Carolinas, I forgot which one, and I loved listening to her talk about the big plantations and Civil War history.

I always got the impression that Mrs. D felt a little superior to us Yankees, but we forgave everything on chicken barbecue day.

Checking my list against everything that had already been done, I didn't see any strawberries in the cooler for the strawberry shortcake that Sarah Stolfus was making.

I went into the diner and found Juanita sitting with her eyes closed and her index finger through the handle of a coffee cup.

"Juanita, are you awake?" I said softly, and her

eyes blinked. "Did any strawberries come from the organic farm?"

Nothing.

I gently nudged her arm. "Juanita? Strawberries? Are there any strawberries?"

"Clyde, you are my life."

*Say what?*

She was dreaming about Clyde, my senior handyman? The two of them fought like heavyweight boxers.

Juanita and Clyde seemed as far apart as crème brûlée and unsweetened gelatin.

That just added more strangeness to a strange day that started with the VanPlanks' checking in.

"Juanita, wake up." I gave her arm a stronger nudge. "You're having a bad dream."

She blinked awake. "What?"

"What did you do with the strawberries?"

"Huh?"

"The strawberries for the shortcake. Did you clean them, slice them, sugar them?"

"I forgot to tell you." She yawned. "They didn't come in."

"I'll give Various Veggies and Fruits a call right now. And I'll take care of washing and cutting them. Go home and get some sleep." I looked over at Cindy. Her head was back down, and she hadn't moved since I last saw her.

Having my employees snoozing at the counter wasn't exactly good for business. Customers might think that the Silver Bullet was a halfway house for chefs with sleeping disorders.

I phoned Ronnie Owens at the organic farm.

"Various Veggies and Fruits. This is Ronnie. How can I bring some sunshine into your life?"

"Ronnie, this is Trixie Matkowski at the Silver Bullet Diner. I received my order—lettuce, carrots, cukes, tomatoes—but I'm looking for my fifty pounds of strawberries."

"Hi, Trixie. The kids and Billy are picking the rest of them now, and Billy will deliver them just as soon as they are finished. I'm thinking it'll be two hours, depending on how much they eat."

"That's fine. How do the berries look?"

"Magnificent."

"Just what I needed. Thanks, Ronnie. Oh, will all of you be coming to the Dance Fest?"

"Wouldn't miss it."

We said our good-byes, and the next call I made was to Clyde. "Clyde, how's the bar set up? Got enough ice and tubs? Is the soda set up?"

"All okay, Trixie. Come out and look. The rental tables aren't here yet, but when they come, we're ready to set up."

"When are the tables and chairs supposed to be here?"

"Three o'clock."

"Call me if there's a problem."

"Will do."

I still couldn't see Clyde and Juanita together,

but I'd been wrong before, like when I gave my heart to Deputy Doug.

*But that'll never happen again*, I thought as I wiped the counter. *There will* not *be another man in my life.*

No. Not even Ty Brisco, although he made my cheeks heat and my heart flutter like a teenager's. I had the constant urge to buy a pink diary and write his name in it with a heart over the *I* on his last name.

I'd put all my energy into making the Silver Bullet and the cottages a moneymaking endeavor. Okay, I wasn't succeeding with the cottages, but the diner was netting enough money for me to keep making payments to Aunt Stella.

I loved this place with my whole heart and soul. Always had, always would. I'd grown up here, and I'd always remember the great times I'd had with my family and friends.

Including Claire Jacobson. I didn't feel I'd come close to solving the mystery of her death, but a couple of things were adding up.

I still thought her murder had something to do with the fact that she was pregnant. Someone didn't like it, and wanted her out of the way.

Was it "B" or someone else?

It couldn't be "B" of the love letter. He adored her. Things change, though, and something could have happened.

I puttered around the kitchen and made up the

orders that the waitresses turned in because I was here and my two chefs had narcolepsy.

Cindy did drag herself into the kitchen when she heard the bell ring. "I'll make up those orders, Trixie. My shift isn't over yet."

"Yes, it is. Go home. Tomorrow will be a big day, and I'll need you wide-awake and alert."

"Thanks. I'll come in early tomorrow."

"I'd appreciate that."

Ray walked in with a gray bin full of dirty dishes and started loading them into the dishwasher.

"How's everything, Ray?"

"I'm not that busy. Is there anything else I can do?" *What a sweet kid!*

"Sure. Why don't you see if you can help out Clyde and Max in the yard? They are overseeing the tent setup and the bar and waiting for tables and chairs. The tables need to be arranged and covered."

Out the back door, I could see a huge white truck roll in. SANDY HARBOR PARTY RENTALS was written on the side in bright balloons.

"There's the truck now with the tables and chairs," I said.

"Cool," he said, and hurried out. I was sure that he'd enjoy working outside for a while. Even computer nerds need sunshine.

I made up more orders. A party of five all wanted corned beef sandwiches. Two wanted mac and cheese. A party of eight wanted breakfast, so

I was busy with launching bread on the Ferris wheel to toast, making omelets, and grilling bacon and sausage. The egg orders were tricky: up, over easy, over light, lightly scrambled, over dry.

A horn blared at the back door just as I finished the breakfast order. I saw a VARIOUS VEGGIES AND FRUITS sign on the van door and surmised that it was Billy Swenti with the strawberries.

Billy was one of my original suspects from the B List. Although I didn't really suspect him, he might still remember some detail about Claire that would help the case. I couldn't wait to talk to him.

Opening the door, I saw a half dozen children sitting in the van. Billy was tall and thin and had a receding hairline, but the majority of his hair cascaded down his back in straggly strands. His jeans were dirty and torn and he wore a black Grateful Dead shirt.

"Are you Billy?" I asked.

"Yep."

"With my strawberries?"

"Just picked. Fifty pounds. Me and the kids did it. They are still warm from the sun." He smiled and I saw that Billy needed major dentistry, and fast.

I waved to the kids who were leaning out of the van window. "Thanks for picking my berries. If you come tomorrow night, you can have strawberry shortcake, and I'm going to tell everyone that you picked the berries just for them."

The pride showed on their cute faces, all races and various ages.

"Ronnie said that he'd bill you," Billy said.

"Okay, but can I have a moment with you alone?" I asked.

His brow furrowed. "I guess so."

He yelled to the kids that he'd be right back and to behave. In my family, that was a signal to me, my sister, and brother to act up.

We stepped into the kitchen of the diner. "Billy, do you remember Claire Jacobson?"

"Yeah. Claire. They just found her body."

It seemed as if each word pained him to speak.

"How well did you know her?"

"Why do you want to know?"

"All those years ago, she was a friend of mine, and I owe her."

He didn't ask me what I owed her but walked into the kitchen.

"I owe her, too," he said. "She came into the grocery store in town now and then. I had a summer job there. She was always with her parents, but we found time to talk. She was easy to talk to, and I needed to talk."

"Did you go out with her?" I asked.

He shook his head. "That was the summer I came out. My parents went crazy, and Claire listened to me. That's all. Why do you ask?"

"Do you know anyone whose name starts with a *B* that she might have been friends with?"

He thought for a while. "Buddy. Buddy . . . um . . . Wilder. He hung around Claire as much as he could."

"Were they going out?" I asked. "Like a couple."

He shrugged. "I don't know. I just saw them together a lot, and I think she liked him, but I don't know if they were a couple. She liked everyone. I hope they find the guy—or woman."

"Woman?" I asked, surprised. I never thought that Billy would think a woman had killed Claire.

"They were all jealous of her."

"Like who?" I think I already knew, but I wanted him to say her name.

He looked at the floor, not moving.

"I don't know if I should name someone. It's not fair to gossip. I know how it feels, true or not."

"This conversation is just between us."

He hesitated for what seemed like hours. Finally he choked out a name.

"Laura VanPlank. She's now Laura Tingsley. She hated Claire because Rick liked her."

I knew that.

"Were Claire and Rick a couple?" I asked.

He shrugged. "Locker room talk had him with Claire. And I think he wanted to be with Claire, but Laura was always in the way. She clung to him like a spider clings to a web."

"Thanks, Billy." I held up a finger. "Wait a second. I want to pack up some chocolate chip cookies for your hard workers."

I gave him a bag of Mrs. Stolfus's cookies and walked him out.

"See you at the Dance Fest. The last one I went to was the one . . . the one . . ."

"The one where Claire disappeared," I said.

"I'm hoping, probably like half the town, that this new Dance Fest will erase that one."

"Me, too," I said.

"And now another guy turned up dead in one of the cottages."

"Yeah."

"Maybe the Dance Fest can erase that one, too."

What was wrong with my brain? I never even gave it a thought that my Dance Fest was the first one in ages. I remembered that Aunt Stella gave them up because of Uncle Porky's health, but I wondered if another reason, of equal merit, was Claire's disappearance.

Something near the cottages caught my eye. I put my sunglasses on and saw Carla VanPlank standing on a small step stool and looking into the windows of Cottage Eight.

What on earth?

The windows were shuttered from the outside, but only a hook and eye anchored them to each other. She must have unhooked a set of shutters.

What nerve!

I hurried off to the cottages and approached her. "Carla, what on earth are you doing?"

"I'm just looking. No harm done."

"What are you looking for?" I tried to keep my voice even, but I was livid.

"I don't know yet, dear. I'll know it when I see it."

"Like what?"

"Oh, I don't know. I guess I wanted to see if Phil Jacobson left anything behind."

"As you can see, everything was taken by the police."

"Not his typewriter," she said.

"Apparently, that wasn't important to the police." I took a deep breath before the top of my head blew off like a volcano. "Mrs. VanPlank, please get down from that stool immediately. I don't want you falling. I don't want you hurt."

I held out my hand to help her down, and she finally took it.

Whoa! I just remembered something she'd said.

"Wait one second, Carla! How did you know that the man who was murdered in this cottage was Phil Jacobson? His name was not released by the police yet. I repeat: not released."

She seemed totally unconcerned and waved a hand across her face. "Oh, I heard it somewhere. Small town, you know."

"Not that small."

She grinned. It was a strange, lopsided grin and her eyes looked glassy. Was she drunk?

Something was wrong with her. Maybe she needed to go to the doctor.

I took her hand and helped her back to her cottage. I knocked on the door, and finally her husband, Grant, answered. "Mr. VanPlank, I think something is wrong with your wife. She was standing on a chair, looking in on Cottage Eight."

"*What?* What were you doing that for, Carla?"

"Because I wanted to." She sniffed. "If you can do anything you want, Grant, so can I. And I wanted to see the inside of that cottage."

"Don't start with me again. I want to have a nice, peaceful day. I'd like to enjoy my daughter's company, my goof of a son-in-law's inane ramblings, and even your company, dearest wife. For a while yesterday, I thought we might have buried the hatchet and were making some progress on our marriage."

"You're dreaming, Grant."

"I guess I am."

"Well, I'll let you two go," I said. "I have work to do to get ready for the Dance Fest."

"Thank you, Trixie."

"No problem. Maybe you should take her to the doctor."

He nodded, but I didn't think he was going to exert himself.

I walked to the diner, thinking about the episode with Mrs. VanPlank. She had a lot of nerve looking in the window of Eight.

And she knew that it was Phil Jacobson who was murdered there.

I dismissed her from my thoughts until I could tell Ty what she'd said. I had a lot of other things to think about.

I really hoped that the Dance Fest would be a success. I wanted a huge turnout because I was going to eavesdrop like crazy.

# Chapter 16

"Anything I can do to help?" Ty walked up on my back porch as I was enjoying the breeze and the white caps that were forming on the lake.

"Everything's all ready for tonight. There will be some last-minute things to do, like barbecuing the chicken, but I have time for that yet. I don't want it to be dry."

There were about four hours to go before I needed to spring to attention as the Dance Fest attendees would be arriving. Right now I needed to get off my feet and relax.

Buddy Wilder's group was playing another round of volleyball. They played so much volleyball I wondered if they were training for the summer Olympics.

Ty sat in the Adirondack chair next to me, and I was glad I had taken the time to put on makeup and curl my hair. I was also experimenting with a new lipstick that was guaranteed not to drip off my lips if I was working in a hot kitchen.

"I'm getting nowhere on the murders, Trixie. I can't help feeling that I'm overlooking something important, but I can't think of what."

"All roads seem to lead to Laura VanPlank Tingsley. She was jealous of Rick paying attention to Claire. Also, she couldn't have children and I think she knew that Claire was pregnant and thought that the baby was Rick Tingsley's. And I think that Phil was murdered because he was onto the killer. He was trying to lure him or her out but got killed. But there's no 'B' anywhere in my theory."

Ty snapped his fingers. "I got a call from the state police today. Ballistics tests showed that the gun found in Cottage Eight under the bed was registered to Phillip Jacobson and that it wasn't fired in ages. Matter of fact, it looked like Phil never cleaned it. It wasn't the murder weapon in either of the murders."

"You found a gun in Cottage Eight?" I was so surprised, you could have knocked me over with a pastry bag. "Gun? You didn't tell me you found a gun!"

He ignored my shock and anger.

"It seems that Phil Jacobson brought one with him, but when he needed it, it was under his bed, the queen bed."

"You found it under the bed in Cottage Eight?" I asked.

"Yep."

"And you didn't think to tell me that either, huh?"

"I just found out that it wasn't the murder

weapon in either murder," he said. "I'm telling you now."

"Of course it wasn't the murder weapon. Phil wouldn't kill his own sister, for heaven's sake. He was too young, and how would he drag her body into the cave?"

"It might have been planted on him for some reason. We have to cover all bases, Trixie. You know that," he said.

Right now I was so mad at him, I could happily toss him off my porch, headfirst.

I sat stewing in my own anger. I was going to solve these two mysteries without him. He didn't need me, and I didn't need him.

I watched as Grant VanPlank and Carla Van-Plank walked behind Cottage Eight. I don't know why they showed such interest, but I perked right up. So did Ty.

"What are they doing?" he asked.

"Snooping. That's what everyone does with Eight."

"They'd better not go in. Even though the cottage was released by the state police, I kept the tape up for a reason."

"They're not going in. They're just walking around."

Interesting.

It was interesting that they were even walking together since they didn't seem to get along. To me, it seemed that Carla wouldn't, or couldn't, forgive him for blowing his senatorial run.

Tonight I was going to find out if Claire was the one that Grant had had an affair with. Was he also the one that "B" beat up for stalking Claire?

I didn't know how yet, but I was going to polish my high school acting skills for tonight. After all, I was in the chorus of *Bye, Bye, Birdie*—back row, first one on the right, nondancing part.

Ty cleared his throat. "You're mad at me."

"Ya think?"

"Look, Trixie, I—"

"Stop." I held up a hand. "I know that you don't want me helping you. I know that you're trained, and I'm not. I know about confidentiality, but it's not your cottages that are empty. It wasn't your friend who was shot."

I stood up. "I have to take a shower and change. Then I have to check that everything's on schedule for the Dance Fest."

"But, Trixie—"

"Gotta go!" I twirled like a newbie on a dance show and hurried into my house.

I was going to wear a new pair of black jeans and a royal blue sparkly top.

The front doorbell rang, and I saw that it was mail delivery. Oh! It was the embroidered golf shirts that I'd bought for Ray, Clyde, and Max. And I bought my waitresses white blouses with the same logo.

They could wear them for the Dance Fest.

I called Ray on his cell phone and left him a message to come over. He could deliver the new uniforms to my staff. We were going to look fabulous tonight.

Out my picture window, I could see Ray running over as if he were on the track team. I didn't mean for him to break speed records getting here.

He took my steps two at a time. I opened the door and invited him in for some water and a towel to wipe his face. He was panting and sweating like a racehorse.

"Ray, I got the guys embroidered shirts and the waitresses embroidered blouses. Would you deliver these? They'll sort out the sizes themselves."

"Yeah, sure."

"There's a shirt for you, too."

"For me? I just started here."

"But you're a part of the team, Ray, and you're doing a fabulous job."

Suddenly I had a scathingly brilliant idea. "Um, Ray, how good are you at running people's names on the computer and finding out . . . things about them? Old things."

"I'm outstanding."

"This is nothing illegal. Nothing I want you to hack. I just want you to use whatever sites you think have the most information. I'll give you the names, and you dig up the dirt. I mean, you dig up old things about them of interest. For the guys, I'm looking for anyone with a *B* nickname."

"Okay."

His eyes sparkled. He was ready to go.

"My laptop is on the kitchen table. Let's rock."

I found my B List and added more names to it. Rick and Laura VanPlank Tingsley, Grant Van-Plank, Carla VanPlank, Antoinette Chloe Switzer Brown and/or Brownelli.

That was the list of everyone who knew Claire. In the case of the VanPlanks, I just threw them in to see what skeletons Ray might find.

"This is just between us, Ray, and you have to hurry. The Dance Fest is about to kick off."

"Yeah. My parents and my girlfriend are coming."

"Great. You'll have to introduce me."

"Yeah." The whine of my laptop booting up seemed to hypnotize Ray. He sprang into action and started typing faster than the speed of sound.

After my shower and after redoing my hair and makeup, I found Ray still typing.

"I printed off the most interesting stuff. It's on the printer tray," he said, not looking up.

I skimmed the pages. There was nothing exciting. Ray kept typing and printing and I kept skimming.

"Ray. I'm sorry, but I have to go. It's time to barbecue the chicken and make the chef salad."

"I'm almost done."

"Okay. Keep going. Finish up and bring me the printouts. I'll pass out the tops to the staff." I picked up the box and headed for the front door.

"All right."

When I walked out the door, I noticed that Ty was still sitting on the porch.

He gave me the once-over and whistled long and low. My mouth went dry.

"You clean up nicely," he said.

"Thanks." I grinned, loving the look on his face. "What have you been doing here? Thinking?"

"Yeah. I was just thinking about the case."

"Me, too, but I can't deal with it right now. I hope to have hundreds of people coming to the Dance Fest. Oh my goodness, Ty. I hope we don't run out of places to park."

"I have it covered. Vern McCoy is going to let the latecomers park up the road and on the bank of Route 3."

"Chelsea is going to take payments at the door and hand out wristbands. She's going to check licenses, too. A green wristband means they can drink. Red means that they can't."

"Got it," Ty said. "How about if I make sure that everything's always full at the buffet?"

"Antoinette Chloe's going to do that. She's been a wonderful help, even though I have to constantly remind her to take her hats off so she doesn't deep-fry the menagerie on top."

"What do you want me to do?"

"You can provide security, make sure that no one leaves the grounds for a bonfire somewhere else, and make sure that no one gets that close to our bonfire."

"Will do." He gave me a sharp salute. "Let's go. I can barbecue the chicken for you in the meantime."

"Thanks. Then I won't smell like a smokestack, and I can do other things." I slipped a clean apron over my outfit. I didn't want anything to happen to it.

I did some odds and ends and in between I thought about the case . . . and Ty. And how he looked at me.

Ty? Why was I thinking about him?

I found my notebook and flipped it open.

Juanita was still going to stay on chef duty just in case we got some customers who weren't interested in the Dance Fest. I told her to try and talk them into the Dance Fest and/or the buffet.

If they didn't want the buffet, she'd have to cook off the menu.

Ty and I walked together but parted when Ty kept on going to the diner and I stopped to check everything on the grounds. The band was setting up, and I introduced myself.

"I'll trust you to get things hopping, right, guys?"

"I'm Frankie Rudinski, and I guarantee that the neighbors will complain to the police—if you had any neighbors." A short, rotund man with friendly eyes, a perfectly bald head, and a huge smile stepped forward and took my hand. "Stella and Porky always danced to the first dance—a polka. Are you going to carry on that tradition, Trixie?"

I thought for a moment. Who on earth could I get as a partner? Ty was my first choice, and I'd bet my bank account—as anemic as it was—that he could do a mean two-step, but what did a Texas cowboy know about doing the polka? Clyde or Max could probably bounce around a bit with me.

The polka was exhausting, but I was up for it. I was in fairly good shape from all the work that I'd been doing, and I was continuously in motion, mostly doing the Diner Shuffle. The Diner Shuffle had to be a form of aerobic exercise. If not, it should be!

Just hearing that polka beat brought back so many memories of wonderful times, family times.

"Um . . . I'm not very good at doing the official polka steps, but I can bounce around with the best. And I'd love to kick off the Dance Fest."

"Whoeee!" he said. "We're ready whenever you are. It's been a long time!"

I laughed. They hadn't lost their energy, just most of their hair, over the past twenty-five years.

One guy was positioning a chair and unlocking a big case. He pulled out a cherry red accordion. I remembered Aunt Stella playing the accordion with Frankie and the Polka Dots. It was always the highlight of the summer for me.

I wished she would have been able to come.

I waved good-bye to Frankie and the Polka Dots, checked in with Clyde and Max, and peeked at the tables under the tent. Someone had picked wildflowers and set them on each table.

"Who picked the flowers?" I asked Juanita later.

"Ty. He went to the meadow early this morning and picked them. I put them in vases."

"He did? Really?"

Ty never ceased to amaze me, but he didn't seem like the wildflower-picking type. I wondered if he had an ulterior motive. Maybe he was looking for more clues or more loose manuscript pages from Phil's typewriter. It had been windy. Maybe some pages that we'd overlooked before had blown around.

Ty hadn't said a word to me, but that didn't mean he hadn't found something.

My cheeks heated. I was getting mad at him all over again over nothing.

Out the back door, I noticed Buddy Wilder in the parking lot. He was getting something out of the van that he drove here in. I'd been waiting to catch him alone. *Now's my chance!*

"Later, Juanita," I said, running out the back door of the diner. I slowly walked toward him and feigned surprise when he noticed me.

"Buddy! Hello. How are you enjoying your stay here?"

"It brings back old times."

"I know. That's one of the reasons why I love this place so much. Such good memories, and some awful ones, too. Claire's murder, for one, and then Mr. Burrows." I shook my head. "Horrible."

"I know. I sit on the beach, and I can remember Claire and Phil building sand castles."

"Who was she in love with, Buddy? You?"

He shook his head. "I tried like hell, but I couldn't get anywhere with her."

"Did that make you mad?"

He made a face and stared down his tanned nose at me. "What are you asking me? Was I mad enough to kill her?"

He spoke through gritted teeth, and I thought he was going to get physical. I stepped back. "I didn't mean that, Buddy."

He shook off his anger, and I could see him transform back into the charming con man that he allegedly was.

"I could have any girl I wanted. I moved on. Besides, no one could stay mad at Claire for long. She was the sweetest. But maybe too sweet, and more than a little too naive. I was worried about her because she didn't know how to handle all the men who came sniffing around her."

"Who were the sniffers, Buddy?"

"Some old guy. Matter of fact, he's staying here. I almost fell over when I saw him."

"Grant VanPlank?"

"Yeah, that's his name, but he wasn't the only one."

"Rick Tingsley?"

"Yeah. He hung around her like a love-struck puppy."

"Did she like him?" I asked.

He shrugged. "Yeah. I think she did."

"Who else?"

"All the males in Sandy Harbor High School. They all loved her. She was a friend to all," he said. "But someone obviously didn't like her—probably a woman."

That was an offhand remark and just what Billy Swenti had said. Interesting.

"Like who?"

"Laura VanPlank, the snob. She was the direct opposite of Claire. I felt bad for Ricky. She sank her claws into him and never let go."

"What about Antoinette Chloe?"

"She was the exception. She was Claire's only gal pal."

"Oh, wait. Wasn't Antoinette Chloe with Sal Brownelli back then? Wasn't she worried that Sal would be attracted to Claire?"

"Nope. Sal only had eyes for Antoinette Chloe and vice versa."

Good for ACB. She was secure in her muu-muus.

"Were you questioned by the cops back then, Buddy?"

"We all were, but mostly we had to prove that we never left the bonfire all night."

*But someone else could have arrived at the bonfire who was not part of the senior class and killed Claire!*

I reminded myself that Claire was just considered a missing person back then. That's probably what the one Sandy Harbor deputy was going on twenty-five years ago, but now everything had changed.

"Thanks for the information, Buddy. Sorry if I upset you."

"It's old news, but it seems like just yesterday. It was like the end of innocence for the class of eighty-nine, know what I mean? Growing up here was idyllic, easy, for the most part. Some of the kids' folks were farmers, and they had to work hard, but we also played hard. Fishing, boating, swimming, tubing—we did it all, but I can't think of one of us who would kill someone."

Buddy looked close to tears, and I hoped that the allegations against him were false. But that was up to Ty and the New York City Police Department to figure out.

"Buddy, I don't want you or any of your friends to pay for the Dance Fest. It's on me."

"That's very generous of you, but I won't hear it. I know you are losing business because of Mr. Burrows's murder, and I want to support businesses in Sandy Harbor."

"You're sweet, Buddy." I took a deep breath, convinced that Buddy wasn't a suspect, or had I already ruled him out?

Still, Buddy didn't give me any information that I didn't already know; he just seconded my conclusions.

But he did get me thinking that someone else could have been at that bonfire. A nonsenior person. An uninvited person with killing on his, or her, mind.

I saw Grant walking with Carla again. They looked up and waved to me, then stared at Cottage Eight. They were very interested in that cottage. Even when Grant sat on a chair by the water, Carla still seemed morbidly interested in the cottage.

Ray jogged toward me wearing his new golf shirt and carrying a handful of white paper.

Oh! That reminded me that I forgot to pass out everyone's "uniform." I picked up the box that I'd left on a chair and gave it all to Juanita to do. I needed to see what Ray found out.

Cars were coming down the main road that led to the diner, and Vern McCoy was blowing his whistle and parking them in the parking lot and a nearby field as fast as he could. As I waited for Ray, even more cars came, making a solid line down the road and onto the highway.

It was going to be a great turnout.

Ray handed me the stack of papers from my printer.

"Anything exciting, Ray?"

"Nah. I didn't think so, but you might. I think that one *B* nickname turned up."

I looked at the top printout. "Bond is Grant VanPlank's middle name," Ray said.

"His middle name is Bond! Really? That's interesting."

I didn't see Claire or anyone calling him by his 007 middle name. But maybe he'd been much more dashing and debonair back then and charmed her.

"And also, I don't know if it's a big deal, but some reporter from Central High School's newspaper, called the *Bobcat Bulletin*, said that—" Ray took the stack of papers from me and leafed through them. "Uh . . . said that Rick Tingsley should be called Boomer for the way he knocked over 'Central High's Bobcats like bowling pins.'"

"Boomer, huh?" That definitely could be a big deal. It was good to have a hacker on your side.

"Was that an expression way back then?" Ray asked.

"How do I know, Ray? I was ten at the time."

"I wasn't even born yet!"

The nickname apparently never caught on, because none of his classmates ever called him that.

This was so overwhelming, and I felt so useless. I pinched the bridge of my nose, trying to get rid of Headache Number Twenty before it camped in my temples.

I should have read up on Grant VanPlank on the Internet more. I'm sure I would have found out that his middle name had started with a *B* a long time ago. Instead I took the low road and read all the gossip about his various affairs.

My only excuse was that I had a lot on my mind, or what was left of it.

I wondered if Ty knew about Grant's middle name. He probably did.

But I'd bet that he didn't know that Rick Tingsley was Boomer with a *B*.

People filed in as I leafed through the papers. When I looked up again, the tent was packed and I heard my name announced by Frankie. The Polka Dots were doing a drumroll.

I tucked the papers into my back pocket and hurried to the dance floor. I'd forgotten to ask Clyde or Max to dance the first dance with me.

As I stood there with the drum still rolling, I felt as if every pair of eyes were on me, which they were.

It was a beautiful night. The sun had set in an orange-purple glow, and now the inky sky was littered with bright stars. The air was warm and the smell of the lake was in the air.

The sides of the tent had been rolled up so everyone could enjoy the beautiful evening. If it turned too cold or started to rain, they could be rolled down. The tent glowed from the little white lights that were strung up and the bigger white lights over the buffet tables.

I was proud of the fabulous job that my staff had done. Even Antoinette Chloe, who was not part of my real staff, had worked hard and had shown a definite talent for short-order cooking.

As everyone continued their applause, I stalled for time to lower my heart rate. Then I thanked everyone for coming.

"Everyone has welcomed me to Sandy Harbor and has supported the Silver Bullet Diner. There have been some awful things that have happened recently, but soon the sheriff's department will get to the bottom of what occurred, and Sandy Harbor will be all right again. I'd like to thank everyone for coming to the first Dance Fest in twenty-five years. And I'd like you all to know that there will be a Dance Fest every Saturday until Labor Day. Thanks, everyone! Now dance, have a fabulous time, and don't drink and drive. Select a designated driver or let me know, and I'll find someone to drive you home!"

Frankie announced that I'd kick off the party with a polka, just as Porky and Stella Matkowski used to do.

I felt a little sad that neither of them was here to enjoy this. I missed them both dearly.

As tears pooled in my eyes, I tried to inch my way off the dance floor until strong arms stopped me and whirled me around.

Ty!

He turned and turned me in perfect time to the beat. If this was a Texas two-step, I was boot scootin'.

"Ty, how did you learn how to polka?"

"My mother was Polish. Karpinski. I grew up being everyone's partner at weddings when a polka was played."

"No way that you're half Polish!"

"Way."

"Karpinski?"

"Karpinski. Sophie Karpinski."

I knew now why I'd liked him right from the start. I tabled this exquisite piece of information for later.

The printouts from Ray were stabbing me in the back, and the fact that Grant Bond VanPlank was a definite suspect was making me breathless and flushed. Thank goodness there was a breeze to-night.

I waved my arms for everyone to join us, and the dance floor was soon packed. "Ty, I have to sit. I'm pooped."

"Okay." He put his hand at the small of my back as he often did and led me to a chair just off the dance floor. Suddenly my feet didn't hurt, my breath wasn't ragged, and I could have walked around the whole grounds with his hand on my back.

"Thanks for bailing me out of that, Ty."

"My pleasure."

Oh, wow. Did he have to say that so sexy with his low, sweet Texas accent?

I sat in the chair and pulled the printouts out of my pocket.

"What's all that?"

"Something that Ray did for me. Ty, I think Rick Tingsley called himself Boomer or maybe Claire called him that first. Yes! Claire went to Central High in Rochester. The Bobcats! The Sandy Harbor Trout played the Bobcats, so she would have read about Boomer and the bowling pins in the *Bobcat Bulletin*. Oh, and Bond is Grant VanPlank's middle name. And Carla knew that Burrows was really Phil Jacobon."

I looked at the clear, crisp typing on the page. I could even see it in the dim light of the lanterns and torches around the dance floor.

Oh my! I gripped the arms of the chair to keep from falling to the floor.

Type, type, type!

Ribbons on old typewriters. Ink cartridges on the new computer printers, faxes, and copiers.

Ribbons on old typewriters.

Ribbons on old typewriters!

"Ty, I gotta go!"

# Chapter 17

I kept to the shadows and snuck to Cottage Eight. My heart was pounding so loud I could be another drummer in Frankie's band.

I pushed the tape away from the door and opened it. It was so dark, I couldn't see a thing inside, and I didn't want to crash into any of the boards that we'd stacked up or step on a nail.

I flipped on the switch and unplugged all but one lamp so no one would notice the light leaking out of the cottage.

Why didn't I bring a flashlight? Why did I still not own a magnifying glass? It would have come in handy tonight.

I knew the answer to both of those questions. I was impatient.

I went to the typewriter, now on the kitchen table.

Then I manually rolled the left spool of ribbon to the right spool. There had to be information on here. Good information.

When I held the typewriter ribbon to the light, it would tell me what Phil was typing!

If it was like the ribbons of old, there would be three rows of type on it. When one row would finish, it'd kick over to the next row. The print on the one page of Phil's manuscript that I'd seen was dark, so maybe he'd used a new ribbon and it wouldn't be struck over a lot.

I couldn't wait to look at the spool, so I sat down at one of the kitchen chairs, unwound the right spool, and held the ribbon to the light.

It was rather slow reading, and the black ribbon looked like a mound of thick spaghetti on the floor, but I read:

> *I found Claire's diary under a loose floorboard under her bed. In it, she wrote "I hope that Boomer will still love me after I tell him that I'm pregnant. I'm really very excited to have his baby—our baby—but I doubt if my parents or his parents will be happy.*
>
> *"And the woman who calls herself Boomer's girlfriend has something to think about. I've heard it through the grapevine that Laura VanPlank can't have children because of an accident. I don't want Laura hurt because of my feelings for Boomer, but I want him to be a father to our baby. We'll be a family, but first, he wants to get a job and get some money."*

Boomer was Rick Tingsley! I knew it. He was the "older man," by a whole year!

There was more, but the loose floorboard had gotten to me. I had to find the diary. Maybe Phil had put it back, thinking that it was safer there until he could get it to the police or finish reading and writing about its contents.

It was so dark, I had to turn another light on in the smaller bedroom that had two sets of bunk beds. That's where Claire and probably Phil had slept when they were kids. I got down on all fours to look for a board that might be loose. My inky fingers felt all over every crevice and plank of open space. I pushed the right set of bunks out of the way and looked for anything unusual—other than dust elephants—that might be there.

Nothing.

I pushed that bunk bed back and went to the other. I got that out of the way and knelt back down.

Oh!

With what little fingernails I had, I picked at a board that was just a bit out of sync with the rest and managed to pull it up, along with the board next to it and the next.

Then I saw a little pink leather book with gold lettering that said DIARY. It had a little flap with a tiny lock. I picked up the diary and looked at it. There was a small indention in the gold-tipped pages. Gently, I pulled out a tiny rusted key.

My heart was pounding so hard I had to sit down. I shut the light off and went into the kitchen. Stepping over the ribbon on the floor, I sat down, ready to unlock the secrets from Claire's diary.

My hands were shaking. I couldn't do it. I had to boot up or something.

Finally I took the little key and unlocked it.

There it was, on the inside cover, written in curlicues and hearts and other girlish doodles:

*Ms. Claire Tingsley*

*Mrs. Rick Tingsley*

*Mrs. Richard Tingsley*

*Mr. Richard and Mrs. Claire Tingsley*

*Boomer Tingsley and Claire Jacobson Tingsley and son or daughter*

Oh my! Boomer was really Rick Tingsley.

Did that mean that Laura killed two people?

Something was still tweaking me about Laura. She was a woman who just about fell apart when her cook and waitress were late. Did she have the guts to pull off two murders?

I remembered how her high heels were killing her feet that day in her kitchen. She didn't even dare to take them off for fear that she'd suffer the disapproval of Carla.

Poor Laura. Even if she was successful in getting into the White House via Rick—which was highly unlikely—Carla would want to redecorate and would kick the antiques to the curb.

Carla. I hated to think this, but my housekeeping cottages were way below her standards. She wanted to leave Laura's beautiful four-hundred-square-foot contemporary, which, rumor had it, the VanPlanks had paid for, to sleep in my rustic cabins? Then again, I'd caught her staring into Cottage Eight. This cottage! Phil Jacobson's cottage at the time of his murder.

What was she looking for?

I looked at the diary in my hand. I think I knew.

Suddenly the vapors of a gallon of Chanel No. 5 surrounded me. There she was, Carla VanPlank, in black flats with a big, ugly gun pointed at me.

*Oh, crap!*

No one knew where I was.

"Don't move, Trixie. Don't move a muscle or I'll shoot you. Put the diary on the table."

"How can I put the diary on the table and not move a muscle, Carla?"

"Shut up. You know what I mean."

"I would think that you'd be better at this by now. You killed Claire and Phil, didn't you?"

"I said shut up!"

She had crazy eyes. Crazy eyes and pink pearls.

"Carla, don't do anything stupid." I shook my head. "Oh, wait. You already did."

"I said shut up. Hand me the diary."

"I wish you'd make up your mind."

"Shut up!"

"Why? Tell me why. If you're going to kill me, I have a right to know," I said, glad that I was still sitting or I'd faint dead on the floor before she had the chance to kill me.

"She got in the way."

"Of what?"

"Of Laura marrying Rick Tingsley."

"I don't get it," I said, stalling for time. Besides, I wanted to hear her say it from her own candy apple red lips.

"She was pregnant. You know that by now. You've been snooping enough. Laura can't have any children because of her car accident. Of course, Rick would marry Claire since she was pregnant, and that would have ruined all my plans for my daughter."

"So you waited until Claire left the campfire, followed her, and shot her."

"Yes. It was noisy with the firecrackers that someone threw into the bonfire, so I shot her and dragged her body into the woods and hid it. The next day, I buried her in a cave that I knew was there."

"You knew she was pregnant because you and Laura were in Dr. Francis's waiting room."

"Claire had the stupid sonogram in her hand when she left Dr. Francis's examination room. She was so excited, she dropped it. I picked it up and saw that it was a sonogram picture."

"And you knew the father was Rick?"

"Yes. I'd seen the way he looked at her. The same way my 'husband' looks at other women."

"And you wanted Laura to marry Rick and push him into politics just like you did with Grant?" She was blabby and maybe had had too much to drink, and I wanted to stall her. Maybe Ty, or someone, would see the lights on in the cottage.

"Yes. Rick is slow and dull compared to Grant, but he's more malleable."

"And what about poor Phil Jacobson?" I asked. "You knew that it was Phil Jacobson who was murdered in Eight because you did it. Everyone else thought that the victim was a man named David Burrows. His real name hadn't been released yet."

"Phillip was going to expose me."

"How did you know that?"

"By a lucky coincidence we were both in the newspaper office at the same time. I was waiting for Joan Paris to lunch with her—I wanted her to do a special interview with the mayor about his run for senator. Phil was asking about archives relative to Claire's murder. He didn't see me, but I saw him. I knew immediately who he was. It was that cowlick on the back of his head. He had that as a boy. And his creepy eyes. Claire had those eyes."

*Their eyes have nothing on yours about now, lady.*

Was anyone going to look for me? I was running out of questions. I could hear Frankie and the Polka Dots from here. No one would hear a gunshot.

"You don't really want to kill me, Carla."

"Oh, I sure do. I really do. And your time's up."

"I don't think so, Carla. Put the gun down."

"What?

"In the bedroom is Deputy Ty Brisco with a tape

recorder. Everything you say will be held against you in a court of law. Oh, and you have the right to remain silent." I put my index finger over my lips. "I really think you should remain silent."

"I don't believe you that Ty Brisco is in the other room. He'd come out to rescue you, wouldn't he?"

Good question. *What do I do now?* There was nothing that I could use as a weapon within reach. There was cutlery in the drawer by the kitchen sink.

"Uh, Carla? Could I have a last request?"

"No!" She cocked back the lever thing on the gun. The metallic sound bounced around the room.

This was it. It was the end of the line for Beatrix "Trixie" Matkowski. Aunt Stella would have to come back from Boca and sell the Silver Bullet and the twelve little cottages. Oh, and the Big House. That would have to go, too.

And I wanted my first Dance Fest to be a success.

I wondered if my staff would miss me. And my cute Dance Fest outfit was going to be a bloody mess. Well, maybe the blood would be hidden by all the sequins. That would be good.

I'd like to die with dignity, but I was just about to cry like a baby and pee my new jeans, not necessarily in that order.

"Look, Carla. Every person about to die in every movie and TV show and on death row gets a last request. Now, come on, all I want is a glass of water. I'm really dry, and I love the Sandy Harbor water—I really do."

"Dammit, get a glass of water and shut the hell up."

"Gee, thanks, Carla. But first, I have to find a glass that I like."

"I don't care if you drink out of the faucet. Just hurry up."

I pulled open cabinets and drawers, talking and moving and trying to distract her. I yanked out a cast-iron frying pan—my favorite cookware—and threw it like a Frisbee in her direction.

Yes! I stunned her enough that she fell on the floor. The gun went off, and the blast sent shock waves through my entire system.

I looked down, expecting to see something wet and red spreading on my new top. Nothing.

Happy that she'd missed, I dove on top of her skinny frame and designer pantsuit and heard a *whoosh*. I think I collapsed her diaphragm like a sponge. She went limp, and I yanked the gun out of her hand. It was still warm from the shot. I aimed it at her heart.

"Let me know if it was all worth it when you're sitting in prison. Do you think they'll classify you as a serial killer? You have two murders under your silver belt and one attempted murder for *moi*. That's quite a legacy, Carla."

She let loose a streak of swearwords that no First Lady should ever say.

The door flew open. It was Ty pointing his own gun and looking like a cowboy from the Wild West. Only a good guy. He wore a white cowboy hat. He stood in the doorway for a second, analyzing the situation, then stepped next to me. He pried Carla's gun from my stiff fingers and slipped it into the waistband of his jeans but still aimed his at Carla.

I let my sore arms relax at my sides.

"Want to tell me what's going on, Trixie?"

"Carla killed Claire because she was pregnant by Rick Tingsley. Laura can't have kids. Rick was going to marry Claire and ruin Laura's chance at being the First Lady of the United States. If I was a shrink, I'd guess that Carla was living her life through her daughter because Grant VanPlank has terminal zipperitis and will never be elected by sensible voters."

I took a breath. "And she killed Phil because she thought he was going to expose her. And she was going to kill me because I found Claire's diary and read the typewriter ribbon." I pointed to the floor. "I didn't finish reading it, but you can."

"That's quite the . . . the . . . summation."

"Ty, I think you should handcuff Carla now because she's getting her designer outfit all dirty on the floor and because I'm going to faint soon, and I want to see her arrested and in handcuffs. The silver cuffs will match her outfit perfectly."

Ty cuffed Carla on the floor, then helped her to stand. He read her the Miranda warning, which he knew from memory, and it was all very cool.

Carla started crying, and her makeup ran down her face.

Deputy Vern McCoy ran into the cottage, looked at Ty and Carla, and said, "I'll take her down to the lockup. What do you want me to book her for?"

Ty looked at me and grinned. "Tell him, Trixie."

"Two counts of premeditated murder and one count of the attempted murder of a terrific chef."

"Vern, Trixie and I will be right behind you. Trixie will have to give her statement, but there's one thing I have to do first."

Vern clasped the chain that connected Carla's handcuffs and steered her toward the cottage door. Looking over his shoulder, he said to Ty, "Yeah, what's that?"

Ty smiled at me and wrapped his arm around my waist. He probably didn't want to have to pick me up from the floor when my adrenaline tanked and my knees gave out.

"I'm going to dance another polka with Trixie."

# *Epilogue*

Hi, Aunt Stella!

I have to tell you some things, and I know that e-mail is the best way to reach you, you *bon vivant*!

First, the Dance Fest was a success. The arrest of Carla VanPlank (you remember her) for the murders of Claire and Phil Jacobson (and the attempted murder of me!) spread like wildfire, and finally Ty stepped up to the microphone and told everyone at the Dance Fest what had happened.

Instead of a downer, Ty stressed that the Dance Fest should be a celebration of Claire and Phil's life and that the black cloud had been lifted from Sandy Harbor, thanks to me!

I got several minutes of applause and a standing ovation. When they kept yelling, "Speech," I took the microphone and told everyone that Cottage Eight would be taken down and in its place would be a garden for Claire and Phil Jacobson.

I'm sure that you'll agree that this is the best for Cottage Eight. I'm thinking of building Cottage Thirteen, but some people are superstitious. Maybe I'll just call it Cottage Twelve and a Half!

The faux-reverend Buddy Wilder asked me if he could lead everyone at the Dance Fest in a prayer for Claire and Phil, and I handed him the mike. He said a nice prayer, gave a little eulogy, and it was quite lovely. When he was finished, Ty whispered in his ear, and they both stepped away from the dance floor and walked over to the state police car, where Buddy was handcuffed and taken away.

I gave a signal to Frankie to get the Polka Dots polka-ing, and he did, and everyone swarmed the dance floor. This will be a Dance Fest that Sandy Harbor will be talking about forever.

I found it interesting that Buddy's pals that drove with him from New York City, and saw him arrested, didn't leave the Dance Fest but were dancing away as Buddy was driven away.

Juanita, Cindy, and my waitresses along with Clyde and Max really pulled through, keeping the buffet hot and plentiful. Ray Meyerson (I think you know his parents) is working out fabulously and during the Dance Fest, he was busy busing tables and keeping the trash cans empty.

In conclusion, Aunt Stella, the first Silver Bullet Dance Fest in twenty-five years was very entertaining with two arrests. Around it all, Frankie and the Polka Dots were thumping out their polkas, but it wasn't the same without you playing the accordion.

How I'd love to hear you play again!

By the way, I danced the first dance (a polka, of course!) just like you used to do with Uncle Porky. I danced with Ty, who surprised me with how good he can polka for a cowboy from Texas, but his mother was Polish (Karpinski), and she taught him. Cool, huh?

I got my mother upset when I told her about Carla VanPlank holding a gun on me. I don't know how I did it, but thank goodness for cast-iron frying pans. I threw it at her as hard as I could, and it knocked the wind out of her.

I guess when there's a stressful situation, you get strength from somewhere, and I did. I wasn't going to let her shoot me when I had so much to do yet.

And dancing with Ty was something special. After Doug's betrayal, I never thought I'd trust another man again, but Ty is different. He makes me laugh, he challenges me, and makes me crazy all at the same time. He's fun to be with.

Love you,

Trixie

I hit SEND just after I deleted that stuff about Ty. That was the kind of thought that was meant for a diary—a little pink diary with gold-tipped pages, a gold lock, and a tiny rusty key.

I was going to keep Claire's diary after it was released from evidence. Ty said that I could have it as a memento of Claire since she didn't have any family remaining.

And that was sad. A life so promising, cut short over such stupidity.

But I'd read every word she wrote and remember what it was like to be so young and so in love. I'd experienced that for a while with Deputy Doug, a brief while.

I smiled as I headed to the kitchen of the Silver Bullet. It was time for my shift, and I couldn't wait to start making the orders and feeding everyone. There's nothing like great diner food. It's comfort food.

And a lot of people in this world need comfort.

The Silver Bullet and the Sandy Harbor Housekeeping Cottages (minus Cottage Eight) is my legacy. And soon the families would return and enjoy the lake and the grounds and my cooking.

Life is good.

*Family (and Friends'!) Recipes from the Silver Bullet Diner, Sandy Harbor, New York*

# Texas Sheet Cake

### From my friend Michele Masarech

Michele is a friend of mine who lived across the street in the old neighborhood. She's a very busy nurse who has been to Texas once, but she makes this cake for most every event because her time is limited and it's easy and fast to make for a crowd. She said that over the years, she's perfected the original recipe. Everyone at the Dance Fest raved about this cake, and Ty absolutely loved it since he's from Texas!

1 cup butter
1 cup water
½ cup cocoa
1 cup sour cream
1½ cup coarsely chopped walnuts
1 tsp. vanilla
2 cups sugar
½ tsp. salt
2 cups flour
1 tsp. baking soda
2 eggs (slightly beaten)

Preheat oven to 350 degrees Fahrenheit. Bring butter, water, and cocoa to boil in saucepan. Remove from heat.

Add remaining ingredients, mixing after each addition.

Pour batter into greased and floured 12½″ x 17½″ x 1″ baking pan.

Bake 22 to 27 minutes.

## *Frosting (spread on hot cake)*

½ cup butter
1/3 cup cocoa
4 cups confectioners' sugar
1/3 cup milk
½ to 1 cup ground nuts

In saucepan, bring butter, milk and cocoa to boil.

Add confectioners' sugar, adding more if needed to make it of spreading consistency.

Spread frosting on hot cake.

Sprinkle with ground nuts.

### Mrs. D's Dixie Barbecue Sauce & Marinade for Chicken

Mrs. D was from one of the Carolinas, I can't remember which one, but she passed away many years ago. Every time I make this, I think of her and the fun neighborhood barbecues.

½ cup oil
1 cup vinegar
2 Tbsp. salt
2 tsp. poultry seasoning
¼ tsp. pepper
1 egg

Put everything in blender and let mix. Cover chicken with mix. Use remaining for basting on barbecue. If there's not enough, make another batch!

## Dick Green's Coleslaw Dressing

Dick Green is a very sweet guy that I used to work with when I was a tour guide in Philly. He made this for a work party, and I just had to have the recipe. I have to confess that I dislike coleslaw, but I love making it, and everyone tells me that this coleslaw recipe is the best.

> Medium head shredded green cabbage (can mix in some red cabbage for color)
> 1 cup shredded carrots (about 2 to 3)
> 1½ cups mayonnaise
> 2 Tbsp. sugar
> ¼ cup cider vinegar
> ¼ tsp. celery seed (or oregano)
> ½ tsp. salt
> ¼ tsp. black pepper
> 1 small grated onion (if you desire)

In large bowl, combine ingredients, then mix in cabbage and carrots. Cover and chill 2 to 3 hours before serving.

## Joan Wojcieson's Coleslaw Recipe
### Handed Down from Her Grandmother

Joan is a dear friend of mine from the old neighborhood. This recipe is a little twist from the standard coleslaw recipe because the dressing is heated and Grandma Wojcieson used to buy bagged coleslaw and then dress it.

*2 1-lb. packages coleslaw*
*2 chopped onions*
*1 cup sugar*
*1 cup vinegar*
*1 tsp. celery seed*
*1 tsp. salt*
*1 tsp. dry mustard*
*¼ tsp. pepper.*
*1 cup vegetable oil*

Bring onions, sugar, vinegar, celery seed, salt, dry mustard, and pepper to boil.

Remove from heat and pour in vegetable oil.

Pour over coleslaw, mix, and let set for at least 24 hours in fridge before using.

Joan says that this lasts a long time in the refrigerator.

## Trixie's (Really Easy) Pulled Pork Recipe

*There are many, many recipes for pulled pork, but
mine is the absolute easiest. You won't believe this!*

Boneless roast pork shoulder
Salt and pepper to taste
1 to 2 bottles barbecue sauce

Get a boneless roast of pork shoulder (the cheapest
one possible).

Cut it in half or leave it whole to fit it into a
Crock-Pot (depending on the size).

Cook on high all day (8 or more hours) with some
salt and pepper, draining some of the juice now
and then.

When it is done, pull it apart with two opposing
forks.

Pour in your favorite barbecue sauce until it's
well coated.

# Mom's (Rose's) Bite-Sized Cheesecakes

*I've kept this recipe since I was in St. Margaret's Grammar School. My mother and I used to make these two-bite cheesecakes for every one of their numerous bake sales.*

¾ cups sugar
2 packages (8 oz. each) cream cheese
2 eggs
1 Tbsp. lemon juice
1 tsp. vanilla
box vanilla wafers

Beat all ingredients until fluffy. Place 1 vanilla wafer in lined cupcake pan (use small liners).
Fill ²/₃ full with cheese mixture.
Bake for 15 to 20 minutes at 375 degrees.
When cool, top with spoon of pie filling.*

*Or whatever you'd like to top the cheesecakes with. For the Dance Fest, I used a dollop of lemon curd and 3 to 4 fresh blueberries because it was blueberry season. Sliced strawberries would work or any kind of fresh berry or even fruit jam.

Ready for another helping of
Christine Wenger's Comfort Food
Mysteries?

Don't miss

*DINERS, DRIVE-INS AND DEATH*

Available from Obsidian in January 2015!